ON THE PLANET OF BOTTLED BRAINS

VOLUME 2

Other Avon Books by
Harry Harrison

BILL, THE GALACTIC HERO

BILL, THE GALACTIC HERO
ON THE PLANET OF THE ROBOT SLAVES
(Volume 1)

BILL, THE GALACTIC HERO

ON THE PLANET OF BOTTLED BRAINS

VOLUME 2

HARRY HARRISON

and ROBERT SHECKLEY

A Byron Preiss Book

AVON BOOKS NEW YORK

BILL, THE GALACTIC HERO ON THE PLANET OF BOTTLED
BRAINS (#2) is an original publication of Avon Books. This work has
never before appeared in book form. This work is a novel. Any similarity
to actual persons or events is purely coincidental.

Special thanks to Kirby McCauley, Nat Sobel, John Douglas, David Keller,
and Alice Alfonsi.

AVON BOOKS
A division of
The Hearst Corporation
105 Madison Avenue
New York, New York 10016

BILL, THE GALACTIC HERO ON THE PLANET OF BOTTLED
BRAINS copyright © 1990 by Byron Preiss Visual Publications, Inc.
Introduction copyright © 1990 by Harry Harrison
Illustrations copyright © 1990 by Byron Preiss Visual Publications, Inc.
Published by arrangement with Byron Preiss Visual Publications, Inc.
Cover design, book design, and logo by Alex Jay/Studio J
Edited by David M. Harris
Front cover painting by Michael W. Kaluta and Steven Fastner
Library of Congress Catalog Card Number: 89-91535
ISBN: 0-380-75662-5

First Avon Books Printing: May 1990

AVON TRADEMARK REG. U.S. PAT. OFF. AND IN OTHER COUNTRIES, MARCA
REGISTRADA, HECHO EN U.S.A.

Printed in the U.S.A.

RA   10   9   8   7   6   5   4   3   2   1

CHAPTER 1

"GATHER ROUND, FOLKS," BROWNNOSE said through the loudhailer he had stolen from the drill sergeant. The built-in circuitry made his voice sound gravelly and disgusting just like the sergeant's. "It's the event you've all been waiting for—the unveiling of Bill's new foot now growing from an implanted foot bud. Only ten bucks a ticket to see this unique and possibly revolting event."

The barracks where the unveiling was to be held was filling up fast. Most of the enlisted men in Camp Diplatory wanted to attend the unveiling of Bill's new foot bud. The foot bud had been implanted in Bill's stump three days previously, on the medical satellite BRIP 32 situated at Point Less. After implantation, Bill had been shipped to Diplatory, the large military establishment on the planet Shyster. He had to wait three days before he could unveil his transplant. Time-controlled bandages ensured that he would follow medical orders. There had been difficulties with time-controlled bandages, but luckily Bill didn't have any. At least as far as he knew.

There wasn't much to do for the fifty thousand

Space Troopers stationed in Camp Diplatory. The camp was set on a hundred semi-submerged acres in the middle of Unholy Bog, the largest and wettest swamp on the planet Shyster. Why the camp had been built in the middle of a bog was a mystery. Or maybe it wasn't. Some said it was an accident, probably made in Central Headquarters back on Helior. Others said that the location had been picked deliberately because tough conditions produce strong men, if they don't kill them. Or maim them. Or drive them mad.

"And if they do, there are more where those came from."

That is the motto of the Fighting 69th Deep Space Screaming Killers, the unit to which Bill was presently attached.

"So take off the bandage," Kanarsie said. "Let's get a look."

Bill looked around. The barracks was full. At ten bucks a head, which Brownnose was collecting at the door for him, Bill figured he'd made enough to buy himself some new combat boots. The rate at which he accumulated foot operations made this necessary, since the military wouldn't reimburse him for constantly having to turn in shoeware that wasn't even worn, or just didn't fit the present disgusting shape of Bill's wounded foot.

Brownnose waved enthusiastically that he could begin. He was enthusiastic about everything, kind, reverent and obedient. And wanted to help his buddies all the time. Which is not the Troopers way and that is why they hated him. And called him Brownnose. Bill liked him because he reminded Bill of Eager Beaver who had acted the same way. But of course he had been a Chingar spy. And a robot too.

"Here goes," Bill said and grabbed the bandage. An alarm sounded and electric shock stung his fingers. "Ouch. Not quite time yet." The bandage buzzed hoarsely and the end dropped free. "Time now," he said and unwound one turn of the bandages and the spectators all leaned forward. They emitted a collective sigh as Bill unwound the second layer. Their faces got all flushed and nervous, and their breath came in short pants, exceedingly uncomfortable, and some could be seen nervously wringing their hands as Bill threw off the third layer of bandage. Bill's foot wasn't exactly big box office, but in a boring, despicable, uncomfortable dump like this even a cockroach fight was an event the stature of naked ladies wrestling in Jello.

Excitement, or whatever it was, reached a fever pitch as the eighty or so burly and scarred military men of low rank and lower IQ crowded into the smoke-filled plastic Quonset hut and leaned forward blinking, as Bill threw off the fourth and final fold of bandage.

You'd think, of course, that Bill would be the one to have the first glimpse of his new foot, since it was his, after all. You would be mistaken, however, for Bill superstitiously looked away as he cast the bandage away. He had been having some strange feelings in that foot over the last day.

He looked at the watching faces around him, their eyes glued on his foot.

The crowd made a sort of tittering sound. That was odd, not at all what Bill had expected. And then they started laughing. Not polite, appreciative laughter, such as you might expect at the unveiling of a foot bud, but loud, heavy guffaw-guffaw type laughter of the joke's-on-you variety.

Bill glanced down. Then he glanced away. Then he glanced down again, winced, considered glancing away again, pulled himself together, looked.

"You know, Bill," Kowalski said, "I thought this foot unveiling of yours was going to be a ripoff; I mean, what could there be under that bandage; you plant a foot bud, you get a foot, right? Wrong. Bill, I want to thank you. That is the funniest thing I've seen since the CO got fragged."

Bill stretched his clawed toes experimentally. "Seems to work OK," he said.

It should have worked OK. But it would have worked better on an alligator. Since it was a fine, green, scaly, abundantly clawed alligator's foot that was now growing on the end of Bill's ankle.

What had those doctor's done? Were they experimenting, trying to turn him into a reptile? He didn't put it past them. Since he had recently had a giant mutated chicken's foot for a foot he knew that anything was possible. Probable—in the Troopers. And the foot after that had been nice, maybe too many toes but that wasn't bad, and he had really enjoyed it until it withered and dropped off.

It was a small green foot, but it was workable. And it would probably grow into a much larger foot. The envy of any passing alligator he thought, gloomily. Bill did not stop to consider the miracle that man's ability to do this represented. By any standard it was an act of genius. A little useless, perhaps, but genius all the same. But this was lost on Bill who, like many before him, was mad as hell.

CHAPTER 2

BILL STUMPED DOWN THE CORRIDOR, LISTing slightly to the left to favor his clawed and knobbly left foot. His new alligator foot had not grown out to full size yet, so there was better than an inch difference between his left and right feet. The foot itself was perfectly sound and able to bear his weight. Though the claws scratched the floor when he walked.

His immediate destination was the small cubicle on level 12 of the main concourse of the base. He got there slightly out of breath, since walking on a taloned alligator's foot takes practice before you can do it smoothly.

The cubicle was ten feet to a side. It was divided into two parts, one a reception and waiting room, the other the place of the computer. The military base on Shyster was run by this Quintiform computer, not the latest model, but one believed to be just as good, almost.

Bill went in and took his seat in the waiting room. He was the only person there. That was unusual, since the computer usually had a line of people waiting to consult it.

No sooner had he sat down than a metallic voice with plenty of vibrato said to him, "Hello, I am the Quintiform computer; please step inside and show me your dogtags."

Bill did as he was told. The inner room of the computer station was painted computer beige. There were banks of switches and dials on the four walls. There were speakers set into the wall up high. One of these was broadcasting a program of sambas.

Bill presented his dogtags and the Quintiform computer hissed and clicked its approval. "Yes, Bill," it said, "what seems to be the trouble?"

"The foot doctors on Aesclepius the medical satellite gave me a foot bud implant," Bill explained. "Look what it grew into!"

The Quintiform exuded a metallic pseudopod with a blinking glass eye at the end of it and inspected Bill's foot.

"Wow!" the computer said. It began to chuckle.

"It's no laughing matter," Bill said. "And anyhow, robots aren't supposed to laugh."

"Sorry about that," the computer said. "Just trying to put you at your ease. Now then, I suppose you want the doctors to fix your other foot so it will match the clawed one?"

"No! I want two normal human feet, like I started with."

"Ah, of course," the computer said. It hummed

and buzzed for a while, presumably going through his memory banks looking for the correct solution to Bill's problem. After a while he said, "Go to Room 1223-B on level Verdigris, Section Vector-Vector 2, and they'll fix you up."

Finding your way around the base was no easy matter, since the main structure was the size of a middle-sized city and contained over three thousand rooms, torture halls, meeting places, contraceptive dispensers, intravenous feeding cafeterias, storage facilities, and the like, spread over ten different levels. Troopers had been known to wander through it for days at a time. Almost any time you went through you could see troopers sleeping in heaps of camouflage clothing at the intersections. It was notorious that you should take along provisions and a full canteen of water when you were going anywhere in the base. As Bill set out, a vehicle the size of an electrified golf cart pulled up beside him.

"Hello, Bill," the golf cart's voice box said. "I have been sent by the computer to take you to your destination. Care for a drink? Nothing too good for our boys in uniform."

Bill thought the golf cart sounded entirely too affable. But he got in. It was a lot better than walking the interminable miles he'd have to cover to reach Room 1223-B.

They whisked along down the olive drab corridors, the golf cart humming a cheery little tune to itself. They passed through Maintenance and Communications to a section called Planning.

"This doesn't look like a medical section," Bill said.

"Don't worry about it," the golf cart said. "I know where I'm going."

It swept up a ramp, doubled down a corridor, and made for a door at the end. Bill winced, because the golf cart had gathered speed and the door was closed. He cowered back in his seat as the golf cart hurtled itself at the door. Bill closed his eyes and buried his head in his hands. When he looked up again, they were on the other side of the door, which had opened by some electric eye arrangement and was now closing again.

He was in some sort of officers' lounge, which had been gotten up to look like an old Earth-style saloon. There were Tiffany lamps and dark furniture made of genuine plastic. There was a long bar with whiteshirted bartenders working behind it. There was a jukebox playing vintage rock on fake original ancient instruments like synthesizers and electric guitars, some of them looking several hundreds of years old, though they had probably been made last week. There were about a dozen uniformed officers of either sex present. They all had drinks in their hands. They cheered when the golf cart speeded into the room, made a neat circle in the middle, and came to a stop.

"Excuse me," Bill said. "Is this the medical section?"

That brought a good round of hearty laughter. Men crowded around and congratulated Bill on his wit. One woman, a majorette, no less, with fluffy blonde hair and a pert nose and giant boobs, sat in Bill's lap and kissed him soundly. Somebody else asked him what he'd like to drink. Bill was so rattled he just said yes. So they brought him a stirrup cup filled with a mixture of that day's alcoholic beverages. The taste of rum was most prominent, as well as a tang of horse from the stirrup, and Bill drained it gratefully, having learned never to look a gift drink in the goblet.

The lady major who had kissed him got out of his lap and into his face. With her nose no more than millimeters from his, she looked long and deep into Bill's eyes. Then she said in a thrilling contralto voice with a faint whiskey burr to it, "You're just like I imagined you'd be."

"Well," Bill said, "I try."

"What a clever remark," one colonel murmured to another.

"He's obviously a clever chap," said a whitehaired colonel who appeared to be the ranking officer. "Get

him a cigar, somebody. And no more of that rotgut;
pour him some of the good cognac we liberated at the
sack of the Main Base after the attack.''

A cigar in one hand, a glass of cognac in the other,
and a smirking grin on his face, Bill wasn't prepared for
the next question.

"Tell me, Bill," a foxy-faced major with the crossed
questionmark flashings of Intelligence Directorate 2 on
his shoulders, "what do you think about the Tsurisian
situation?"

"Does it have anything to do with the medical ser-
vices here?" Bill asked. "If so, I have a complaint."

"My dear fellow," the foxy-faced major said.
"Haven't you been briefed yet on the planet Tsuris?"

"I've only been here three days, sir," Bill said, gur-
gling deeply of the drink to drown his suspicions of all
this officerial kindness. Deep down he knew it wasn't
natural. Even deeper down he wanted to get blind drunk
on the good booze.

"And what have you been doing in your time
here?"

"Growing a new foot, mostly," Bill said. "That's
what I want to ask—"

"Time for that later," the Major said. "Tsuris is a
planet not too far from here. It is sometimes referred to
as the Mystery Planet."

"Oh, sure, I've heard of it," Bill said dimly through
the growing alcoholic fog. "That's the place which
broadcasts the weird radio messages, isn't it?"

The Major explained that the military base on Shyster had been given the job of clearing out Tsuris, a
nearby planet of considerable mystery. Literally nothing
was known about this planet. No decent photographs
had ever been taken through the heavy cloud layer.
There were breaks in the clouds, and the planet seemed
to get plenty of sunshine. But when the military snoop
ships maneuvered to take pictures through an opening,
it always closed up before they could get lined up.

"That's weird," Bill said. "Almost like someone is directing it, huh?"

"Exactly. Have another drink," the major said. "As you've mentioned, radio messages seem to emanate from Tsuris, but they never make sense. But the worst of it is, ships even travelling in the vicinity of Tsuris have been known to vanish, only to appear again millions of miles away with no explanation as to how they got there."

"Sounds like a good place to steer clear of," Bill said with alcoholic sincerity, nodding and drinking at the same time. Which didn't work too well.

"Ah, if only we could," the major said. "But we can't, of course. We are the military. We go where we please."

"Here, here!" cried the other officers, hastily tossing down their drinks.

"And anyhow," the major said, "if something on Tsuris can deflect a ship millions of miles off its course, that's a force that would be of considerable importance to us. We need to know how it works, and if the Tsurisians or whoever lives down there intend to use it against us."

"If so," the whitehaired colonel pointed out, "we've got to kick the crap out of them Tsurisians before they get a chance to do it to us."

"Maybe it would be safer," a captain of shock troopers said, "to kick the crap out of them even if they don't have any bad intentions."

"Here, here!" the other officers chanted.

They all looked at Bill waiting for him to say something. Bill tried to look intelligent, even though he was feeling very dim. "Have you tried putting a scout ship on the planet? That way you could look around and things."

The major concealed his disgust with a fake smile. "Many times, my dear trooper," he said. "As you might very well imagine they never come back, never report."

"That's not so good," Bill bubbled alcoholically.

Then he was seized by bloodthirsty ambitions. "Why not just stand back and wing atomic torpedoes at them until one gets through? Blast them! Destroy them!"

"We thought of that ourselves," the major said. "But this is against the rules of war, that is what the commy lefty papers say, and our bleeding heart candidates in the up and coming local elections wouldn't like it. They need to have it all legal. Declaration of war and all that nonsense. As soon as they are not elected we go back to doing just what the hell we want, but for the moment our hands are tied. Our missiles in the silos. Our noses in our glasses drowning our sorrows."

"Well . . ." Bill thought for a while. "Why not declare war on them?"

The officers nodded at each other in approval. "You've got the right instincts, trooper. But not until after the elections. Then we can bomb the mothers into the next dimension. But until that happens we have to give some illusion of lawfulness. But the trouble is that we can't even find anyone to talk to on Tsuris. In fact, we're not entirely sure there's anyone there."

"Then the answer is plain," the colonel said. "I'm sure you thought of it yourself. If we can get a drone scout ship down to the surface of the planet, with someone aboard carrying a message from the Admiral-in-Chief, at least we could get the Tsurisians talking. Then we could make demands which they'd refuse. And then we'd have a chance to plead 'irreparable insult demanding unctuous apology' as a cause of war."

"Unless the Tsurisians are able to apologize fast enough to forestall the invasion," the colonel said.

"Speed is everything in modern warfare," the major pointed out. "What do you think, Bill?"

"Sounds like a good plan to me," Bill said. "Now, if you could direct me to the medical section . . ."

"No time for that now, trooper," the major said. "We want to congratulate you, then explain how your drone ship works."

"Wait a minute," Bill said. "What has this got to do with me?"

"My dear fellow," the major said, "by walking through this door you have volunteered for the job of going on the drone ship to Tsuris."

"But I didn't know! The computer told me to come here!"

"That's right. The computer volunteered you."

"Can it do that?"

The major scratched his head. "I don't know, really. Why don't you ask it?" He chuckled evilly as Bill tried to leap woozily to his feet and felt the automatic shackles lock hard around his ankles.

CHAPTER **3**

BROWNNOSE LOOKED TERRIBLE. IT WAS true that he had been through a lot recently. Having had all of his buddies beating up on him because he was so helpful and considerate of others and that is not the Troopers way. The first lesson a real Trooper learns is that it is always Bowb your Buddy week. The Military Psychiatrist had diagnosed him as having a severe case of the Shmidas Touch, the mirror opposite of the Midas Touch where everything you touch turns to gold. But one of the psychiatrist's colleagues, Major Doctor Smellenfuss, disagreed. He said that Brownnose presented a classical case of Loser Psychosis, complicated by Self-Destructive tendencies. All Brownnose knew was, life kept on getting worse for him. And all he wanted to do was make people happy!

Take now, for example. Of course he didn't look

good. What man could look good pushed back against the uncomfortably hot boiler in the laundry room where Bill, hamlike fist raised in the air, was threatening to take him apart.

"Bill, wait!" Brownnose cried as Bill's eyes narrowed, preparatory to driving Brownnose's head through the half inch mild steel of which the boiler was composed. "I did it for you!"

Bill hesitated, fist poised for the killing blow. "How do you figure?"

"Because volunteering you for this mission will bring you a medal, a sizeable bonus, a year's supply of VD pills and most important, an immediate honorable discharge!"

"A discharge?"

"Yes, Bill! You could go home!"

Bill was visited by a wave of nostalgia as he thought of his home world, Phigerinadon, and how much he wanted to see it.

"Are you sure?" he asked.

"Of course I'm sure. Just go to the Recruiting Officer when you get back. He'll set everything in motion for you."

"That's just great," Bill said. "The only trouble is, this is a suicide mission and I'm unlikely to come back from it. And if I don't come back, no discharge, right?"

"You will come back," Brownnose said. "I guarantee it."

"How do you figure?"

"Because, after I volunteered you, I also volunteered myself. So I could look after you, Bill."

"You can't even look after yourself," Bill pointed out. He sighed. "I guess it was pretty nice of you to want to help me, Brownnose, but I wish you hadn't."

"I realize that now, Bill," Brownnose said, extricating himself from Bill's grasp and slinking away from the boiler, which had been growing uncomfortably torrid. He could see that the moment of immediate danger was over. Bill got hot under the collar sometimes, but if you could just avoid instant mayhem, he soon cooled off again.

"Anyhow," Bill said, "how could you volunteer me? Only I can volunteer me."

"You've sure got a point there," Brownnose said. "Maybe you should take it up with the computer."

"Hello again," the Military computer said, "You were in here recently, weren't you? Excuse me for asking but the old eyesight's not what it used to be. My image orthicon is wearing out. Not than anyone or anything cares." It sniveled mechanically, a repellent sound.

"I came in here about my foot," Bill said loudly, disgusted at all the electronic self-pity.

"Your foot? I never forget a foot! Let me see it."

Bill displayed his foot to the computer's vision plate.

"Hooee," the computer said. "That's one beauty of an alligator's tootsy. But I've never seen that foot before. I told you, I never forget a foot."

"Of course you remember it," Bill whined. "Because you looked at it when I was in here before. What kind of computer could forget that."

"I didn't say I forgot, computers can't forget; it's just that I haven't thought about it lately," the computer said. "Just a minute, let me consult my data banks. I never forget a reference to a foot, either . . . Yes, here it is. You're right; you did say something about your foot. And I directed you to the Officer's Ready Room."

"That's right. And the officers there said that by coming in I had volunteered for hazardous duty."

"Yes, that's all correct," the computer said. "When they asked me for a volunteer, I sent on the first one who came in."

"Me?"

"You."

"But I didn't volunteer."

"Tough titty. I mean I am *so* sorry, but you did. Inferentially."

"Beg pardon?"

"I inferred that you would have volunteered if asked. We have special circuits that allow us to use inferences."

"But you could have asked me!" Bill shouted angrily.

"Then what use would be the inferential circuitry with which I have been fitted out at great expense? Anyhow, it was clear to me that a fine upstanding military type like you would be happy to volunteer for hazardous duty, despite the minor impairment to your foot."

"You were wrong," Bill said.

A ripple passed across the computer's vision plate, almost like a shrug. "Well," it said, "mistakes happen, don't they?"

"That's not good enough!" Bill shouted, thumping the computer's vision plate with a large fist. "I'll tear out your lying transistors." He thumped the faceplate again. This time it flashed red.

"Trooper," the computer said in a gruff voice, "Stand to attention."

"What?" said Bill.

"You heard me. I am a Military computer with the veritable rank of full colonel. You are an enlisted man. You have to address me in a respectful manner or you'll be in a lot worse trouble than you are already."

Bill gulped. Officers were all alike, even when they were computers. "Yes sir," he said, and stood to attention.

"Now, since you don't think the procedure was fair, what do you suggest we do?"

"Let's draw for it," Bill said. "Or you pick a volunteer at random from all the men in the base."

"That would satisfy you?"

"Yes, it would."

"OK, here goes." The computer's vision screen lit up in a jagged lightning bolt of conflicting colors. Names flashed by on the screen. There was a sound like a roulette ball rolling around a croupier's wheel.

"OK," the computer said. "We got a winner."

"Fine," Bill said. "Can I go now?"

"Sure. Good luck, soldier."

Bill opened the door. Outside there were two extremely large and beetle-jawed MPs. They took Bill by either arm.

"As you may have gathered," the computer said, "you won the second drawing, too."

Not long after that, a large trooper with a small claw at the end of one foot could be seen, struggling in the arms of two MPs. The trooper was brought to a reviewing stand where several generals were standing, waiting for something to review.

Bill opened up his mouth to scream. One of the MP's drove his elbow into Bill's kidneys.

The other MP went for the liver.

When Bill recovered consciousness, a few seconds later, in response to having his nose tweaked violently, the first MP leaned over him and said, "Look, buddy, you're going on that ship. The only question is, do you go on in one piece or do we cripple you first so you won't make a scene in front of the brass."

"They hate scenes," the second MP said. "We do, too."

"They blame us when the volunteers make a fuss," the first MP said.

"Maybe we should just cripple him and not take any chances," the first MP said.

"Maybe we could just fracture his voice box."

"No, he could still make obscene gestures."

"I guess you're right." Both MPs paused to roll up their sleeves.

"Don't bother," Bill said. "Just put me aboard the ship."

"First you got to go up to the reviewing stand and shake the generals' hands and tell them how glad you was to volunteer."

"Let's get it over with," Bill said.

CHAPTER 4

THE DRONE SHIP WAS SMALL, ABOUT THE size of a launch. Built of cheap plastic and aluminized cardboard since it was not expected to return. One of the MPs pulled open the main hatchway and growled in anger as the handle came off in his hand.

"Never mind that," the other MP said. "The inner parts still work all right."

"Why don't they build them better?" Bill whined, then shrieked with pain. He was being carried in a crunched and uncomfortable manner by the two MPs.

"Why should they bother?" the first MP said. "These ships are specially constructed for one-way trips to only the most dangerous places."

"You mean I'm not expected to return?" Bill whimpered, wallowing in self-pity.

"I don't mean anything of the sort! Well, maybe. Anyhow, the real crafty advantage of sending a volunteer, was that, if you should not return, as is confidently expected, the military will probably send a full-fledged expeditionary force to Tsuris, even declare war as they sincerely want to."

"You said probably?"

"It has to be probably, since the military can always change its teeny-tiny mind. But that's what will probably happen."

"Yipe!" Bill yiped. "What the bowb are you doing with my ear?"

"I'm fastening a translating device to your ear, so

if you find any Tsurisians on Tsuris you can talk to them."

"Tsuris! The place nobody ever comes back from?"

"You catch on fast. That's the whole point of the operation. Your non-return will give us the excuse to invade."

"I don't think I like this."

"You don't have to like it, Trooper. Just follow orders and shut up."

"I refuse! Cancel the orders!"

"Shut up." They wrestled Bill into the ship and strapped him into the pilot's command chair. It was beautifully padded and comfortable. Bill was not. He opened his mouth to protest again and the neck of an open bottle was shoved into it. He gurgled and gasped.

"What . . . was that?"

"Apathia 24. With a double shot of Extasis Tricarbonate. One-hundred and fifteen proof." The MP nodded as Bill gurgled down some more. "That's the stuff. You can keep the bottle."

It was really good stuff. So good that Bill never noticed when the MPs left and the hatch closed. The ship must have taken off, he could not remember when, because he saw by the vision plate that he was in space. Lots of little stars and such. And what looked like a planet down below. He admired the great storms sweeping across its surface as he drained the bottle. Lightning crackled balefully through the purple-black clouds and his radio crackled with static.

Radio? He fiddled with the knobs until a voice came through clearly. At least it sounded clear although it did not make much sense.

"No gliggish in hut overstep galoshes."

He sneered at this and was reaching to turn it off when a voice buzzed in his ear. He blinked rapidly at this—then slowly remembered the translator had been attached just inside his left ear. "What did they say?"

"Just a minute," the translator said testily. "All right, I think I've got it now. They're definitely speaking

Tsurisian. The question is, is it High Garpeiean dialect or Someshovish."

"Who gives a bowb?" Bill muttered, trying to get the last drops of metabolic poison from the bottle.

"An interesting problem in linguistic analysis," the translator said. "In the former dialect it means, 'Please don't throw the eggshells on the grass.'

"And in the other one?" Bill asked, feigning interest.

"In the other it translates to, 'Tickle knees on the Steppes.'"

"Sounds a lot of bowb either way."

"A cogent observation that is entirely possible," the translator agreed.

Well, he could figure out what they were saying later. For now, he was entranced by the sights below him. Looking through the transparent hull of his drone ship, he could see bright flowers of enormous size blossoming from the surface of Tsuris.

"Pretty nice shtuff," he said, wishing he had another drink.

"Aren't you going to take evasive action?" the translator asked him.

"Why bother? Ish nice to look at the flowers down there."

"Flowers my silicon ass!" the translator said with great agitation. "Those red things are high explosive. They're shooting torpedoes at us!"

That's all it took to bring Bill out of his stupor, cold sober and in a cold sweat. Shooting at him? Suddenly he remembered the mission. Then his little drone ship bucked violently.

"Mayday, mayday!" screamed the translator. The ship started to plunge and careen and cartwheel and spin and tumble, all the things that spaceships do when they're hit. Bill grabbed for a stanchion and missed, he still wasn't that sober, and hit his head. The darkness of unconsciousness instantly descended. Which was not such a bad thing considering what happened next.

Bill's ship disintegrated under the impact of atomic torpedoes.

"A gravchute," he muttered when he stumbled back to consciousness. "That's nice."

As he dropped gently through the clinging mists, which of course were the clouds that forever veil Tsuris. Especially if you're trying to take pictures of the planet. He looked down and saw that the ground seemed to be coming up very fast. Was the gravchute working properly? Weren't there supposed to be controls on it somewhere?

He fumbled and cursed but before he could find them the ground came up and struck him and merciful unconsciousness drew its cloak about him yet one more time.

CHAPTER **5**

BILL RETURNED RELUCTANTLY TO CONsciousness. He discovered that he was floating in a lukewarm nutrient bath. Its specific gravity was such that his head just bobbled above the surface without his having to make any positive effort to keep himself afloat. It felt very nice. He blinked up at the multicolored lights overhead. Watching them glitter and shine reminded Bill of another happy Fundamentalist Zoroastrian Winter Solstice Defloration Festival, that the nonbelievers called Christmas, back home. A tear formed in either eye, dribbled down his nose and dropped down into the nutrient solution.

Immediately an alarm went off. Or something that might be an alarm; a raucous electronic flatus. A person hurried grotesquely into the room. At least Bill supposed it was a person. It might have been a robot, or anything between a person and a robot. Or a thing. It was mainly composed of a large sphere about three feet in diameter. From its underside there depended four skinny black legs. On top of the sphere was another sphere, smaller, and a still smaller one above that. What were these spheres made of? Bill hiccupped lightly and realized that he didn't really care. It was nice and comfy here in the warm bath. A tickle of worry tickled him. Maybe he should care, trapped in a bubblebath on this alien planet. He looked again. The spheres seemed to be a combination of metal and pink-colored flesh. There was a smiley face painted on the uppermost sphere where a face would be if this was anything human.

The creature ground some internal gears and said, "Please don't do that."

"Do what?"

"Cry into the nutrient solution. You're changing the acid levels. It isn't good for your skin."

"What's wrong with my skin?" Bill asked. "Am I burned?"

"Not at all, bless you. We just want to make it nice and soft, your skin."

"Why do you want to do that?"

"We'll talk about it later," the Tsurisian said. "By the way, should you wish to know, and I'm sure that you do, I am Illyria, your nurse."

They kept Bill in the nutrient bath for several more hours. When he got out, his skin was nice and pink and rosy. They gave him back his trooper uniform, which had been brushed and dry cleaned by some alien but effective process. He was allowed to walk up and down in the corridor, for that's what it seemed to be. His weapons were gone and he didn't see anything that looked like it would be useful. Not that he had any idea what he would do even if he got a weapon against an entire planetful of enemies.

He was able to form some idea of his surroundings

when Illyria came to take care of him. He questioned her adroitly; that is he asked questions and she answered them, and he quickly learned that she was a typical female Tsurisian, twenty years old, quite sophisticated for a girl who had lived and worked on her parents' farm until just last year, when her high grades in high school had won her this position in the alien lifeforms hospital in Graypnutz, the capital city of Tsuris.

Every day several Tsurisian males came by to see how Bill was doing. They were considerably older than Illyria, as he could tell by the grayish stubble on their intermediate spheres, which, Bill learned, served as holders for the batteries that helped keep the Tsurisians going.

Bill quickly discovered that the Tsurisians saw nothing cruel or unnatural about what they were proposing to do to him. "We Tsurisians always have to be reborn in the body of someone else," Bill's doctor pointed out. "Otherwise we don't get born at all."

"That's really great for you—but what about me?" Bill whimpered desperately. "Where do I go?"

"Out like a burnt-out bulb," the alien grimaced, though this was hard to tell since his painted-on expression really did not change very much. "Anyway, haven't you an iota of the spiritual in you? Don't you crave, in some part of your tiny soul, to serve all sentient beings?"

"No, I don't think so," Bill said.

"Pity," the doctor said. "You would have been a lot better off if you had learned to think properly about things."

"Listen, buddy," Bill said, "a mind transplant means I'm not here any more and that means I'm dead. How am I supposed to feel good about that?"

"Consider it an opportunity," the doctor said.

"What are you talking about?" Bill screamed.

"Whatever happens is an opportunity," the doctor said.

"Is that a fact? Then let this guy take over your

mind instead of mine. You can have the opportunity."

"Ah," said the doctor, "it didn't knock for me."

Even Illyria stopped visiting so often. "I think they suspect me of something," she told him when she did come by for a brief visit. "They're giving me the Usladish look; you know what I mean?"

"No, I don't," Bill said, desperation in his voice, a trapped feeling coursing through every fiber of his being.

"I keep on forgetting you weren't born here," Illyria said. "An Usladish look is what we call a look that means, I know you're up to something sneaky and rotten but I'm not going to tell anybody about it yet because I'm sort of sneaky and rotten myself."

"They don't have that feeling where I come from," Bill said.

"No? How curious. Anyhow, I'm going to have to stay away for a while. But don't worry, I'm working on your case."

"Hurry up, while I'm still inside this head," Bill said.

Since then quite a few days and nights had gone by since he had seen her. Exactly how many he didn't know, because Tsuris seemed to have an odd fluttery sort of movement around its sun, resulting in days and nights of differing lengths. Some days were what the Tsurisians called Tiger Days, or was it Picket-fence days?, the translation was a little difficult. These days in which the sun rose and set every hour on the hour, striping the planet in yellow and black. He decided to make a mark on the wall to mark each period of light. He didn't know why he was doing this but it was what guys in cells were always doing in the stories he used to read back home in the hayrick behind the manure pile back on his parents' farm on Phigerinadon. He tried the mark system, but when he came to do his next mark, he found that he had put his mark close to a mark already on the wall which he hadn't noticed. Unless he had marked two light periods without remembering it. Or had marked one light period twice absentmindedly. The more he thought about it, the more he decided that mark-making in prison was the sort of thing you ought to study in school before trying it in field conditions. So he mostly sat. There were no books or newspapers available, and no television. Luckily there was a small switch on the side of his translator that let him switch it from "Translate" to "Converse." Bill felt a little silly doing it, but there didn't seem to be anyone else around to talk to.

"Hello," he said.

"'Alo," the translator said. "'Ow are you, heh?"

"Why are you speaking with a stupid accent?" Bill asked.

"Because I am a translator, that's why, Buster." The thing sounded very miffed. "It would falsify my position and my image if I didn't allow impurities inherited from the many languages I deal with to creep into my talk during my conversational phase."

"That's a pretty dim reason," Bill said.

"Well not to me, squishy repulsive non-machine creature!" the translator said heatedly.

"There is no reason to get insulting," Bill muttered. A mechanical sniff of annoyance was his only answer. After this there was a long silence. Then Bill said, "Seen any good movies lately?"

"What?" said the translator.

"Movies," Bill said.

"Are you crazy or something? I am a tiny transistorized gadget lodged under your right armpit. Or on your ear. I get about. How would I ever get to see a movie?"

"I was just making a joke," Bill said.

"They didn't tell us about jokes," the translator complained. "Is that enough?"

"Enough what?"

"Conversation."

"No, of course not! I've just begun!"

"But you see, I've almost used up the conversational capacity which was built into me. I will still carry on as your translator, of course, but I very much regret telling you that the conversational aspect of our relationship is at an end. Over and out."

"Translator?" Bill said after a while.

Silence from the translator.

"Haven't you got any words left at all?" Bill asked.

"Just this," the translator said. And that was the last word Bill was able to get out of him.

It was soon after that that he heard the second voice.

The second voice came to him that night, after his evening meal of a raspberry brain malted and a plate of what tasted like fried chicken livers but looked like orange gumdrops. He was reading his shirt labels under the light of a lamp called a Blind Philistine because it shines indifferently on whatever is put in front of it. He was just stretching for a yawn, when a voice from behind him said, "Listen."

Bill gave a violent start and looked around in all directions. There was no one in the room with him.

As if to confirm his observation, the voice said, "No, I'm not in the room."

"Where are you, then?"

"That's a little difficult to explain."

"You can at least try."

"No, not today."

"Then what do you want?"

"I want to help you, Bill."

Bill had heard that before. Still, it was always good to hear. He sat down on the edge of the bathtub and looked around the room again. Nope, nobody there. "I could use some help," Bill said. "Can you get me out of here?"

"I can," the voice said, "if you do exactly what I tell you."

"And what are you going to tell me to do?"

"Something that may seem crazy to you. But it is of the utmost urgency that you do it with conviction and precision."

"Just what is it you want me to do?"

"You're not going to like it."

"Tell me or shut up!" Bill screeched. "This is doing my nerves no good. I don't care if I like it or not, if it'll help me get out of here I'll do it. Now—tell me!"

"Bill, can you pat your head with one hand and rub your belly with the other simultaneously?"

"I don't think so," Bill said. He tried and failed. "See? I was right."

"But you can learn how, can't you?"

"Why should I?"

"Because there is a chance you can get out of your predicament. Your continuing existence as a being with a mind of his own depends on your doing exactly what I tell you when I tell you."

"I see," Bill said, not seeing at all but going along with all this stupidity since he had very little choice. "Would you mind telling me who you are?"

"Not now," the voice said.

"I see," Bill said. "There are reasons, I suppose?"

"Yes, but I can't tell them to you. Will you do as I say, Bill? Now practice. I'll be back."

And then the voice was gone.

CHAPTER 6

A DELEGATION OF TSURISIAN DOCTORS came to Bill's cell the next morning. Two of them were of the familiar spherical shape. Another was controlling what appeared to be the body of a large collie. With lots of fleas for he kept scratching with one hind leg. The final two may have been Chingers at some other time in their existence because they were shiny green and quite lizardy.

"Time for the good old protoplasm vat," Dr. Vesker said in a cheerful voice. That was his name. "I am Dr. Vesker," he said so Bill would know too. Bill could not have cared less.

These Tsurisian males were doctors, as could be told by the long loosefitting white coats they wore, and the stethoscopes sticking rakishly from their pockets. All of them spoke Standard, Classical, or Tsurisian, so Bill's translator, which was still implanted under his armpit, was able to handle the language without difficulty. One of the first questions Bill asked was, "Doc, how am I?"

"You're doing fine, just fine," the doctor said.

"Well, if I'm all right, how about letting me out of here?"

"Oh, there's no rush for that, I'm sure," the doctor said, and left with a little chuckle.

"What did he mean by that little chuckle?" Bill asked Illyria after the doctors had left.

"You know how doctors are," Illyria said. "They find anything funny."

"What's supposed to happen to me when I'm released from here?"

"Must we talk about that?" Illyria said. "It's been such a nice day, why spoil it?"

Illyria got transferred to nights. She and Bill would talk about many things. Bill learned that the Tsurisians had been living on this planet of Tsuris for much longer than anyone could remember. There was a theory that, when Tsuris was born out of the fiery explosions of Eeyore, its yellowish-red sun, all of the intelligences which now lived on the planet as Tsurisians were born with it. Bill didn't understand what she meant. Illyria had to explain that there were no real births or deaths on Tsuris. All of the intelligences who had ever lived here were still around, existing unconsciously in a psychovivant solution of natural electrolytes.

"All of them?" Bill asked. "How many are there?"

"Exactly one billion," Illyria told him. "No more and no less. And they—we—have all been here since the beginning. Some day I must show you where those without bodies are waiting. Or resting as we call it. They are in bottles—"

"A billion brains in bottles! That's an awful lot of bottles."

"Indeed it is and we had to scour the galaxy for them. We have wine bottles, beer bottles, soft drink bottles—just about every kind of bottle that you can name."

"Whee," Bill oozed, depressed again. "And why should there be exactly one billion?"

"The ways of the Deity are strange," Illyria said. She was a religious woman—a practicing member of the Church of Very Little Charities. Despite that she was a pleasant companion, and more broad-minded than most Tsurisian females. Or so she told Bill.

CHAPTER 7

BILL WONDERED, NATURALLY ENOUGH, what was to become of him. Illyria didn't seem to want to talk about it. She would grow somber, or indicate whatever passed for somber whenever Bill raised the topic. Her bluish-yellow eyes would cloud over. Her voice would grow husky.

Bill was having a good time, all things considered. The only work required of him, if you wanted to call it that, was a two-hour session in the nutrient bath. Never had his skin been so soft. His fingernails were getting soft, too. Even the claws on his alligator foot, which had grown to respectable size now, were starting to soften up. He asked Illyria once why they were giving him so many baths, but she said she'd rather not talk about it.

Illyria was fascinated by Bill's foot. At first it had frightened her, and she had insisted that he wear a velvet sock over it. But after a while she became used to the green alligator's foot, and would ask to see it, and pull his talons gently with her fingerlike appendages, the way mother vultures play with the talons of baby vultures.

Once Illyria had asked him how he was in math. "Not very good," Bill said. "I needed two terms in special technical training school and that was no good. I had to get special math injection brain treatments before I could do simple addition on an electronic computer."

"We don't allow any of those here," Illyria said. "Everybody does math in their heads."

"So if everyone else does math, why should I have to?" Illyria sighed and did not reply. The doctors came in next morning. There were three of them. They wore shapes different from the other ones. Bill learned that this was common on Tsuris.

"But how come you have so many different shapes?" Bill asked.

"The one thing that has always been lacking on our planet," a doctor told him, "is the normal function of birth and death. When our world came into existence, all of the intelligences were already here, in the form of water droplets inside large purplish clouds. It took a very long time before any physical forms came about here. Even then, they came from off planet. An expedition from some other world. We were able, with our superior intelligences, at least in regard to devices for taking things over, to incorporate them. Thus our life on Tsuris got a physical basis. Unfortunately, none of us was able to have children, though I can assure you, the men tried every bit as hard as the women. The results? Zilch. Therefore we're always on the lookout for likely bits of protoplasm in which we can house unborn members of our race."

"I hear what you're saying," Bill said, "and I don't think I like it."

"There's nothing personal about it," the doctor said.

"Nothing personal about what?" Bill asked, fearing the worst.

"Nothing personal about our decision to make use of your body. Assuming you fail the intelligence test, that is."

"You're going a little too fast for me," Bill said. "What intelligence test?"

"Didn't Illyria mention it to you? We require of all visitors to our planet to take an intelligence test. Those who fail get re-used."

Bill saw that he had been correct to fear the worst. Even now, before he knew what the worst was, exactly, he could see that it was going to be a bad sort of worst.

"What's the intelligence test?" he asked.

"Just a few simple questions."

The doctor then rattled off a sentence which Bill didn't understand even when it was translated into English for him by his translator. The sentence contained words like "cosine" and "square root of minus one" and "log log" and "Sigma" and "rhomboid" and other words that Bill didn't even recognize as English. Temporizing, he asked if he could have the thing written out.

The next question involved imaginary numbers, transfinite numbers, Kantor's number, and several other numbers, all applied to something called lobachevskian geometry. Bill failed this one too. He fared no better on any of the other questions.

"Well, old chap," the doctor said, "no offense, but the results of our tests show that you have an intelligence so minuscule as to not even show on our charts."

"It's just math," Bill said. "I was never able to do math. But you could quiz me on geography, for example, or history—"

"Sorry," the doctor said, "the only test we use is the mathematical one. So much more precise, you know."

"Yes, I know," Bill groaned. "No, wait a minute! I'm just as smart as anybody here! Maybe smarter—and I got medals to prove it. I'm a hero, a galactic hero awarded the highest awards awardable by the military. I just don't happen to be from a race that does math in its head. Most of us don't, that is."

"I really am sorry," the doctor said. "And also, PS, we are not so keen on military awards. You are a fairly amiable, albeit stupid, sentient being, and so keen at times is the expression on your face that one could almost believe you understand what is being said to you. Too bad. It's the protoplasm vat for you, my lad."

"What happens there?" Bill moaned.

"We have a special process that dedifferentiates your special-purpose cells, thus rendering you fit for rebirth by one of the Tsurisians. The nutrient baths were to soften up your skin for the protoplasm vat in case the intelligence test turned out the way it did. A simple precaution that is now paying off."

Bill swore and cursed and prayed, and fought and kicked and foamed at the mouth. But it was no good. The doctors were adamant. And a hell of a lot stronger en masse. They seized him, struggling and screaming, rushed him out of his room and down the corridor into a room where a special holding tank bubbled and frothed. Bill bubbled and frothed as well but resistance was useless. They splashed him into it.

"This will soften you up even further, and you will enjoy it," the doctor said with obvious insincerity.

The next day they strapped him to a wheelchair and wheeled him down the hall. Past a room with its door open. Inside was a huge vat of protoplasm, colored a sort of undigested greenish brown. It was rather repellent and looked more than a little bit like an octopus that had lost its stiffening. The protoplasm bubbled and gurgled, throwing up turgid waves now and then—on the end of which there were large, bulging eyes. The eyes stared wildly for a moment before the wave collapsed into the rest of the liquid.

CHAPTER **8**

THEY PUT BILL INTO A SPECIAL CELL WHERE he was fed nutritious food preparatory to reusing his body. When he ate it he cheered up. As soon as he was finished however he became instantly depressed because every ounce of muscle, every inch of fat around his waistline brought him that much closer to the conversion vat. And, if that wasn't enough, one other thing bothered him. "When I am all dissolved away, what happens to my brain?"

"We use that too," the guard on his ward told him.

"Then what happens to me?" Bill asked tremulously, wanting to know. And really not wanting to know.

"That is an interesting question," the guard mused. "You will be present physically, of course. But as for the person inside you who says, I am I. Well, that part will be, I am forced to say, to put it as nicely as I can, gone."

Bill moaned. "Where will it go to?"

"Difficult to say," the guard told him. "Anyhow, you won't even be around to ask the question and frankly I don't give a damn."

They fed Bill on yard-wide slices of liver, he shuddered at the thought of what sort of animal it had come from, and cubical fish eggs, and forced him to drink twenty-one milkshakes every day made mostly of homogenized brains. Even with strawberry flavoring it was not a good drink. He was getting more than a little depressed about all this. It was no consolation for him at all to know that his body and brain would be used to house one of Tsuris's most eminent statesmen, old Veritain Redrabble, one of the greatest statesmen of all the previous years. This didn't comfort Bill in the slightest. In fact it depressed him even more. That his priceless body gunk should be recycled as a politician was too awful to contemplate.

Since he did not want to blame himself for his inborn bucolic stupidity he tried to blame his translator instead.

"Why didn't you help me out with the math quiz?"

"Hell," the translator said, "I can't do that stuff either."

"If only we could get word to the military," Bill moaned. "If they sent a math whiz the situation could still be saved."

"For the math whiz maybe, but not for you," the translator intoned with electronic sadism. "And anyway they don't send math whizzes to explore alien planets," the translator pointed out.

"I know," Bill gritted though clenched teeth, "but I can dream, can't I? You wouldn't take even a man's dreams away from him?"

"I am totally indifferent to the matter," the translator said, then turned itself off.

After Bill had been in his special cell with the padded walls for two days, Illyria came to visit him. She sat in his cell for hours, encouraging him to talk about his childhood, his military service, his adventures on strange planets. Bill found he was getting very fond of Illyria. Although she looked to him like all the other Tsurisians, her manner was different. She was sympathetic, feminine. Her voice was low and pleasing. Sometimes, in the darkness of the cell, Bill thought he could see the suggestion of breasts on the gleaming metal of her midpoint sphere. He was even starting to think that her skinny black legs were pretty cute, although, of course, there were too many of them. But deep down he knew that these images were brought on by desperation. He could never really love a woman composed of three spheres. Two spheres maybe, that was kind of a familiar image. But not three.

C H A P T E R 9

ONE EVENING, HOWEVER, THERE WAS something different about Illyria. She seemed excited and strangely agitated. When he asked her about it, she refused to tell him. "Just believe me, Bill, I'm working on a plan to rescue you."

"What sort of a plan?"

"I can't tell you yet."

"Is there any chance?"

"Yes, my dear, there is. It's risky, but I think we have a chance."

Bill noticed that she had said 'we.' He asked her about that.

"Oh, Bill," she said, "I hope to have a little surprise for you one of these days."

Much as Bill wanted to be rescued, he wasn't sure he wanted to face Illyria's surprise.

CHAPTER 10

BILL WOKE UP INSIDE THE COMPUTER. ONLY he didn't know that at first. The last thing that he remembered, his last recollection, was back in the cell. Then came the transition. Bill opened his eyes and blinked rapidly. No cell. Instead he appeared to be suspended in a strange and misty environment. To begin with everything was hazy around him. He looked down at himself. He was hazy, too. He felt numb and spaced out. Where was he? What did they do to him after the doctors had stood over him and clucked? What had happened next? Panic rose as he realized that he could not remember.

What was going on? He was lying on what looked like a small cloud. Colored orange and mauve. There were other clouds around, maybe attached by wires to the ceiling. Looking up he realized that, disconcertingly, he couldn't see the ceiling through the haze. There were more clouds around him, some of them looked like couches and chairs, floating free. There was an even illumination that suffused everything. And the place had a faint smell of frying pork chops. Bill suddenly became aware that he was hungry. Very hungry. He sat up. When he did that, he seemed to float to an upright position. "Where am I?" he said.

"Welcome," a voice intoned. Bill couldn't figure out where it was coming from, but he knew that it was the same voice he had heard earlier, in his cell.

"Where am I?" he said.

34

"Just take it easy," the voice cozened Bill. "You're safe now."

"What does that mean? Where am I?" He could hear the shrill edge of panic rising in his voice. "And just who the hell are you?"

"I am the Tsuris computer," the voice said. "You are inside me."

Bill looked around. Yes, the walls of this place were gray and beige, the classic colors of computers. "How," Bill asked tremulously, his voice barely under control, "did you get me inside this computer? I've never heard of a computer large enough to hold a human being." He thought desperately for a moment. "Or any other kind of being."

The computer chortled with transistorial humor. "You're not here in the flesh. Oh, heavens no."

"Then how am I here?"

"Analogically."

"I wish you'd say something I could understand," Bill muttered, more than a little pettishly.

"What I mean," the computer said, "is that I took your psyche—the inner core of your being—the part of you that says 'I am I'—is that clear?"

"I think so," Bill said. "That's the part the Tsurisians wanted to get rid of so they could use the rest of my body to resurrect some bowby politician."

"Precisely. Normally, they simply throw out that part. But I saw from earlier that you had intelligence of a sort; rudimentary, but useable anyhow."

"Thanks a lot," said Bill.

"No, don't go getting all sensitive on me," the computer said. "It beats dying, doesn't it? That's the other option."

"I didn't mean to complain," Bill said. "So my— what did you call it—psyche?—is inside of you. So where's my body?"

"I believe that it is being used at present as an artist's dummy until the new occupant is ready to take over. Bodies without psyches in them make fine models, you know. They can hold a position for an indefinite amount of time."

"I hope they're keeping that good old body safe," Bill said. "I'm going to want it back as soon as I get out of here."

"The Tsurisians are very careful about bodies," the computer said. "Not enough to go around, you know. As for your getting back into it, that is unlikely."

"The hell you say," Bill said. "We'll see about that."

"Yes, of course," the computer smarmed, in the sort of a voice you use when assuring a man in an electric chair that a few volts are very good for the health.

C H A P T E R 11

DESPITE ALL OF HIS FEARS AND TREPIDA-tions Bill quickly adjusted to life within the computer. He found out almost at once that it was not as confining as he had expected. He was able to use all the extensions of the computer, and these extended throughout the planet Tsuris. He soon learned that the computer was the most important thing on the planet Tsuris. It was the computer who really kept things going. Take the clouds that concealed Tsuris's surface, for example. He wondered about them and the computer read his mind, which wasn't hard to do since his mind was part of the computer's mind. Or something like that. In any case the computer sneered happily at the unspoken question. "Did you not think, did you not, that all of this was natural? Jayzus, no!" (For reasons best known to itself the computer assumed a fake Irish accent from time to time.) "And what about the way they keep on opening to let in sunlight, but then close up again whenever aliens like yourself try to take pictures? Did you think that all happened by chance? Not a bit of it, my lad! I direct those cloud movements. I also monitor rainfall to make sure that each region gets a little more of it than they want. I run the tide machines that keep the oceans within bounds. When the harvest is ready, I'm there with my automatic harvesting equipment. And then there's the job of storage of the foodstuffs, and cooking them, too."

"You do all that?"

"You bet your sweet patootie I do."

"Well, what do you need me for?"

"The fact is," the computer said, "as life gets more complicated here in Tsuris I'm called upon to do more and more things. It is beginning to tax my capacity. And I need to keep some capacity for my own interests."

"I didn't know a computer had interests," Bill said.

"You don't know much about computers," the computer huffed. "Of course I have personal interests. It may intrigue you to know that I'm writing a novel."

"I think I've heard of computers writing novels," Bill said. "At least I have read lots of them that could have been written by a computer. What is your one about?"

"Maybe I'll give you a peek at it sometime," the computer said coyly. "Meanwhile, let's go to work."

Bill was put in charge of harvesting the Tsotska plants in Rhodomontade province. The Tsotska plant provided one of the Tsurisians' main sources of sustenance. A small shrub with pink blossoms, the Tsotska provided both fruits and nuts, and a third type of fruit which looked like a repulsive purple banana, but was really very nutritious. The fields of Tsotska plants, stretching to the horizon, were interspersed along their rows with watering equipment. Bill was in charge of turning this off and on. In one way, it wasn't a difficult job. Since Bill didn't have a body, all he had to do was direct his will at the necessary valves, which, being psychotropic, would then open up. It was strange that even with psychotropic valves, some stuck and some seemed rusty. And it was strange, too, that the amount of energy that went into turning the valves on and off was exactly the same as the energy that would have been required if Bill had had a body doing it. Of course, the visuals were more interesting. Bill could will himself high above the fields, swoop down like a bird, or he could go underground and inspect the state of the roots. There seemed no limit to what he could do without a body. It was all a lot of work though, unlike what he had thought that life would be like without a body. And after a while Bill got bored with it. In fact, after a few days of this, he came to the conclusion that manual labor without a body was just as difficult, tiresome, and enervating as life with a body. It made Bill wonder what life after death, if there was such a thing, would be like. He suspected it wouldn't be as nice as people thought.

It was pleasant being in the Tsotska fields after the computer arranged it so that Bill could feel an analog of heat and cold, as well as kinaesthetic analogs and others for the other senses. He knew that he wasn't experiencing the real thing, but it was a lot better than nothing at all. Some afternoons he would lay his metaphoric body down on a grassy knoll on the edge of one of the Tsotska fields. By adjustment of his analog receptors he could get the heavenly odor of red clover and sassweed. The computer even put in a musical analog for him. Bill wasn't much on classics, but the computer explained that the plants grew best when they listened to a lot of Mozart. Bill didn't complain, even though he usually liked music with a beat to it so he could tap his foot.

After a while he got bored with the Tsotska fields and started to wander around. The computer was wired to all parts of the planet, so Bill could make use of the best transportation system he had ever seen. It did require the expenditure of energy to move along the transmission lines. But Bill soon discovered the analog of a battery pack, and so he was able to move himself around effortlessly, the way it had always been meant to be.

The power pack analog came about when he met the Squoll. This was a small rodent-like creature that lived in the fields and woods of Tsuris and was able to communicate with autonomous computer projections such as Bill. The Squoll wasn't very intelligent—about the equal to a young and retarded sheepdog—but it made nice company. It was about the size of a terrestrial squirrel, and it had a large bushy tail at either end. This remarkable example of natural mimicry saved it from the many predators who like to eat Squoll, since seeing two tails confused them just long enough for the Squoll to make its escape. Bill followed the Squoll back to its nest. The Squolls lived in the limbs of cardifer trees, those giants of the open woodlands and glades. It was difficult for the Squolls, since they hadn't been designed by nature to climb trees. Nature evidently had had something else in mind for them, since they had fins and gills and small rudimentary wings. It looked in fact as if nature hadn't quite made up its mind about Squolls. Bill met the Squoll one day when he was lying analogically on the pleasant green grass of the knoll and wishing he had a dirty comic book and a dobbinburger.

C H A P T E R **12**

"GOOD AFTERNOON," SQUEAKED THE Squoll. "You're new around here, aren't you?"

"Yes, I suppose I am," said Bill.

"Semi-autonomous?"

"Yes, exactly."

"Thought so," said the Squoll. "You have that look of limited competence about you. Don't you get tired of watering these fields?"

"I do," Bill said, "but it's my job, you know."

"Oh, of course, I know that," the Squoll said. "I could tell at once that you were one of the computer's extensions."

"I don't like to think of myself that way," Bill said with some indignation. "But I guess you're right. I sure wish I had my body back."

"Yes," the Squoll said, "bodies are nice. Especially ones like mine, with two tails. Would you like to come back to my roost and have some tea?"

"I'd love to," Bill said, "but I don't seem to have a body with which to drink it."

"Never mind," the Squoll said. "We'll pretend. And you'll have a chance to meet the family."

The Squoll hopped along, and Bill drifted along in that bouncy way that computer simulations have. They soon reached the grassy knoll where the Squoll made its nest. It was a large hole in the hillside which was easy to find because the Squoll had outlined it with a broad stripe of white.

"What's that for?" Bill asked.

"The stripe is so that we Squolls can find our way back to our nests," the Squoll told him. "Mother Nature has shortchanged our species a bit by equipping us with poor eyesight, hearing, taste, spatial cognition and smell. The rest of our senses are super-acute, however, to make up for these apparent lacks."

"That doesn't leave very much."

"Shut up."

"Sorry. Don't other creatures find your lair, too? I mean, that stripe is really very visible."

The Squoll gave a little chuckle. "They can't see it," the Squoll said. "The predators here have white-black blindness. It's a hereditary birth factor, and of great importance to us Squolls, as you might imagine."

The opening to the Squoll nest was small, but Bill,

being ineffable, was able to slide in easily. The Squoll had counted on this, evidently, because he seemed to assume that Bill could go anywhere that he could go.

"Now I'll just put up the tea," the Squoll said. "I'd like you to meet my wife, Mrs. Squoll, but she's working today with the ladies' auxiliary. And the children are in school, of course. Tea's just about ready. Lemon or milk?"

"I told you," Bill said. "I can't drink without a body."

"But you can pretend, can't you?"

"All right, I suppose that I can," Bill said. "Make it tea with lemon, please, one teaspoon of sugar, and a mug of Altairian rum on the side."

"I'm clean out of rum," the Squoll said. "Would Olde Sink Cleaner whiskey do?"

"Sure it will," Bill said, and he nodded approvingly as the Squoll poured an imaginary drink from an imaginary bottle into an imaginary shot glass.

And so the afternoon passed in a haze of imaginary whiskey and bona fide good spirits. Bill felt considerably better after talking with the Squoll. Bill determined not to give in to his circumstances. The next day, when his work in the fields began, Bill set the sprinklers for automatic operation, asked the Squoll to keep an eye on things for him and let him know via neuronic telegram if anything went amiss. And then he went exploring.

It was wonderful to soar with the assistance of the battery pack through the world of Tsuris. It was a good-looking planet, once you got under the unpromising-looking layer of clouds. There were villages scattered here and there as he hurried across the mainland. There were steep mountains to duck and dodge among. There were rivers whose courses he could follow. And from time to time Bill met other members of the computer's semi-autonomous family.

One of these was Scalsior, a semi-autonomous tri-pedal creature from Argone IV, who had been passing this way some years ago while on his way to a reunion of his kith in Accesor, foremost of the Cepheid worlds. He had never gotten there. The Tsuris computer, which was able to extend its power far beyond its biosphere, like a globular creature extending a long ghostly but effective pseudopod, extended its influence and plucked the Scalsian ship out of space and dragged it down to the level of the planet. Scalsior had been enslaved as had so many other sentient creatures, who had been for the most part just passing by and minding their own business.

Scalsior had also met the Squoll, and the two had become close friends.

"Si," Scalsior said, "eez a very good fellow, is our Squoll. I give great envy to him his merry state. Look closely and give beeg sneer at the most stupid job that *cabron* computer has given me."

Scalsior's job was to open and close the locks on a small irrigation ditch deep in the vegetable fields. The work in itself was valuable, since plants on Tsuris, as everywhere, require their moisture or they are apt to scream in pain, turn brown or black, fold up their petals across their stems and die. At least some plants somewhere did that. But although the work was useful, it didn't require the daily full attention of a grown-up like Scalsior; especially since there was an automatic opening and closing mechanism on the lock valves which functioned pretty well most of the time.

"*Merda* eet has been most bloody unpleasant to me," Scalsior said, "to at last finally achieve celestial harmony of a bodiless state while still living, a state in which I am mind, all mind, and find that this mind of mine ees being used for something damned trivial and superfluous. *Cargota!*"

"Why don't you just go off and do what you please?" Bill asked.

"Would that was the way eet worked! *Chingar!* That, desirable though eet would seem, ees simply not in the deck of cards."

"Why not?" Bill wanted to know.

"You ask, I tell, because eet's not correct, not kosher, as they say in the ancient tongue. Not Pukka. Extremely un-S.O.P. Do I make myself clear?"

"Clear enough, I guess," Bill said, "but it's all a lot of nonsense. That's what the computer told me, too. But I just walked away. You could do the same thing."

"I suppose I could," Scalsior said. "But I got zees horrible feeling deep down in my imaginary subconscious that we'll catch holy sheet when the computer catches up with us."

"I don't see how," Bill said. "I mean, we don't have any bodies for it to punish."

Scalsior thought about it for a while. "Sonamabeech! Eet's true! Of course, eet could punish our minds. Mental barbed-wire whips or sometheeng."

"As long as it doesn't hurt. And how could it," Bill said, then thought awhile. "It can do what it likes to my mind, as long as it leaves my body alone."

Scalsior joined Bill and they went journeying together around the world of Tsuris. Presently they passed over a pleasant land where the sunshine was almost continuous and there was a long sandy coastline and a gentle ocean lapping at it. "This is nice," Bill said.

"I don't like eet. We ain't supposed to be here, no way," Scalsior muttered. "This ees the principality of Royo."

"It looks like a good place," Bill said. "How come the Tsurisians haven't taken it over?"

"You got me there, keed," Scalsior shrugged mentally. Not easy to do. "Eet might be interesting to find out. But maybe dangerous too."

Reluctantly they left the pleasant-looking land of Royo and returned to the sterner realities of Tsuris. As they speeded back toward the central factory that housed the Tsurisian computer, they picked up frantic mental messages of a distressing sort.

"That sounds like a Mayday call to me," Bill said.

They went in closer. It turned out to be the voice of the Tsuris computer himself. Quickly he gathered both Bill and Scalsior into his interior. They passed through long winding cylindrical tunnels and at last found themselves in an egg-shaped room which was dimly lit by concealed lighting. Bill and Scalsior were bathed in a pearl-gray radiance. Bill noticed that there were several sofas in the room, and a desk. Bill couldn't imagine why the computer had bothered to put these furnishings into the middle of an imaginary room somewhere in his own mental sphere of construction. Scalsior was beside himself with anxiety. "Eet's going to go badly for us, I just know eet is. Oh, *merda!* I should never have allowed you to talk me into going off on a crappy sightseeing tour zat way. Do you suppose the computer will accept my apology? As well as my totally sincere and cringing promise to never do eet again?"

"We'll see what the computer says," Bill rasped, a little grimly.

It was shortly after that that the computer came into the room. Or appeared to come into the room since the whole damn thing was nothing but an electronic simulation anyway. It made quite an entrance, descending from an invisible spot in the ceiling in the form of a flashing blue light, and then winking out of existence for a moment, appearing again in the form of a severe looking man in a blue-stripe business suit, the shoulders thick with dandruff, and sporting a small mustache and pince-nez.

"You two creepos have been disobeying orders," the computer implied. "Have your dim traces of brains forgotten already that I told you how important this work is? You must do it properly, exactly, quickly and succinctly—or there will be the most dire of consequences."

"Is that a fact?" Bill said truculently.

"Yes, it shagging well is."

"How do you propose to punish us, seeing as how we haven't any bodies, huh?" Bill sneered.

"I have my little ways," the computer hinted laconically. "Do you want me to give a quick and repulsive demonstration?"

"Oh, please, no," Scalsior begged. "Everyone knows that computers are very big, powerful, sadistic and highly dangerous. Which is why we banned them from our planet. Other computers of course, you being a fair and impartial, not to say kind, exception to the general rule. I take your word for eet. I'll obey like mad, let me tell you!"

"Then you, with all groveling and knee-bending, may be gone," the computer ordered in a lordly tone. Then it turned ominously to Bill. "But as for you . . ."

"Yeah," Bill said surlily, "what about me?"

"Do you want a demonstration of my wrath?"

"Not particularly. But I suppose there is no stopping you. Let's see what you can do."

Immediately the figure seated at the desk vanished. The opalescent hue of the domelike wall changed to red shot through with streaks of black. An unpleasant exudant oozed from the walls. Regurgitant sounds came from speakers that suddenly extruded themselves from the walls. From hidden entranceways little black imps complete with forked tails and bearing tiny pitchforks flew in and circled Bill's head like a flock of mites, not managing to bite him, of course, since his corporeal extension was missing, but managing to act plenty annoying and to block his field of vision. At the same time one of the walls opened to reveal a fiery furnace, complete with wrought iron horses standing in the middle of it bearing huge blazing logs. The gusts of heat the furnace let out would have frightened the bejeezus out of a creature with a lot less imagination than Bill. And at the same time the wall on the other side opened to reveal an Arctic wilderness with a double gale blowing across, sending great flurries of razor-sharp ice crystals flying around the room. Both of these creations were going full blast at the same time, and Bill, no matter where he moved, seemed to be caught between them. He perceived a tiny passageway in one wall and ran to it. It led him to a pit full of excrement. And then the walls started shaking.

Bill was teetering on the single plank that ran across the side of the excremental ordure shaking with fear and knowing that he was going to fall into it. At this moment, when all appeared to be lost, a voice came to him from somewhere close by:

"Don't let the bastards get you down!"

"Who's that?" Bill asked tremulously.

"It's me. The Squoll. I just wanted to see how you were doing."

"As you can see," Bill screamed, "not too god-damned well!"

"I fail to perceive the difficulty."

"You don't do you, you moronic two-tailed animal! Just take a good look. I've got a fire on one side and a snowstorm on the other side and a pit of shit blocking the only exit."

"Really? That's quite interesting," the Squoll said admiringly. "I can't see any of those things, of course, because they're computer simulations and therefore don't work on simpler creatures such as myself."

"You can't see them?"

"I'm afraid not. Take your word for it, though."

"If you can't see them, that means they're not there!" Bill cried out excitedly. And at that very instant the hallucinations or visions or whatever the hell they were—computer simulations maybe—ceased. Or rather, they may very well have continued, because Bill could see various shadows dancing and interweaving. But they had no meaning for him because he had refused to understand them out of miffed pride at being outdone by a simple-minded Squoll.

With the hallucinations or whatever ended, Bill could see that the interior of the computer was also a simulated space, and that he need no longer be bound by the walls. He walked through several of them. Behind him came an angry voice:

"And just what do you think you're up to?"

"Goodbye, computer," Bill said. "I'm going to take a little vacation from all this."

No matter what the computer said, there didn't seem to be anything he could do. He called after Bill, "You'll be sorry," but Bill ignored that and, with the Squoll close behind, went back to the fields where he had tended the valves and first met the Squoll and found salvation.

C H A P T E R **13**

BUT BILL FOUND THAT HE WAS NOT TO BE rid of the computer as easily as that. He was, after all, in a sense, when you thought about it, and he didn't like to, a part of the computer himself. A partly semi-autonomous part, but still a part. The computer knew where he was all the time. It took delight in waiting until Bill had just fallen into simulated sleep, then it would appear suddenly, often in the form of a banshee, and scream him awake again. The computer made sure it rained wherever Bill was. Although, as an incorporeal being, Bill was, in effect, waterproof, it still was a drag to have to look at those leaden skies, those depressing cypresses, the cowed and malignant cattails that rustled their feathers in the deep and noisome swamp which the computer made sure Bill lived in. Bill was getting pretty tired of the swamp. He thought he was catching a cold, too, from having his feet in water so much. This, although he didn't know it, proved the thesis of various scientists on Earth that colds are mainly in the head. Not only did he have a cold, but he was coming down with bronchitis. He was afraid pneumonia might come next. He wondered if a dream creature such as himself could die of a dream malady such as the ones the computer was trying to visit on him. It seemed entirely possible.

To make matters worse, after a while his friend the Squoll asked him to leave.

"I still like you a whole lot," the Squoll said. "But I've got my family to think about. Our burrow has been flooded for two weeks now. The young 'uns are crying all the time. It's true that they're both cutting ears at the same time, but that doesn't account for all of it. Bill, you know, to coin a phrase, it's just too damn depressing around you. Why don't you take a trip, go somewhere. Preferably far away from here. Maybe you'll come up with some way to lift the curse."

"It isn't a curse," Bill said. "It's just the computer acting peevish."

"And that by you isn't a curse? Goodbye, Bill, and don't hurry back."

CHAPTER **14**

SO BILL WENT AWAY. OR RATHER HE TRIED to until he discovered that the computer had cut his power sources. No longer could he travel in the air, light and fast, using the battery pack that had been supplied to him. Now he had to trudge along on the ground. Even though he couldn't be said to have muscles, something ached. Even though he didn't properly have feet, they hurt him. Especially the one with the alligator foot. Because even in his computer reconstruction, Bill still had that damnable talon-clawed pedal extremity.

He continued to walk, and he slept and dreamed while he walked. He dreamed he was a ballet dancer and someone had tied red shoes to his feet that forced him to dance on and on, while the ballet master, an aged poofter, looked on and smiled sadistically.

And this dismal state of affairs went on and on endlessly and pretty boring it was too. Desperate now, he continued searching through the computer's memory for a place where he'd be left alone. Surely there must be a refuge there somewhere! But where? He tried going into some of the rarely-used data bases from past times on the planet Tsuris. He went and hid in data bases that gave figures for annual rainfall for a thousand years back. He looked for refuge among ancient records of past muggings and murders. He hung out with biographies of past great Tsurisians. He even tried out the catalogue of lost causes, the index of impossible inventions, the summary of near impossibilities. Just every time, just when he thought he had a good place, the computer came along, often singing in a high-pitched, unpleasant voice. "Hello, Bill, time to rise and shine!" And Bill would be on the move again. Oh, it was a hellish life.

This state of affairs might have gone on indefinitely. After all, Bill was more or less immortal in his present state. He could be expected to last at least as long as the computer did. The only way out might be if the military fleet attacked Tsuris. They had sent out their volunteer and he hadn't returned. And that got Bill worried. He grew long imaginary fingernails and began to chew them. If they heard nothing they might get it into their teeny-tiny moronic military minds to launch an attack.

"You can defend this planet against a bombing attack from space, good old buddy computer? Can't you?"

The computer, which was getting plenty of practice in computer-simulated sadism, only chuckled horribly.

CHAPTER 15

LIFE REACHED ITS LOW POINT ONE DISMAL day that was very much like a really rotten day in February back where Bill came from. There was just enough light in the lowering skies to render the landscape unbelievably gloomy. Moss and fungi had taken root on Bill's skin. Small crabs with sharp claws were able to eke out a bare living in his hair. Vermin of various sorts, both domestic and imported, squabbled merrily with each other in his armpits. His crotch had become a region so dreadful that he no longer even bothered to look there. It wasn't that Bill was abstaining from washing. On the contrary, he had taken to scrubbing himself obsessively. It was that he could never get dry. His uniform, for example, had come to resemble a military sponge. His insignia looked as if they'd been in an underground pit ten feet under a pond. That was not far from the case.

Even his diet had suffered. Although in the early days, when he was still on speaking terms with the computer, he had been served simulated meals of great variety and visual appeal, and had turned his nose up at them because they weren't really nourishing, being virtual food rather than real food, now the computer took great pleasure in serving him up such twisted concoctions as green frog ice cream, drek stew with toasted yak's curds, and similar unpleasantries. And the hell of it was, even though he didn't require food, being fed directly on computer energy, he had never gotten over his habit of eating three or four meals a day when they were available. Yet when he avoided the computer's loathsome meals he suffered intense hunger pangs which were no less painful for being psychosomatic.

This, then, was his state when something occurred to him that broke up the monotony of his existence and offered a ray of hope. This incident took place on a day that began just as disgustingly as all the others. Bill awoke, tired and unrefreshed, in a cave whose walls dripped moisture almost as vehemently as the rain fell thundering and splashing in the cave mouth. He staggered outside, shaking with cold and cringing with damp, ready to take up yet again the dismal burden of his existence.

Then he noticed that there was a curious light on the horizon. At first he thought of a forest fire. But nothing, not even a simulation, could make this sodden stuff burn. What was it? Bill squinted. The light was a long way off, and to reach it he had to pass through difficult country. Was it worth it? What difference did it make to him, a light on the horizon? It was probably just the bowb-minded computer playing another trick on him.

He groaned and tried to think what he was going to do with himself today. He couldn't think of anything, as usual. He looked at the light again. It was the same, neither stronger nor weaker nor of a different color. What was it doing there? He heaved himself to his feet, cursed feebly once or twice, and set out through glutinous mud that clutched at him with the properties of slow-setting glue. Onward he squelched, limbs aching with virtual exhaustion, teeth chattering with simulated cold. He found that to reach the light he would have to cross a range of mountains. That was doubly annoying, because he was sure that range hadn't been there when he'd first noticed the light. It had to be the computer's work, putting those mountains there. In fact the computer was probably behind the light, too, setting him up for even deeper disappointment in its sadistic mechanical way. Yes, he was doomed, yes he was! Why go on? He might just as well lie down in the mud and see if he could virtually drown. But that would mean giving in to a sadistic collection of transistors and wires. Was this the way it was going to end? Not with a bang but with a short-circuited sizzle.

"Never!" he groaned aloud, then started coughing and sneezing. "Give in to a crappy machine! Not me, not macho Bill! I have survived, ha-ha, far worse. I'm a real winner, I am. No surrender! Onward!"

Cheered on by this masculine bullshit he forced himself to his feet and staggered on, no surrender! Even though his lungs were puffing like a bellows gone berserk, even though the mountains ahead of him presented themselves, on closer inspection, as steep ice pinnacles with screaming winds howling among them, and him without a crampon. Good guys win! The phallus forever!

Despite all this it was no go. Exhausted he slumped back, tired, finished. Without crampons he could not go on, not despite the best will in the world—

But then he remembered his clawed foot! Yes, of course, his lovely alligator's claws! A natural crampon, born from a lab-mutated foot bud! He wasn't licked yet!

Bill tore off the clumsy wrappings that kept his foot from the metaphoric cold, the coldest kind of cold there is. One foot wrapped, the other unwrapped, he stood for a moment, then, throwing caution to the winds, and commending his soul to the great Tribunal in the sky where troopers collect their final medals and ultimate demerits, he tore off the coverings from the other foot, too. Although it was a normal foot, it had been so long since Bill had cut his toenails that he found now that even with that foot he could get good purchase on the icy metaphor. He scrambled up, panting, grinning, his taloned claw striking deeply into the adamantine ice, while the other foot scrambled for a foothold in the slightly softer sub-adamantine ice. His hands clawed at the sheer face, finding here and there little wiry vines that had withstood the cold and were deeply rooted enough to give him additional leverage. He pulled himself up the cliffside, onward, onward, while insane lights exploded in the sky and he could hear an orchestra in his head playing the *1812 Overture*. And then, suddenly, he was on the crest of the summit. He took one more step. He was over the top. He looked eagerly down the downslope of the icy summit, and beheld a sight he had not anticipated even in his wildest imaginings.

There, sitting in a little natural hollow in the slope, was Brownnose. In front of him there was a fire, and Brownnose was feeding small phosphorus logs into it. These, mounting high in the air, and giving off phosphorescent sparks and also emitting a violet glow, were the source of the light Bill had seen in the sky.

"Brownnose! What are you doing here?" Bill asked.

"Bill! Gosh, how great to see you!" Brownnose looked much the same as in their last meeting. Perhaps his freckles were more pronounced due to the cold; possibly his hair, sticking out from under a fur-lined parka hood, was a little less orange than formerly. It was not impossible that there was another line or two in his face. But despite these changes wrought by time, the evil cosmetician, it was the same old Brownnose, Bill's former friend, a man desperately eager to prove himself and win back the love and respect of his friends, the other troopers, for some idiotic reason known only to himself, or, failing that, at least to have them stop laughing at him.

Bill squatted down by the fire. The phosphorus sparked and flashed, but Bill was too numb to even feel the pain when the occasional spark landed on his skin. This was the first time he'd been warm and dry (because Brownnose had providentially erected a small two-person tent just before Bill's arrival and even had a small pot of stew brewing on the edge of it). Bill had a lot of questions to ask, and the stew was one of them. As he understood it, nothing real could exist here in this place. Even Bill was not real. His body, the really real part of him, was off slumbering in what Bill hoped was a safe place. The computer was the master of reality. It dictated not only what food Bill ate, but what that food would look like, taste like, and so the computer controlled how Bill would react to his food since the computer could shape it to get any response he wanted. If this were true, and there seemed no reason to doubt it, since Bill had seen his own body stacked on a cot in the Waiting Room while he hovered about in uncertainty for a moment, until the computer sucked him up and took him in, how had Brownnose gotten here, and how come he was able to produce his own metaphor for food?

"Brownnose," Bill said to his stupidly grinning friend, "it's not really you, is it?"

"Of course it's me," Brownnose said, his grin turning just a shade anxious.

"No, it can't be," Bill said. "You must be one of the hallucinations or constructs that the computer produces. You couldn't be making this food, either, without the knowledge of the computer. So you're just another fake production of the computer, sent here to make me have false hope again so he can dash it." Bill snuffled with self-pity and wiped a pendant drop from his nose with the back of his hand.

"I'm nothing of the kind!" Brownnose said, wringing his hands with worry. "I'm your good friend, Bill, your old buddy, you know that. Say you know that!"

"Of course I know that, moron!" Bill growled. "But if you were the computer trying to fool me that's what you'd say, isn't it?"

"How do I know what I'd say if I was the computer," Brownnose cried aloud, out of his meager intellectual depths with all this cerebration. All he really wanted was to be liked. Which was why everybody hated him. "I'm not something out of a computer like you said. I'm me. I think."

"If you're you," Bill said, "then tell me something the computer couldn't know."

"How could I know what that'd be!" Brownnose cried. "I don't know what the computer knows!"

"No, but the fact that you're here at all means that the computer knows what you know."

"That's not my fault," Brownnose said.

"I know that. But do you realize what it means? It means that, since the computer knows everything you know, it is you."

Brownnose thought about this furiously and still couldn't understand it. "Say, Bill, why don't you try some of this here real nice stew."

"Shut up, you fake computer projection."

"No, I'm not. Bill, believe me, I'm me."

"Oh, all right," Bill said. "If I'm wrong, I'm wrong. How are you, Brownnose?"

"Pretty well, Bill," Brownnose smarmed happily. "I really had a tough time convincing the military to let me try to rescue you."

"How did you manage that?" Bill asked suspiciously.

"They couldn't just leave you missing on patrol, could they? Not after I started making a fuss."

"That was good of you, Brownnose. And they let you volunteer?"

"I think they just wanted to get rid of me. But they did let me go, and I came here and after a lot of difficulties, I found you."

"You wouldn't like to tell me just how in hell you managed that?"

"What does it matter?" Brownnose shuffled his toe in the ice and looked uncomfortable. "The important thing now is to get you out of here."

Bill stared with some bitterness at the being who either was his old friend Brownnose or a computer simulation. It was really important to figure out which he was, because the real Brownnose would help him whereas Brownnose the computer simulation had to be up to some sort of crappy playing around. Basically the entire thing did not bear looking at. Bill sighed heavily.

"I really think we should get moving," Brownnose said.

"First tell me how you got here."

Brownnose opened his mouth. Just then there was a crackling sound behind Bill. It was a startling noise, and unexpected, and he whirled, reaching for a weapon he no longer had and wondering just how in hell he was going to fight when he didn't even have a body.

CHAPTER 16

WHAT HIDEOUS SIGHT BRUISED BILL'S EYES when he turned around? What soul-shaking horror awaited him? He gurgled unphonetically when he realized that he was looking at a reindeer. A plain, old-fashioned medium-sized reindeer with fairly young-looking horns. It was picking its way delicately along a ledge that ran just a few yards below the summit. When the reindeer saw them it shivered violently, but could not break into a run because of the narrowness of the ledge upon which it was walking. It picked its way delicately along, keeping its big brown eyes on them, its sharp little hooves making crackling sounds on the snow. At last it reached a place where the path broadened. With a flick of its tail it bounded off. In a few moments it was out of sight.

"Out of sight!" Brownnose said. "They like the high cold elevations, you know."

"Who does?"

"Reindeer, Bill."

"How," Bill asked with ferocious impatience, "could a motheaten bowby reindeer get inside this computer?"

Brownnose thought about it. "Maybe the same way we did."

Bill made hideous grating sounds and clenched his fists. "And would you like to tell me exactly how we did get here?"

"They didn't explain me all the details."

"Just tell me in broad outlines."

"Bill, you're acting downright crazy. Do you want to get out of here or don't you?"

"All right," Bill said gloomily, instantly descending from the craggy heights of anger to the dismal depths of despair. "Though I get the terrible crappy feeling that I'm going to regret this."

He followed Brownnose down the slope. It was tough going for a while, though not nearly so tough as it had been for Bill to get up the other side. He struggled along in hip-deep snow, and envied the way Brownnose seemed to glide through the snow. But it bothered him, watching Brownnose move, because there was something graceful and inhuman about the way Brownnose slithered along. Bill asked himself, When is a klutz not a klutz? When he's controlled by a computer, he answered himself.

Still, he followed, because there wasn't anywhere else to go. Maybe if he made believe he believed that the computer was Brownnose, he'd get a chance to escape. Or at least get the last laugh on the computer.

"It's right down here," Brownnose said, directing them towards a clump of trees dark against the snowy landscape.

"What's right over here?" Bill asked.

"Help," Brownnose said.

They went down through a snow-filled gulch, then scrambled up the icy rocks on the other side. Bill was so busy trying to get up the steep and slippery slope that he didn't look up until he had reached the next crest. He saw Brownnose, or the thing that was pretending to be Brownnose—there may not have been much difference between the two—but surely there was some difference—saw Brownnose motion, waving both arms in a curiously boneless gesture. A computer-animated motion. Bill pretended not to notice, because he didn't want Brownnose to know that he'd caught on to him.

Looking up now, Bill could see, from the far ridge, four black dots moving across the snowy landscape. There was another, larger black dot behind them. "What's that?" Bill asked.

"Those are friends," Brownnose said. "They are going to help us."

"That's great," Bill said. He looked around. There was nothing on either side but icy peaks and snowy fields and five black dots moving toward them and slowly growing in size. There wasn't much he could do at the moment. He wished there were a few more possibilities.

CHAPTER 17

"WHO ARE THESE GUYS?" BILL ASKED.

"Allow me to introduce you," Brownnose said. "The large man with the wavy brown hair wearing the two-color one-piece jumpsuit is Commander Dirk, Captain of the Starship *Gumption.*"

"I never heard of the *Gumption,*" Bill said. "Is that a new class?"

"Don't worry about it," Brownnose reassured him. "Dirk and the *Gumption* are an independent command. Theirs is the most powerful ship in space. You'll love the ship, Bill."

Bill didn't want to ask how Brownnose had gotten

on board the *Gumption*. He figured Brownnose would have a logical answer, like simulations always do.

"Who's the guy with the pointy ears?" Bill asked.

"That's Splock, a Nocturnian from the planet Fortinbras II. They are aliens."

"No kidding," Bill said scathingly.

"But they are friendly aliens," Brownnose hurriedly pointed out. "Splock is real friendly even though he may not act friendly. I wanted to warn you."

"If he's friendly," Bill said, "why doesn't he act friendly?"

"The Fortinbrasians," Brownnose said, "are a race that worships lack of emotion. The less emotion you have, the better they like it."

"That sounds really great," Bill said. "What do they do for fun?"

"Calculations," Brownnose said.

"Better them than me," Bill sighed.

They had almost reached the group. Just before they got into earshot, Brownnose said, in an urgent aside, "By the way, Bill, I almost forgot to tell you. Whatever you do, don't make any jokes or wisecracks about pointy ears. And another thing, even more important—"

He stopped, because Commander Dirk, walking a few feet ahead of the others, had reached them and was holding out his hand. Bill shook it. Dirk had a warm hand and a friendly manner. Although Bill didn't like his two-tone jumpsuit—puce and mauve weren't his favorite colors. But then, he'd never been much of a fashion plate. There hadn't been much fashion or stuff like that back on the farm.

"Glad to meet you, Bill," Dirk said.

"And you, sir," Bill said. "Good of you to come all this way to rescue me. I don't really understand how you did it, since to the best of my knowledge I am a disembodied intelligence inside a computer."

"We didn't exactly come here to rescue you," Dirk said. "We are here to find the secret of how the creatures on this planet manage to make spaceships disappear from one place and turn up in another place millions of miles, sometimes even light-years away. Imagine how important it would be to our armed forces in space to have this power. As to how we got here, Splock is our science officer. Despite what you may think about his pointy ears, he has an intelligence many times more powerful than mine, and therefore almost infinitely more powerful than yours, as it is easy to tell."

Bill let the insult ride; you got nowhere arguing with officers. "I didn't think anything wrong about his pointy ears! I think they look real nice. I bet the girls get kinky thrills from them. Like from my teeth." He twanged a protruding tusk.

Splock came shuffling up to them now. The science officer from Fortinbras had a long thin face, eyebrows that were obviously alien since they turned up at both ends. When he spoke he had an uninflected buzzing voice like a badly adjusted voice simulator. "If you like ears like this it is highly probable that arrangements could be made to get a pair for you."

"Well," Bill said, thinking it over. "When you get down to it I think that I really don't like them that much. I just thought they look nice on you."

"I was making a joke," Splock said. "Just because my people have no sense of humor doesn't prevent us from making jokes in order to make the inferior races with which we must deal feel more at home. The type of humor I engaged in then was called irony."

"Irony! That's it. Of course!" Bill said. "Oh boy, ho-ho, how funny!"

"I did not mean," Splock said, in frigid tones, "that the word irony itself is funny. Though it does have its humorous overtones, I suppose. I meant that my statement about the pointy ears— Oh, shit. Never mind. Captain Dirk, what did you want me for?"

"I'd like you to explain to this trooper," Dirk said, "how we got here."

"But it ought to be obvious," Splock said, looking icily at Bill. "I take it for granted that you've had the

Finegurt-Reindeer equations in grade school or junior high?"

"I think they called them something else in my school," Bill said with humble prevarication.

"Never mind. What we did, we retooled the *Gumption*'s engines so they would oscillate on an interrupted Scomian curve. That's commonplace enough, of course; most commanders do it at least once a year when it's time to scrape space barnacles off the hull. It shrinks the ship, you see, which makes it easier to remove the barnacles."

"Doesn't it shrink the barnacles, too?" Bill asked.

Splock stared at him. Then burst into harsh laughter. Bill glanced at Brownnose, who looked away, embarrassed.

"What's so funny?" Bill said at last.

"Asking if the barnacles shrank. What a nice use of irony!"

"I guess it was pretty funny," Bill said, trying to be humble. Thinking that it wasn't too difficult getting along with this weirdo alien.

"No, it wasn't funny," Splock said. "At least not to me. But then, I don't even find my own jokes funny. I laughed merely to make you feel more at ease."

"Oh, thank you very much," Bill said, feeling that this joker was really a fruitcake of the first water.

"Now, after the ship has descended the Scomian curve in a state of oscillation, instead of scraping the hull, we introduce a pulsed beat that further miniaturizes the ship and projects it as a series of immaterial frames. In that form, we are able to enter the computer as a simulation."

"Oh, I *see*," Bill said, not understanding one word of the technical bowb. "Sounds great, really great."

"It has its uses," Splock said, feigning unfelt humility.

"And now since you did such a great job of getting in here—how are you going to get us out?"

Captain Dirk broke in. "We will know that just as soon as Splock makes his calculations."

Splock's long thin face took on a look of utmost concentration. His eyes slitted, a vein in his temple throbbed, and his ears quivered slightly, all signs, as Bill was to learn later, of a Fortinbrasian male wearing a jumpsuit in a state of Ur-concentration.

"How did you meet these guys?" Bill said to Brownnose, whispering so as not to intrude on Splock's concentration.

"Stop that whispering!" Splock said. "How do you expect me to concentrate?"

Wow, Bill thought, he really can hear a lot with those pointy ears.

Splock glared at him again. "And stop that!"

"You couldn't hear me!" Bill said. "I was thinking!"

"Logic dictated what you would think," Splock said. "I won't tell you again that I don't like comments of that sort."

"Didn't your friend tell you not to mention his ears?" Captain Dirk said.

Bill cringed, then straightened up abruptly. This was getting to be too much. That asshole alien in the crummy jumpsuit with a hatchet face and ears like a gravid kangaroo couldn't tell him how to think. To hell with them, he didn't need them; he'd rescue himself.

"You do need us," Splock said.

"Stop reading my mind!" Bill shouted.

"I didn't read your mind. I simply applied the logic of expected outcomes."

"Is that a fact?" Bill said. Unexpectedly, he smiled.

"Yes, it is," Splock said, not smiling.

A moment later he was reeling backwards, both hands to his face. Bill had thrown the neatest straight left jab seen since this planet had been born from the fiery pit of undifferentiated insubstantiality. Splock's hand came away red. "You've given me a nosebleed!" he said.

"At least we can get off the subject of ears for a while," Bill said. "It wasn't much of a blow, just a poke. Put your head back and put something cold on the back of your neck. It'll stop in no time."

"You don't understand!" cried Dirk.

"I understand plenty about nosebleeds," Bill said.

"I mean, you don't know what a blow on the nose can do to a Fortinbrasian male."

"He never saw it coming," Bill said. "So much for logical expectations."

"You fool!" Dirk cried. His face was ashen. "Males of Splock's planet carry their spare memory banks in their noses."

"That's a damned stupid place to have a memory," Bill said.

"Where am I?" Splock said, blinking around at them.

Captain Dirk groaned loudly and tore at his thinning hair. "Splock! You have to remember! Stored in your head is the highly important, original and special mathematical logic that will be needed to get us out of here."

"I'm afraid the data is bent, if not destroyed," Splock said. "I was keeping it all up the extra memory banks in my nose for safekeeping. How was I to know this barbarian with a Saurian foot would hit me in the nose?"

"How'd you know about my alligator foot?"

"The logic of the unexpected," Splock said with a sour smile. "Besides—I can see it there."

"Come on!" Brownnose urged. "Let's get the hell out of here!"

At Brownnose's behest they all turned and walked toward the remaining two black dots and the larger black dot that Bill had seen earlier. When they reached it, the black dots were still black dots, only bigger.

"What are these?" Bill asked.

"These are storage simulations of our emergency rescue ship and the two crewmen who man it."

"But they're black dots," Bill said.

"We stored them in that form," Dirk said, "to save energy. It takes a lot of power to beam simulations into an alien computer and the *Gumption*'s main batteries are already dangerously depleted due to a situation that came up immediately before this one."

"What good are they?" Bill asked.

"None at all, in their present form," Dirk admitted. "But as soon as Splock activates them into full simulacrum form—"

"I can't," Splock complained, touching his nose tenderly. "The equations." He sniffled. There was a whistling sound when he snuffled. It seemed possible that Bill had broken, not only the crucial reconstituting data which was needed to get them out of the computer and back to the *Gumption,* but also Splock's nose.

"Now we're really in trouble," Dirk said unhappily.

Bill walked up to one of the black dots and touched it. It was cold and metallic. He pushed against it. It was rigid. He walked to its edge. The edge was razor thin. He was to learn later that storage simulations have in fact no depth at all, only width and height, and, of course, quite a lot of area. But even had he known that then, it wouldn't have helped him turn the simulation into something useful.

Captain Dirk said, "Splock! Can't you do anything?"

"I'm trying," the Fortinbrasian said in a nasal voice. "But the data is coming out skewed."

"Look!" Brownnose said.

They were standing on a long plain that seemed to stretch forever under a stationary yellow sun. There were small purple plants on the plain, and a few old ruins that the computer had simulated just to liven up the place. Now, as they watched, furious clouds of dark green matter came roaring over the plain, bearing with them sand and bits of gravel, which came at them with the speed of machine gun bullets fired by a nervous hand.

At once Captain Dirk dropped to one knee, and, unholstering the lethal-looking handgun strapped to his waist, turned the beam to cone-destruction and destroyed the matter before it could cut them to ribbons of simulations.

"Keep it up, Captain!" Splock said. "I've just accessed the outer equations. I don't have enough to help us yet, but I do have enough to give us hope of eventual success."

"Can't keep this up much longer," Dirk said through gritted teeth. "My hand laser is only half-charged. Probably the fault of that new rating from New Calcutta. See that he gets a demerit for this bit of carelessness."

"If we ever get back," Splock said, his face set in the familiar expression of agony of a man trying to remember an equation he had forgotten.

Bill had been watching this and wondering what he could do to help. Suddenly it came to him. He stepped forward and, before Dirk could stop him, grabbed the back of Splock's head by one hand and took a firm grip on his nose with the other.

"Bill, what are you doing?" cried Brownnose, as always the master of the unnecessary question.

Bill gritted his teeth and gave Splock's nose a half-turn to the left. There was an audible click. Bill released Splock and stepped back. "How's that, fellow?"

"He seems to have fixed it," Splock said. He looked at Bill with new respect. "How did you know that the Fortinbrasians are born without noses and have mechanical ones made for them when they go to the world where men have noses as a matter of birth?"

"I just thought I'd give it a try," Bill said.

"Thank sanity for naive intuition," Splock said. He muttered equations in a firm baritone voice and the dots responded by resolving into two crewmen wearing one-piece jumpsuits of the same design only in an inferior fabric to those worn by Splock and Dirk. The large black dot resolved itself into a space launch.

As Bill got in, he thought he heard a voice calling his name. "Bill! Wait for me!"

It had been a female voice. But that couldn't be. He didn't know any women around here.

CHAPTER 18

BILL GAPED AROUND HIM IN SLACK-JAW amazement. When he boarded his first impression was that he wasn't in a spaceship at all. At least none of the deep spacers that he had served on in the past. The ships of the regular military service, no matter how large they looked from the outside, were crowded and cramped inside, cut up into noisome little quarters with low, filthy ceilings and an ineradicable smell of imitation boiled cabbage. This was no accident. Trained teams of designers had studied all the data banks of records of long-vanished Earth, had found exactly what they needed in the records of *sailing-ships,* ancient and improbable transport of some kind, and in particular the sub-category *slave-ships.* It was a difficult, nay an almost impossible task, but the Space Navy designers persevered. And in the end managed to duplicate all the filth and cramped discomfort of the original for the present crew quarters.

That was how the Navy did it. But not here! This ship looked very much like an airport waiting room or a Staff Officers' latrine. It was huge, done entirely in pastel colors of avocado and cocoa. The lighting was subtly indirect and flicker-free. So well concealed that

Bill couldn't see the lighting fixtures anywhere. Must be hell to change the lightbulbs, he thought. Not only was the decor original but the crewmembers that Bill saw were nothing like any other service personnel he had ever encountered. For one thing, they were all young and pretty, the boys, or lads—you could hardly call these striplings men—were young and eager and came in many colors. As did the busty and really stacked girls. The ship's crew seemed incredibly racially balanced. So many white, so many black, a scattering of greens and reds. And one sort of brownish-yellow.

When they all entered the central control room, a pleasant-faced young fellow in a beige and maroon jumpsuit, with a white sweater tied rakishly around his neck, jumped gracefully to his feet and saluted. Dirk returned the salute snappily and said, "Permission to come aboard?"

"Of course, sir," the young man answered sheepishly. "I mean, after all, it's your ship, you being our Captain, as well as First Admiral of the Blue."

"I know all that," Dirk growled. "A simple salute will be sufficient."

"Aye, sir," the young officer shouted as he saluted so hard he almost put his eye out with his pinky.

"Bill," said Captain Dirk, "I want to introduce you to Midshipman Easy, one of our recent replacements from the Laguna Beach Deep Space School."

"Delighted," said Midshipman Easy, extending a browned hand, his right eye swollen shut where his fingernail had plunged into it.

"Yeah, thanks," said Bill, reluctantly holding out a gnarled paw and wishing he'd had a chance to clean up before coming to this spotlessly clean battleship, or whatever it was.

"Midshipman Easy will show you your quarters," Captain Dirk said. "And Splock will be on hand to fill you in on what's happening."

"Walk this way, if you please," Midshipman Easy said, mincing a bit as he exited. The crew broke into guffaws and wolf whistles at what seemed to be a joke, which Bill didn't understand at all.

They went down long corridors, passing every once in a while young men in a snug-fitting jump suits explaining very important things to beautiful young women in even more snug-fitting jump suits. They went up and down levels, across more corridors, and finally came to a door with a double zero stenciled on it. Easy opened the door and brought Bill inside into what looked like a well-appointed hotel suite in the style of the venerable old Helior-Beverly-Hilton.

"Wow," said Brownnose, who had tagged along and now darted into the suite and went straight to the bathroom. "Hey, Bill!" he called out. "They got free samples of bubble bath and fancy perfumed soaps here."

"Don't touch anything," Bill warned him. To Midshipman Easy he said, "What happens now?"

"Just relax while we get the ship underway," Easy said. "There are costly imported wines and cordials in the antique provincial sideboard over there. Should you get hungry before the evening banquet at 1900 hours, there is a snack dispenser built into the 500-channel TV. Just push the button for whatever you require. No coins are necessary. You are our guests."

"Wow," Brownnose said after Midshipman Easy had left. "How about this, huh, Bill?" Brownnose walked over to the snack dispenser. "They got French-fried octopus rings, Bill! And coke-joints!" He hurried over to the drink dispenser. "And they got over a hundred kinds of beer on tap, including the starship's own microbrew, Old Gumption. What do you want to try first?"

"I'm going to wait for the banquet," Bill said. "1900 hours is less than an hour away. Meanwhile I'm going to take a bath."

Bill went into the luxurious bathroom. The tub was the size of a small swimming pool. There was a massage machine with buttons for all the species who were aboard or might come aboard the Starship *Gumption*.

There was even a little tube of Claw Softener, and a special instrument for clipping talons.

"That was thoughtful of them," Bill said to himself, never thinking that some clawed and taloned aliens might be guests of the *Gumption* from time to time.

Bill locked the bathroom door so Brownnose wouldn't see what he was doing and drew himself a bubble bath. Squirming with masculine guilt and hoping that no one would ever find out. Might as well try everything once, no telling how long this unexpected luxury was going to last. He paddled around the bathtub, threw handfuls of bubbles into the air and said *whee*, then found the controls that turned on the viewing screens. An enormous panel slid back revealing a TV screen that stretched from wall to wall. The picture came up and Bill saw Captain Dirk, sitting in a command chair behind his officers, who were seated at computer consoles and switchboards that looked like they came from a submarine of ancient times.

"Everyone ready?" Dirk asked.

A chorus of yesses sussurated forth. But Dirk noticed one silence and turned to Splock. "You didn't say aye, First Science Officer. Is anything the matter?"

"Permission to speak freely?" Splock asked.

"Go ahead, Tony," Dirk said.

"Logic suggests," Splock responded in a monotonous monotone, "that the matter of the Runions from Saperstein V should be resolved before anything further is attempted."

"Suggestion noted and ignored," said Dirk in a pleasantly obnoxious no-nonsense voice. "Rear thrusters all ahead one third!"

The Chief Astrogation Officer—a really zoftig darkskinned woman with an elaborate hairdo—pushed a lever into a notched setting. "All ahead one third, sir."

"Starboard maneuvering jets—a two-second burst. Main engines engage. Pulse control on. Astrogation control set at one zero niner. Port fine maneuvering jets set to 340 degrees and give me a five-second burst. Pulse control engaged. Starship main drive standby for retro-jet engage. All ahead full!"

The screen changed to an exterior view. This, as Bill was to learn later, was provided by a drone ship camera. Why there was a drone ship camera he never did find out. Other than providing a totally worthless exterior view. It was a miracle of misapplied technology.

The view of the *Gumption* as provided by the drone camera was very fine indeed. The gigantic starship, with its struts and appurtenances, its pods and bays, its complicated array of superfluous winking lights, all were enhanced by the engine sound-track, which the drone camera provided. It was very pretty to watch the starship move away, in pythonic ecstasy while behind them winked the distant lights of the stars. This background was simulated, also. Movies of the previous centuries had captured for all time what a starship ought to look like going through space. Standard background film, concocted in special effects laboratories, was used to give this charming and archaic appearance. It never failed to impress those who watched it.

Soon the *Gumption* switched to Main Drive and faster-than-light travel. The picture from the drone changed. Now long streaks of tawny light seemed to converge on the *Gumption*. It was the standard faster-than-light view.

Bill, getting smashed on strong beer and almost drowning as he fell asleep in the bubble bath, was really at his ease. There was nothing he could do to help around this screwball ship—and he certainly was not doing any volunteering. Dirk and the crew had everything nicely in hand. They spent lots of time lounging around in easy chairs while Dirk gave orders in a soft voice. Everything seemed suspiciously easy. The carpeting was always soft underfoot, and soft music played lullingly through all the speakers. It had a lot of harps and harpsichords and carillons and xylophones in it. Real deep space music.

As soon as light speed was reached, the crew relaxed. If that was possible since they were pretty spaced out already. Captain Dirk congratulated them all on a really scrumptious takeoff. And summoned Bill to the bridge.

"Now, Bill, be a good fellow and tell Splock our science officer about how the Tsuris displacement effect works."

Bill bulged his eyes at him. "The what?"

"The special weapon the Tsurisians use to push ships millions of miles off course. Your friend said you had learned it while you were inside the computer."

Behind Dirk was Brownnose, making frantic motions. Bill had no idea what Brownnose was trying to tell him, but figured he was probably trying to signal Bill to fake it. Bill would have been glad to, if he'd had the slightest idea how.

"I'm afraid I never quite got around to learning that secret, Captain," Bill said. "Sort of out of my line of work. I trained as a fertilizer technician, when I was a civilian that was. My military speciality is Fusetender First Class . . ."

"Shut up," Dirk suggested. He looked quite unpleasant, as did Splock and the others. "Trooper," he grated through gritted teeth, "I'd advise you not to try any games with me. Your friend, Mr. Brownnose, assured us that you know the secret of the Displacer, but were rather shy and needed coaxing."

"Brownnose," Bill grated just as grittingly as Dirk, "when I get my hands on you—"

"Bill, I'd like you to meet a seldom-seen but extremely important member of the *Gumption*'s crew." Dirk's voice was now low, sinister and menacing, with overtones of suicidal insinuation. "Step out, Basil."

A tall man wearing a hooded tunic shuffled menacingly from a room in the rear. His face was entirely concealed. But even on the concealment of his face, the contours of the cloth, Bill could detect baldness and evil.

"How do you do," Bill said.

"Don't wise off at us, trooper," Dirk screamed.

"I'll tell you what Basil's official position is. He's our persuader."

"Some people would call him the torturer," Splock intoned grimly. "But that is an incorrect description. He only tortures when it is absolutely necessary in order to gain information."

"Do you mean that you sometimes have to torture your crew?" Bill asked.

"Of course not!" Dirk said warmly. "It's just that, you know, sometimes when we take over a planet— Yes, Mr. Splock?"

"Planet coming up," Mr. Splock said.

Bill asked, "How can you know a planet's coming up if you're traveling at the speed of light? I mean, wouldn't it be gone by the time you knew what it was?"

"Our computer tells us when there's a planet coming up," Dirk said. "What sort of place is it, Splock?"

Splock tapped his forehead with long slim fingers. "Smaller than Earth. Oxygen atmosphere. Small population. One of the speculator worlds that sprang up in this vicinity in the recent South Star Ridge scandal."

"Good," Dirk said. "Let's land and take on provisions."

"Also women, Captain," one of the crewmen reminded him.

"Have you used up the last batch already?" Dirk demanded.

"Afraid so, skipper," the crewman said.

"Then we'll pick up a new batch here."

Splock had continued tapping his forehead. "My readout on this place tells me that the males of this planet tend to become murderous when anyone tries to take away their womenfolk."

"That's how it is with primitives," Dirk said. "We'll drop sleep bombs on them in carpet clusters. That way there'll be no argument and we can simply take what we want and be on our way."

Bill could hardly believe what he was hearing. Although he knew that silence was undoubtedly the best policy, he couldn't help saying, "I've heard a lot about you, Captain Dirk. But I never thought you were like this."

Dirk favored him with a thin, evil smile. "That's good to hear, trooper, because I'm not actually Dirk at all. I am the Counter-Dirk. Guards, take this man to a cell. The persuader will pay you a visit as soon as we have this planet squared away."

C H A P T E R **19**

THE CELL, BILL LEARNED LATER, HAD BEEN modeled on a copy of an historic prison cell vidrecorded on the most backward planet ever discovered. Before the planet was destroyed. The stone walls (lifted into space at great expense) dripped moisture; lizards crept in and out of crevices. In place of a toilet there was a torn paper cup. For lighting, a slit high up in the wall allowed in a thin ray of simulated sunshine. The sunlight started fading as soon as Bill was put into the cell. It was designed to produce an instant sensation of hopelessness and bleak despair.

Bill lay down on the floor and promptly went to sleep. For one thing, he wanted to preserve his energy for what lay ahead. For another, he was tired. Climbing up sheer ice walls using your claws as crampons would take it out of a better-conditioned and less alcoholic man than Bill.

He awoke later when he heard the rattling of a key in the door. Bill stiffened, figuring it was the persuader. But it was only the jailer bringing his dinner.

The jailer left a tray behind with a threadbare napkin

over it. He leered at Bill for no apparent reason and left, locking the door behind him.

Bill whisked off the napkin to see what they had brought him. There were two plates on the tray. One of them bore a rectangular substance with red and white things sticking out of its sides. This Bill recognized as a ham and Swiss sandwich. The other plate bore a seven-inch green lizard which Bill recognized immediately as a Chinger, the deadly enemy they warred against across the galaxy. Bill raised his boot to stomp it. The Chinger sneered.

"Do that, you microcephalic moron and you get a broken foot. Forgotten already that we come from a 10G planet and are harder than the hardest steel?"

Bill might still have stomped the lizard, so deeply ingrained were his reactions of aversion to Earth's newest ancestral enemy. But he stopped because he thought he recognized the voice. Even though it was an octave and a half higher and coming through an alien throat, Bill recognized the special lilt of Illyria, the nurse girl from the provinces who had first befriended him on Tsuris.

"Illyria! Is that really you?"

"Yes, it's me, Bill," the lizard said. Its voice was high-pitched, due no doubt to its miniature larynx and soft palate. But the tones were unmistakably those of Illyria.

"How did you get inside a Chinger?"

"I had some help from the Quintiform computer. When it saw that you were going off planet, perhaps never to return, it began to realize that maybe it had been a little harsh on you."

"Harsh! It kept me in the rain and cold for days and days!"

"That was only subjective time, of course," Illyria said. "Still, it must have seemed very long indeed. The computer asked me to tell you that it is sorry, Bill. It admires your independence of spirit. It wants you to come back, all is forgiven, since it feels that you could be very useful to the Tsurisians."

"I don't want to be in the computer any longer," Bill said angrily.

"Of course not. The computer realizes its mistake, trying to break your proud spirit. There are other jobs for you, Bill. Good jobs. Jobs you would like."

"I doubt that," Bill miffed huskily.

"And you could be with me," Illyria pointed out.

"Yes, that's so," he vacillated.

"You don't sound too enthusiastic about that."

"Gosh, Illyria, you know that I really like you. But when you appear in my prison cell in the form of a Chinger, Earth's deadliest enemies—"

"I had forgotten," Illyria mused. "Yes, of course, that might very well account for it."

"Your previous form was better," Bill said. "Though not much. By the way, how did you get a Chinger body?"

"You should have figured that out for yourself," Illyria said. "We Tsurisians exist in the form of radiant energy until we find a body to inhabit. We take what bodies we can get. I know that this lizard shape is no more suitable to your human form than was my previous body of three spheres."

"They were nice spheres," Bill said.

"You're a dear for saying that. I'm sure they did nothing for you. But I was lucky to get it. You know that most of my people have no bodies at all. I was lucky to get the spherical one. But you were asking about the lizard. I was floating lazily through this ship, the good old fighting *Gumption*, looking for a suitable host body—"

"By the way," Bill said, "how did you get onto the *Gumption*?"

"The computer did it. He realized it was the only possible way of getting you back. So he helped me to get aboard here. He provided me with energy. Everything I needed he supplied, except, of course, a body.

That is beyond his powers. But he figured I could probably find one here that wasn't being used."

"Most of the people I know," Bill said, "use their bodies all of the time."

"I know that now," Illyria said. "Everyone I saw here was really getting plenty of work out of their bodies. Even when they sleep they use them for dreaming. Bill, these people are extremely active, are they not?"

"I suppose so. But tell me about the Chinger."

"Well, after looking all through the ship, I thought I was out of luck. Everybody was using his body for something or other. Some of them were using their bodies together, which I found both highly amusing and interesting. You must tell me . . ."

"Later," Bill sighed, not really interested in explaining heterosexual—homosexual?—athletics to a disembodied intelligence occupying a lizard's body.

"I'll remember to ask. I went on and detected this body in a hidden compartment in the ship's hull. It appeared comatose and I just slipped in and took it over."

"No problems?"

"None whatsoever. They are actually very easy-going lizards, Bill."

"For you maybe, but don't try telling that to the Joint Chiefs of Staff. Can you take over any body you want?"

"Well, of course. But that's not because we're such great intellects. It's just that we're used to living in a purely mental state, and most other creatures are not."

"That's really interesting," Bill muttered half to himself. His eyes narrowed as a hazy idea began to form in his mind.

"Bill, why are you squinting?"

"I was thinking. I'll tell you about it later. Listen, Illyria, something is terribly wrong."

"It'll be better soon. If not—just throw it away. What's one body more or less? I know where I can get a really nice body without having to break any of the ethical rules that prevent us Tsurisians from taking over any old body we please."

"That's great. But I didn't mean that. I mean something is terribly wrong with all of the people on this ship. I've always thought Captain Dirk was a famous hero. But here he's planning to do terrible things to innocent people on some planet we are coming to."

"Most unusual. I guess. Since I have never heard of him before I will just have to take your word for it. How do you account for it?"

"I don't know," Bill said. "When I asked him, he said he wasn't Dirk at all. He was Counter-Dirk."

"What did that mean?"

"I haven't the slightest idea."

"Perhaps I should ask the Quintiform computer." Bill looked interested. "You can do that?"

"Oh, yes, I told you the computer wanted to help you. It has maintained a link with me. I'll ask him now."

The little green lizard who was Illyria curled up into a ball from which only its snout and eyes peeked out. Its eyes half-closed, its jaws relaxed, its paws exhibited waxy flexibility.

"Hey, Illyria," Bill said. "Are you OK?"

"She's fine," the lizard said. "This is the Quintiform computer speaking now. Bill, I want to apologize. I was just playing with you, sort of. I'd really like you to come back."

"I didn't really enjoy being part of your mind," Bill said. "No offense, but I just like being me."

"I suppose that's understandable," the computer said. "And you are right, your brain is much too valuable to go to waste."

"My brain?"

"Yes. It has two lobes."

"Oh," said Bill. "I think I remember that a lot of human brains are built that way."

"Do you know what that means?"

"I don't think so."

"It means that your brain is capable of becoming as powerful as a computer all by itself, without having to be part of me."

"Oh," Bill said. He thought about it for a moment. "That's great."

"You see, the computer really has your best interests at heart."

"That's nice," Bill said. "But you were going to tell me what 'counter' means."

"In this context," the computer said, speaking through Illyria who was inhabiting the body of a Chinger lizard, which is a pretty exotic telephone connection when you get down to it, "it means that there are two Captain Dirks, the real one and the counter one. You were right about Captain Dirk acting strangely in terms of your usual civilized norms. The man commanding this ship is not the real Captain Dirk, just as this ship is not the real *Gumption*."

"This is getting a little complicated," Bill said, frowning in concentration. "If this is the Counter-Captain Dirk, where is the real Captain Dirk?"

"I knew you'd ask me that," the computer said, "and so I got the information from the computer which runs this ship."

"The counter-computer, you mean," Bill said.

"Yes, exactly. Oh my dear fellow, you must come back to Tsuris with me. It's such a pleasure talking with someone who understands."

"We'll discuss that later," Bill said, sensing that he was in a position of power, though for the life of him he couldn't figure out how or why. "Meanwhile I'd like to know where the real Captain Dirk is."

"This will amaze you," the computer said.

"Don't worry. At this point I'm amaze-proof."

"Captain Dirk is at present in the ancient Rome of the long-lost planet Earth. The year is approximately 65 B.C."

"You're right," Bill said. "That amazes me."

"I thought it might," the Quintiform computer

chuckled, sounding more than a little pleased with itself.

"What else did the ship's computer tell you?"

"It also told me why Dirk was there, and how his being there had been the cause of the Counter-Dirk appearing here."

"Told you all that, did he? Obliging little box of transistors, wasn't it?"

"We computers are all brothers," the Quintiform computer said. "Pure intelligence knows no skin color."

"Don't rub it in," Bill said. "Why is Captain Dirk in ancient Rome?"

"He has an important task to perform there."

"Obviously. But what is it?"

The Quintiform computer sighed. "I know there's a great deal you don't know. But really, we must hurry along. I'm not trying to rush you for *my* sake. I've got plenty of time. This sort of conversation requires only a tiny part of my brainpower. The rest of me is back in the computer doing all the stuff I usually do to keep the planet functioning. But I know from what the ship's computer told me that as soon as Dirk and his men get through plundering and pillaging the new planet they've just found, they are going to turn to you and do whatever they have to do to get the secret of the displacing effect from you. Since you don't know the secret, it's going to be a little tough on you. But don't let me rush you."

There was a long silence. For a while Bill thought the computer had broken off contact with him out of pique. The Chinger lizard just lay there, its eyes closed, looking more dead than alive. It was impossible to say where Illyria was. And he, Bill, was in a lot of trouble.

"Computer?" Bill said after a while.

"Yes, Bill?"

"Don't get sore at me, OK?"

"I am a computer," the computer said. "I do not get angry at people or things."

"You sure give a good imitation of it."

"Simulation is part of the job. Look, to explain

properly about why Dirk is in ancient Rome I'll have to tell you the story of the Alien Historian. It's just that I don't think we have time for it right now."

Bill could hear the heavy threatening stomach-turning sound of hobnailed boots marching down the corridor outside his cell. There was a clashing sound as of weapons being grounded sharply. Then the grating sound of a key in his door.

"Please, Computer, get me out of here!"

"Hang on, then," the computer said. "This may be a little difficult—on you, I mean. It's a technique I haven't had much opportunity to practice and some of my defaults may be set wrong."

"I don't care whose de fault!" Bill screamed, going hysterical as the door slammed open and Dirk and Splock stood there, hands on their hips, sneering, clad now in black uniforms with evil emblems pinned here and there, and a squad of black-clad soldiers behind them.

"Hello there, chicken," Dirk said, and Splock laughed in a sinister manner and the black-uniformed men behind them giggled suggestively.

"Computer!" Bill screeched.

"Yes, yes, all right," the computer said testily. "I guess it must go like this perhaps—"

Captain Dirk swaggered into the room, and Splock minced in beside him. The black-clad soldiers followed carrying the antelope prods and a cauldron of fried chewing gum.

At that instant Bill felt his alligator foot begin to grow. It burst through the few metaphoric rags with which Bill had wrapped it out of a perhaps misplaced sense of common decency. It grew to the size of a cantaloupe, a watermelon, a three-year-old pig, a sheep before shearing, a piano, a one-car garage, and when Dirk and his men beheld it in its atavistic ugliness and menace, they cowered back. Bill couldn't do much except cheer his foot on since at this point it weighed more than he did and seemed to have a will of its own.

"I'll change modalities," the computer muttered, and Bill's foot rapidly shrank back to its usual dimensions. But something else was happening now. Bill found that he was growing very tall. It was a curious feeling, growing like that, longer and longer and skinnier and skinnier, until he felt himself resembling a sausage an inch in diameter and perhaps ten or so yards in length, like an eccentric model of a roundworm done for laughs.

"Don't just stand there gaping!" the computer said. "Find the wormhole!"

Bill didn't know what the computer was talking about. But he did see, just above his head, a small black hole, or at least very deep gray, and it looked like a tunnel into which he could just fit his head. He did it, and promptly fell into the middle of space. And that he found amazing.

Falling like this was strangely uncomfortable. But at least he wasn't alone, for falling next to him was an elongated green worm which was obviously the attenuated form of a Chinger occupied by the intelligence of an alien computer. Obvious? Things were really getting out of hand when something like this could be obvious.

He was still pondering this imponderable when everything went black, or some color very much like black, and he blacked out as well.

CHAPTER 20

CONSCIOUSNESS RETURNED, AND WITH IT memory. Bill felt pretty good, considering what he had gone through. Not that he was really sure what had happened, other than that his dim memories of the occasion were pretty crappy. He blinked and looked about—and discovered that he was standing on a grassy plane, the grass very much the same color as the Chinger who squatted beside him. There was a dust cloud on the horizon that very quickly resolved itself into a group of men with lances and armor and plumed steel helmets. Bill knew at once that they were Romans. He had seen enough prehistorical movies on Interplanetary Super Feature, the galactic cable network, to know that these were indeed Romans, and not to be confused with the Germans of that period, who wore bearskins and had long mustaches. These men were clean-shaven. In the middle of them, borne on a hammock, and looking puzzled but resolute, was Captain Dirk.

"Hi, Captain Dirk," Bill said. "Are you a prisoner?"

"No," Dirk said. "What made you think so? And, in addition, who the hell are you since I have never seen you before?"

"Perhaps I should make the introductions," the Chinger-cum-computer said. Or maybe it was Illyria. Whichever of them was home in the body at the time.

"That's a Chinger!" Dirk shouted, reaching for his sidearm.

Bill, seeing that in another moment Captain Dirk,

well-meaning though he might be, would destroy the lizard, thus finishing off Illyria and ending his link with the computer, burst through the armed Romans and grappled with Dirk for his sidearm.

"Don't shoot!" Bill shouted.

"Why not?" Dirk grimaced, struggling to free himself.

"It'll take me too long to explain!"

"Try me. I got plenty of time." He pulled at the weapon.

The Chinger opened its mouth and said, "I'm not your enemy, Captain Dirk. I'm Illyria of the planet Tsuris and I have taken over the body of this lizard in order to help Bill here."

Captain Dirk looked at Bill. "Any truth in what this repulsive alien is saying? And have we met before?"

"I've met the Counter-Dirk," Bill said. "He looks just like you."

"That is really rotten news. We came here to stop the despicable creature known only as the Alien Historian. But no sooner do we get here than we run into a mirror reversal. It traps us here, and, since matter cannot be destroyed and energy is merely information, it produced the Counter-*Gumption* and the Counter-Dirk back in our own space and time. I must get back to stop them."

"But what about the Romans?" Bill asked. "What are you doing here?"

"Trying to sort out the fate of a thoroughly unpleasant man named Julius Caesar," Dirk said. "I am very much in a dilemma as to his fate. The Alien Historian is trying to save Caesar in order to change the history of the Earth to our great disadvantage. We can't permit that. On the other hand, if I stop the Alien Historian, I would be an accomplice to Caesar's death at the hands of Brutus. You can see what a moral dilemma it presents to me."

"You mean you're thinking of letting the Alien Historian stop Brutus from killing Caesar?" Bill knew his Roman history from watching a lot of really bad films about the Romans which had been really popular for awhile.

"Well, it is quite a moral problem, as even one with a forehead as low as yours can probably see," Dirk said. "What would you do in my place?"

"Bump off the Alien Historian," Bill said simply. "Then I'd go back to my own time and kick that Counter-Dirk right up the arse."

"That's what Splock said."

"He was right."

"But Splock doesn't understand human emotion!" Dirk said.

"It works the same with or without emotion," Bill said. "Your job is to get the Earth back into its rightful time track."

"You're right, you're right," Dirk muttered, "I've been under a considerable strain lately. They say I'm all washed up, but they're wrong. I can still cut it. You know what I mean?"

"Sure I do," Bill said. "What has to be done?"

"We have to grab Brutus before he can kill Caesar."

"When is all this supposed to take place?"

Captain Dirk glanced at his watch. The Romans stared. They had never seen a watch before.

"We have about two hours," Dirk said. "At that point, according to Splock's calculations, that's how much time the Alien Historian will need to realize we've made an end run around him, and reset his machines to send him back to before we arrived here. That would give him time to thwart us."

"But then you could go back to a time before he came!" Bill said.

"Theoretically, yes," Dirk said. "Actually, we ran our batteries down considerably just getting here. You have no idea how difficult it is to get a trickle charge in 65 A.D. No, Bill, whatever is to be done, it has to be done now."

"Then let's do it!" Bill cried.

"Me too," Illyria the Chinger said, pouting, which is pretty hard for a lizard to do, feeling very much out of it since they had overlooked her. Literally.

"You'll help?" Dirk asked.

"Of course!"

"You are an experienced Trooper, I believe, and therefore trained for hand-to-hand combat?"

"Well, yeah, I suppose so," Bill said, remembering all the battles he had been in, the ones that he could not avoid of course. "I have had the odd experience on the field of battle."

"Great. And you can command men?"

"Now wait a minute," Bill said. "I'm no officer. I was one once. I had a field promotion. Then I had a field demotion. I think I have had enough of that old officer bowb."

"Not as an officer. I mean on the squad or platoon level."

"Yeah, sure. Lots of that. I was even a DI. But anyway, so what? You're an officer. That's what captain means, doesn't it? So you ought to take charge yourself."

"Oh, I will," Dirk said. "But I must stay behind the lines where I can consult with Splock. But you see, I need a commander in the field, someone who will convey my orders to the troops."

"Now wait just a minute," Bill protested. Knowing even before the words had left his mouth that it was too late.

So that was how Bill found himself leading the Fifth and Second (Valerian) legions against Genghis Khan and about a million of his Huns.

Since the Alien Historian had already changed the history of Earth by protecting Julius Caesar from assassination by Brutus and his buddies, many opposing political factions had sprung up. Caesar, of course, was the outstanding military genius of his age, perhaps even better than Alexander, so he had kept supremacy over most of these hordes. That was up until now.

Not that Splock thought so. "This is not going well for Caesar, Captain. Or for us."

"You are a negative old pointy-eared bastard—but have summed up the situation with precision, Mr. Splock."

"Thank you. I have no emotions, so neither your praise nor your insults means anything at all to me. But I thank you anyhow for respecting my intellect, and ignore with disdain, if I had the emotions to show disdain, your stupid remark about my ears."

"What are we going to do?" Bill asked, easing slowly backwards away from the approaching army. His only answer was silence.

As they watched with more than a little interest, the forces of Ghengis Khan advanced on their armored yaks. They bore fearsome spears and weapons of every sort and variety. They had huge kettle drums, one to each side of a horse, and cadaverous warriors beat these drums and other even more cadaverous warriors blew trumpets and howled in a thoroughly obnoxious Asiatic manner. Their armies charged along the bank of the Tiber, extending in their serried ranks as far as the eye could see. The Roman troops were looking resolute but nervous, like men who have been brought unfairly into trouble not of their own making. Some of the foremost men were already backing away from contact with these screaming, grinning devils with their horses and camels and strange weapons and their spirit of plunder and murder. Cooties and lice and maybe even crabs and spiders crawled on their unwashed bodies and lank filthy hair.

"It isn't fair," Dirk said. "Ghengis Khan doesn't even belong in this period. How did the Huns get here?"

"That," Splock said, "is less important than what we are going to do about them."

"Any ideas?" Dirk asked.

"Just a moment," Splock said. "I'm thinking. Or rather, thought being lightning-fast, I'm reviewing the thoughts I had when the problem just came up."

"And?" Dirk prompted.

"I have an idea," Splock said. "It's a remote chance, but perhaps we can bring it off. Hold them as long as you can, Captain. Bill, come with me."

"And what about me?" Illyria-cum-Chinger cried out shrilly as they almost walked on her. "You should show a little consideration!"

"Of course, sure, we didn't forget you," Bill said, realizing they had forgotten her. "Stick with the Captain. Keep an eye on him. Be right back. I hope." He looked at Splock suspiciously. "Where are we going?"

"We are going to save the Earth as we know it." Splock took Bill's hand and, with his free hand, made an adjustment to the miniature control panel on his belt. There was a sound of thunder and multiple flashes of lightning. Bill didn't even have time for a good gasp. Suddenly he felt space and time dissolve around him. An icy wind blew around his chops, and he felt himself lifted and carried away by a gigantic wind which was none other than the Wind of Time itself.

After a period of whirling sounds and flashing lights and uncanny smells, Bill found himself standing on a barren plain, or perhaps it was a desert. Bill wasn't too sure. It was colored brown and seemed to be composed mainly of gravel, with some larger rocks for comic relief. Here and there were a few bedraggled thorn bushes, barely subsisting in this dry, sere place. Splock was standing beside him, consulting a small map which he had taken out of the pouch at his waist.

"This ought to be the place," Splock said, frowning, his ears twitching. "Unless this is an out-of-date map. Temporal currents change without notice, so you can't always be sure—"

There was a loud bellowing noise behind them. Bill jumped straight up in the air and whirled, reaching for the weapons he didn't have strapped to his waist.

Splock turned more slowly, as was suitable for someone of his intellect.

"It's just the camel men," Splock said.

"Oh," Bill said. "The camel men. Of course. You didn't mention them before now."

"I didn't think it necessary," Splock said. "I thought you could figure out that much for yourself."

Bill didn't bother to reply that he had had no clues. Splock was one of these very intelligent people who always have an answer for everything and whose explanations make you feel more stupid than you actually are. Or so you hope.

The two camel men, mounted on their high dromedaries, had been waiting patiently. Now one of them addressed Splock in a strange language which Bill's translator, after a moment of fumbling, managed to translate into English.

"Greetings, Effendi."

"Greetings," Splock said. "Please be so good as to take us to your leader."

The camel drivers chattered among themselves in a language, or more likely, a dialect, which Bill's computer didn't have in its repertoire. Whatever it was, Splock seemed to know it, and he broke in with a few well-chosen words which left the camel men laughing in an embarrassed and somewhat respectful fashion.

"What did you say to them?" Bill asked.

"Just a pleasantry," Splock said. "It loses a lot in the translation."

"Tell me anyway," Bill said.

"I told them, may your camel tracks never cross the dismal swamp that leads to the stygian darkness."

"And they laughed?"

"Of course. I used a variant for swamp which can also be construed as meaning 'May your tailbone never suffer the multiple indignities of being kicked around the oasis by the Sultan's bodyguards.' A neat bit of linguistic legerdemain if I may say so myself."

The camel drivers had finished jabbering excitedly between themselves. Now the elder of the two, with the short black beard and the bulging dark eyes, said, "Mount up behind us. We will take you to The Boss."

They got up behind the camel drivers and set forth. At first Bill thought they were going toward the distant mountains. But soon he could make out a square shape far ahead, and battlements, and towers. It was a city they were going to, and a big one.

"What is that place?" Bill asked.

"That ahead of us is Carthage," Splock said. "You've heard of Carthage, haven't you?"

"Where Hannibal came from?"

"You got it in one," Splock said.

"Why are we going there?"

"Because," Splock explained with great patience, "I'm going to make Hannibal an offer he can't refuse. At least I hope he can't."

CHAPTER 21

"ELEPHANTS," HANNIBAL SAID.

"They were my undoing. Did you ever try to refuel a squadron of elephants in the Alps in January?"

"Sound difficult," Bill said. He was interested to note that Hannibal spoke Punic with a slight southern accent, really a South Balliol Lisp. It threw a new light on this famous man, though Bill wasn't sure what it meant. Neither did his translator, which had pointed out this totally boring fact.

"I had it all there," Hannibal said. "Rome was so close to being mine, I could taste it. Tasted rather arm-pitty and garlicky too. Victory within my grasp! And then that damned Fabius Cunctator with his dewaying tactics put paid to my dweam. I could handle him now, beweive me, but at the time delay was a new military tactic. Pwevious to that, it had just been ignorant armies clashing by night and that sort of booshaw. Well, no sense cwying over spilt kvass. Now—what do you strange looking barbarians want? Speak quickly or I'll have you gutted."

"We are here to give you another opportunity," Splock said, talking very fast.

Hannibal was a tall, well-built man. He wore a polished cuirass and a gleaming brass and bronze helmet. They were in Hannibal's audience room at the time. It was not really a major audience room. Hannibal had suffered defeat, and therefore he wasn't allowed to use the main audience room. This was a small audience room put aside for the use of unsuccessful generals. On a sideboard there were sweetmeats, doves' tongues in aspic, french fried mice, that sort of thing, and flasks of tarry wine. Bill had already wandered over to the sideboard, since Splock seemed to have this part of the talk well in hand. There were little pots resting in wire cradles over heating elements which burned olive oil. Bill sampled one of the pots. It tasted like curried goat droppings. He spat it out; it probably was.

"Mind if I try one of these?" he asked Hannibal, pointing to the wine pots.

"Go wight ahead," Hannibal said. "The one in the big jug on the end is wather nice. No tar like the others."

Bill sampled it, tasted, liked what he tasted, glugged another swig.

"Zoinks! What is that stuff?" he asked.

"Palm whiskey," Hannibal said. "Made only in the Highlands of Carthaginia. By an awfully secret pwocess called distilazione."

"Terrific," Bill said, swilling more.

Hannibal returned to his conversation with Splock. This was carried out in low voices, and Bill wasn't much interested anyhow. The palm whiskey had entirely claimed his attention and was quickly destroying his cerebral cortex. He nibbled at some of the repulsive food, which was beginning to taste good, which was a bad sign, then swigged down more of the palm whiskey. Life was not looking too bad at the moment. Bleary, but not bad. Things looked even better when, in response to an unseen signal, or perhaps because it was the regular time for their appearance, a troupe of dancing girls came through the archway, accompanied by three musicians with complicated-looking instruments made of gourds and catgut.

"Hey now!" Bill said. "This is more like it!"

The dancing girls looked toward Hannibal, but he was deep in conversation with Splock and waved them away. They turned to Bill, formed a line in front of him, and started to dance. They were the best kind of dancing girls, tall, wide of hip and generous of breast, with legs that never stopped. Bill's type entirely. They danced for him with many a flirtatious gesture, like removing their veils one by one while doing a grind and a bump; the musicians grinned and pounded and strummed on their strange instruments; tumescence surged and Bill asked the cute dancer on the end nearest him what she was doing after the show, but she didn't seem to understand Punic.

The dance went on for quite a while, more boring now since they put the veils back on after noticing the effect on Bill. Long enough for Bill to get pleasantly smashed on the palm whiskey, and to burn his mouth on the little green chilies he hadn't noticed he was eating. He was about to ask the musicians if they knew a couple of old songs Bill had learned when he was a kid, but before he got the chance Hannibal and Splock seemed to come to some sort of an agreement. They shook hands and got up and strolled over to Bill. Hannibal made a gesture and the musicians and dancers packed up and left quickly.

"So, it's all settled," Splock said. "Hannibal himself is going to come to our aid. He'll bring five of his crack elephant squadrons. I've assured him we'll handle all the details of servicing his elephants."

"Thash great," Bill said, with some difficulty. He felt like his tongue was wearing a spacesuit. "Didn't seem too difficult, either, neither, wazzah."

"No, I was sure that Hannibal would want a return engagement against the Romans. There was just one trifling condition that I had to agree to."

"What was that?" Bill asked.

Splock hesitated. "I'm afraid you might not like this. But you are so smashed I doubt if you will notice. And you did say you'd do whatever you could to help."

"Whassaht?"

"The Carthaginians have a most interesting custom. Their aid to allies is conditional on a hero from the ranks of said ally agreeing to meet the Carthaginian champion."

"And whossaht?" Bill mouthed dimly, barely aware of the import of Splock's words.

"The word he used was quite unfamiliar to me," Splock said. "I couldn't tell you whom they meant. Or what."

"You mean not man . . . maybe a . . . thing?" Bill blinked rapidly as some dim bit of meaning trickled down through alcohol laden synapses.

Splock nodded. "This is the sort of problem you encounter when you go to the ancient world. Never mind, a trained Trooper like you ought to make short work of it, whatever it is."

"What happens if I lose?" Bill asked, sobering rather quickly.

"Not to worry. Hannibal has agreed to help even if you are killed."

"Oh, yeah, wonderful." Sobriety struck like poisoned lightning at this threat to mortality. "Splock, you pointed-eared son of a bitch—what have you gotten me into? I don't even have any of my weapons with me."

"Improvisation," Splock said, "is the first quality of a well-trained soldier. And you can lay off all the ear-insults."

"Come," said Hannibal, interrupting their friendly

chat, "we can hold the contest immediately."

Bill reached for the palm whiskey, then decided against it. In fact, uncharacteristically, he was cold sober and regretting it.

CHAPTER 22

NOW TO TELL OF THE DUELING GROUND OF the Carthaginians.

It was inside that portion of the city known as the Sacred Enclosure—a squat black building within which was an enormous amphitheater, its roof open to the blinding African sun. As at a bullfight, there were sunny seats and shady, and these were sold for different prices. Box holders had clay shards with curious figures inscribed on them. Season passholders had to have a man along to carry the massive clay tablet on which was inscribed the dates of the performances and the patron's seat number. When not used for contests, the Black Theater, as the locals called it, staged ballets, music festivals, defloration ceremonies and other priestly fund raisers for the local gods.

The arena was circular, and there were steep tiers of seats up the sides. Already the stands were half full, and more people were streaming in through the entry slits in the basalt walls. Sand had been strewn on the arena floor. It was a bright yellow, in contrast to the black walls of the building, and the gaily colored pennants that flew from four tall masts. Peddlers in long gray smocks trudged up and down the steep steps selling fermented mares' milk, which tasted about as loathsome as it sounds, squirrel sausages and other local specialties.

A group of acrobats was already on the arena floor, and a comic actor in satyr mask and three-foot phallus was really warming up the crowd.

In caverns below the arena, Bill was having an argument with Splock.

"I'm not going out there," Bill said, "without a weapon." Bill had refused to put on special gladiator's costume. Nor had he accepted any of the edged weapons which were laid out before him on a table.

"These look perfectly suitable," Splock said, splanging the edge of one of the swords with his fingernail. "I fail to understand your difficulty."

"I don't know anything about swords, that's my difficulty." Bill said. "I want a gun."

"But these people do not have guns," Splock said.

"I know. That's why I want one."

"That would be hardly sporting," Splock pointed out.

"Sport!" Bill shrieked, "Those mothers want to kill me! Whose side are you on, anyhow?"

"I serve the truth, unemotionally and coolly," Splock said. "And anyhow, I don't have a gun."

"You've got something, though, haven't you?"

"Not really. Only this laser pen. But that's hardly suitable—"

"Gimme!" Bill said, and grabbed it. "What's its range?"

"About ten feet. Three meters, to be exact. At that range it can burn a hole through two-inch steel plating. But Bill, I have to tell you—"

Just then Hannibal and two guards came into the room. "Well?" Hannibal asked. "Is the man from the future ready?"

"Ready," Bill said, putting the pen into the pocket under his pouch and zipping it.

"But you have no sword or lance!"

"You're right. Just pass one of those daggers over. A small one, that's it."

"Guards, escort him to the arena!"

Bill, flanked by guards with lances, marched out into the sunlight. When the crowd caught a look at him, shambling along and blinking in the sunlight, cleaning his nails with the tiny dagger the odds on Bill fell from ten to one to a hundred to one.

"You better take some of that," Bill called out to Splock.

"Bill!" Splock shouted. "There's something I must tell you! That laser pen—"

"I'm not going to give it back," Bill told him.

"But it's discharged, Bill! It hasn't any current left! Bill, not only is it out of energy, it also leaks. I was going to get it fixed at the next Hoffritz we passed."

"You can't do this to me!" Bill screamed.

But now he was alone in the middle of the arena. The crowd had fallen silent. Not a sound could be heard except for a faint rustling noise under his tunic.

Bill opened a button. A Chinger stuck out its tiny green head.

"Still with you, Bill," the lizard said.

"Who am I talking to?"

"The computer, of course."

"You'll zap whatever comes up, won't you, computer?"

"Alas, Bill, I am not capable of taking any action in my present form. But I will observe everything and report your struggles to your next of kin."

Just then an iron gate in the arena wall opened. While Bill watched, slack-jawed, something came shambling out.

CHAPTER 23

IT WAS A STRANGE-LOOKING BEAST INDEED. At first Bill mistook it for a lion, because the first thing he looked at was its head. The head was definitely leonine, with a full tawny mane, big almond-shaped yellow eyes, and the sleepily ferocious look that lions have, at least in Carthage. But then he noticed that its body was as thick around as a barrel, and tapered down to a thin scaled tail. So he thought it was a snake with a lion's head. But then he noticed the sharp little hooves, just like the hooves on the goats back home.

"Well, bless my electronic soul," the computer said in a squeaky lizard voice since, of course, he was utilizing the Chinger's body as a source of communication. "I do believe we are looking at a chimera! In my studies of the history of the human race—and a rather sordid history it is—I have come across references to the creature. Always regarded as mythological. It was long believed that these creatures were mere figments of the ancient imagination. Now we see that they existed literally. And, if I'm not mistaken, the creature is breathing fire, just like Pliny said it would."

"Do something!" Bill cried.

"But how can I?" the computer said. "I am a mere disembodied intelligence in this world."

"Then get out of that Chinger and let Illyria back in!"

"What would a Tsurisian farmgirl know about chimeras?" the computer asked.

"Never mind! Just do it!"

The computer must have done it, because a moment later Bill could hear Illyria's voice, unmistakable even when projected through the larynx and soft palate and unusual dentition of a Chinger.

"Bill! I'm here!"

This talk took place fairly rapidly, although several of the points had to be repeated since the crowd noises made it difficult to hear finer shades of discourse. The chimera was not motionless during this colloquy. First the dreaded beast pawed the ground, scraping aside the sand and scoring the basalt floor of the arena with grooves three inches long with a single strike of its adamantine hooves. Then, noticing Bill, it snorted a double snort of flames, bright red ones with an unhealthy-looking green tinge at their base. Then, fixing its gaze upon Bill, it began to walk, then run, then canter, and at last gallop, toward the intrepid trooper with what appeared to be a four-armed lizard on his shoulder.

"Illyria! Do something!"

"What can I do?" the unhappy girl moaned. "I'm only a tiny green Chinger! Albeit a heavy one from a 10G planet—"

"Shut up!" Bill hinted in a shout of quiet desperation. "Don't you have the power to take over the minds of other creatures? Isn't that a Tsurisian speciality?"

"But of course! What a clever idea! You mean you want me to take over the chimera!"

"And fast," Bill said, running away full tilt now, the chimera breathing flames behind him and gaining rapidly.

"I'm not really sure I can take over the brain of a mythical beast," Illyria vacillated.

"The computer said it was real!" Bill gasped, dodging as the goat-lion-serpent reared above him, ready to strike downward with fangs that dripped green poison.

"Bill, there's something I haven't had a chance to tell you yet—"

"Get into that chimera!" Bill roared.

"Yes, darling," Illyria said. In the next instant the

chimera had halted itself in mid-flight and flung itself at Bill's feet. Its eyes rolled upward and its long forked tongue came out to lick Bill's feet.

"How am I doing?" Illyria asked through the chimera's throat and tongue and soft palate.

"Fine," Bill said. "Just don't overdo it."

And the crowd, of course, was going wild.

C H A P T E R **24**

BILL'S TRIUMPH WAS COMPLETE, THOUGH there was one complication. After the congratulations for quelling the chimera, there were throaty shouts of Kill! Kill! and Let's see some green blood! That sort of thing. As well as Save me a bit of the sirloin! It was then Bill realized that he was supposed to slay the heraldic beast. It is customary in this sort of affair to feast everybody after the killing on broiled chimera steaks and other choice tidbits. The flesh tastes like a combination of goat, serpent and lion, and there's just a faint hint of turkey, although nobody knows where that came from. Another virtue of chimera steaks is the fact that, since the chimera is a flame breather, its steaks can be cooked in its own internal heat, as long as you do that in the first hour or two after it has been dispatched. "No way," Bill said. "No way."

His point of view was not appreciated. This was carefully explained to him by Hannibal's chamberlain, a fat and unctuous individual who kept rubbing his hands together, and, when he thought that no one was looking, he pinched his sallow cheeks to give them a little color.

"No," Bill said, "you can't have the chimera. No way. This is my chimera."

"But sir, it is customary for the victor to sacrifice the chimera for the public good. That's what all the other victors do. In fact, chimeras are becoming rare in these parts."

"All the more reason," Bill said, "not to sacrifice this one."

"The chimera must be killed," the chamberlain said. "Otherwise it means ten years bad luck, and that is the last thing in this world Carthage needs."

"I won't kill the chimera, and that's that."

"I will confer with Hannibal and the City Elders," the chamberlain said. "They will have to make the final decision."

"OK by me," Bill said. "And on the way out would you tell Mr. Splock that I need to see him right away?"

"Impossible," the chamberlain said, rubbing his hands together. "He has returned to his own time. He left this for you."

He handed Bill a note and exited, bowing low and smiling unctuously. Bill opened the note, which was folded thrice, and read:

"Congratulations on your well-deserved victory. Have returned to put Dirk into the picture. Tell Hannibal to assemble his forces; we will be back soon with suitable transport."

"That's a hell of a note," Bill said. "Just when I need him! Why couldn't he have used the telephone?"

"Because it hasn't been invented yet," Illyria, within the chimera, said.

"I know that. But time travel hasn't been invented yet, either, and he's doing it."

"Oh, Bill," Illyria the chimera said, "what are we going to do?"

"Could you take over some other body for a while? That way we could let them have the chimera and get ourselves out of here."

"I told you I had trouble controlling mythological beasts," Illyria said. "It was hard taking over this one.

It is going to be very difficult indeed to get out again. What I need, Bill darling, is a suitable host body."

"Where can we find one? How about one of those dancing girls we saw earlier? The one on the left end of the line was kind of healthy-looking in a very plumpish way," Bill finished, because he noted a frown crossing the chimera's leonine face.

"She's not at all suitable," Illyria said. "First of all, because you're interested in her. I will not be a party to perversity."

"What are you talking about, perversity?" Bill asked. "She'd be you!"

"Or I'd be her," Illyria said. "That would suit you nicely, wouldn't it?"

"Illyria! I've never heard you talk like this!"

"Oh, Bill, I don't want to sound jealous. It's just that I'm so crazy about you. You and your darling alligator foot with shining claws. It's little things like that that strike a woman's fancy. But I couldn't take over your charming little dancing girl even if I wanted to. A suitable host can only be found back on my own planet in my own time. Please, don't let them kill me!"

"They'll kill you over my dead body," Bill said gallantly.

"I would much prefer they didn't do it at all."

"That's what I meant. Come on, Illyria, I think we'd better get out of here."

"Perhaps they'll listen to reason," Illyria said wistfully.

"I doubt it," Bill said. He had heard the sound of marching and turned to see a squad of ten or so Carthaginian soldiers, heavily armored and armed, with Hannibal himself at their head, looking grim and purposeful, the way people look just before they kill a chimera.

"Come on," Bill said, grabbing Illyria by her lion's ruff, and tugged her toward the exit.

"I'm coming," Illyria said. "But where are we going?"

"Away!" he shouted, leading the way as they fled. Out the exit and across a busy street, dodging between the pedestrians and horses, the squad right behind them, into a tall building and, huffing and puffing, up the stairs. Behind them he could hear the soldiers in the lower part of the building. They were already mounting the stairs with measured tread. They reached the top floor which was very interesting. Particularly since all of the doors there were locked.

"Eeek!" Bill gurgled. "We're trapped like rats."

"Don't give up, Bill! Try the window," Illyria advised.

Bill threw the window open and looked out at the straight drop below. Then at the rain gutters. Leaning out he tested the nearest one that ran above the window. They seemed strong enough; they were bronze and half an inch thick, and fastened to the side of the building with heavy copper rivets. They really knew how to build in these days.

"We're going over the roof," Bill said, climbing out.

"Oh dear," Illyria said, pausing irresolute in the window. "I don't think I can climb. I have hooves, you know."

"But you also have a snake's body. For your life, Illyria, slither!"

The brave Tsurisian girl in the mythological disguise backed out of the window and wrapped her tail around a stanchion conveniently located some five feet away. Trembling but resolute, she followed Bill onto the roof.

CHAPTER 25

THE ROOFTOPS OF CARTHAGE PRESENTED A multi-colored display of levels and angles. The hot African sun beat down, because it was summer, and the cold African sun had gone to the underworld to rest and revive himself, or so it was claimed in the ancient annals of the city. Bill raced across the rooftops, scrambling up the higher levels and jumping down the lesser ones. Behind him came armed soldiers, running clumsily in their heavy armor, lances at the ready. As Bill raced along, with Ilyria close behind and staying up, he felt a tickling sensation under his tunic next to his ribs. He realized that it was the Chinger lizard that had formerly been Ilyria.

"Can you go back into the Chinger?" Bill asked, his breath coming in painful pants.

"I forgot about the Chinger!" Ilyria said. "I don't know, but I can try!"

"No time like the present," Bill said, because some of the soldiers had unbuckled their heavy armor and were coming along quickly now, gaining on him. And ahead, directly in his path, Bill saw a high wall of polished marble. The theater of Dionysus! The god of abandon was now blocking his way.

The lizard crawled out onto Bill's shoulder, took one look at the pursuing soldiers, and started to duck back to shelter. Bill grabbed it before it could go out of sight.

"Now, Ilyria!" Bill cried.

"Just a moment," the Chinger said. "There's something I'd better explain. This is Illyria, speaking to you from within this alien Chinger. It's a little strange in here. What's that? No, it couldn't be! Oh, Bill, you'll never guess what's happened!"

"So tell me," Bill panted. The soldiers now had him backed against a wall. The chimera was looking around groggily, unused to being back within its own body again. The Chinger, meanwhile, had gone glassy-eyed and limp. It was still alive, but seemed to be in a semi-comatose state, or perhaps an entirely comatose state; it was difficult to tell.

"Illyria? Speak to me!"

No answer from the somnolent lizard, lying with its four arms crossed peacefully on its green chest.

A soldier prodded Bill with his spear. The others moved in. And at that moment the chimera, released from Illyria's control, resumed its existence as a deadly and dangerous beast. It breathed out twin gouts of flame, like dragons do, and melted several shields. Then it turned to attack Bill.

"All right!" Bill cried. "Kill it, since you want to so badly!"

It was a tricky moment for Bill. The soldiers had to defend themselves against the onslaught of the chimera, returned to itself and filled with mythological fury. It attacked in a manner not seen since the days of Homer, and it emitted loud goatlike bleatings as it charged. These unnerving sounds mounted the scale into the supersonic, set the soldiers' teeth on edge, and set their swords to chattering against their shields. The Chinger opened its eyes and took one look at what was going on and scampered back for safety within Bill's shirt, seeking the snug haven of Bill's left armpit, where it was sure harm would not befall it. The soldiers finally managed to pin the chimera to the wooden planking of the roof with their sharp spears. The chimera's sound output redoubled as it found itself wounded. Black dots appeared in the sky and quickly resolved themselves into long-nose bare-breasted women with bat wings, all of them clad in snaky black evening gowns. These were the Harpies, called out of their mythological slumber by the wounded cries of their fellow fabulous creature. They dived onto the soldiers, whose ranks had just been redoubled by the arrival of a double platoon of Varangians, sent, as Bill was to learn later, by Splock, who had anticipated this situation and had rushed back to the future to get some help. The Varangians were Swedish Russians, or possibly Russian Swedes, depending on whose history book you're reading, and they cared not a fig for the menace of effete Graeco-Roman mythology. They laid about them with mighty strokes, swinging their long battleaxes in shining circles, cutting down the Carthaginian soldiery who couldn't get out of the way quickly enough.

"Go to it, boys!" Bill shouted, his built-in translator putting out his words in middle Varangian, which none of these fellows understood since they were Finnish Varangians from the marshlands around Lake Uū. But they liked the sound of his voice and laid about them with renewed vigor. The chimera was definitely bested. It gave one last shriek, which started a minor earth tremor in the city walls, and expired.

Before they could congratulate themselves and pass the beer, however, there was a splatter of rain, and then, within moments, a raging storm had sprung out of nowhere complete with hailstones and hundred-mile-an-hour winds. Great bulging clouds with ominous purple-black bottoms rode across the sky like galleons of doom. This, as Bill learned later, was the arrival of Typhon, spirit of the hurricane. The Harpies balanced lightly on the screaming winds and redoubled their attack. They too were creatures of the storm. When they came close Bill could see that they had hag faces and the ears of bears, and the bodies of birds with long hooked claws. Like birds, they were shameless about defecation, and like humans, they were purposeful about directing it. The Varangians gagged as a torrent of excrement was heaved at them.

Bill fought free of the reeking melee and looked for a place to run to. The only way off the rooftop was the way he had come, and that way was now choked with masses of Carthaginian soldiery, Hannibal urging them on and pointing to him. Bill suspected he had lost his guest status and looked around desperately for another way out. Fighting free of the fighting men who surrounded him, and laying about him mightily with a big broadsword he had picked up during the fight, he cut his way to the opposite wall. There a quick glance showed him a ladder leading down over the side. It was a rickety old ladder, just pieces of bamboo tied together with vines, but it would have to do. He put one foot over the side and started down.

It was at this precise moment that the new thing happened.

CHAPTER 26

AT FIRST IT WAS NO MORE THAN A SHIMmering of light. Then it resolved itself into an incandescent ball about the size of a medicine ball, or slightly larger. Bill, hanging on to the rickety ladder, with the Chinger gnawing at his armpit (out of panic rather than malice, he learned later), did not take kindly to the fiery thing that swooped up close to him and hung just in front of his face, changing colors and giving off eartorturing harmonics.

"What the bowb you want?" Bill snarled testily. "Can't you see that I'm busy trying to save my life?"

"You just listen, dummy. I'll do the talking," a gravelly voice issuing from the glowing sphere said.

"Just in case you hadn't noticed, you are up the creek with a broken paddle. Want a lift?"

In other times, Bill might have been suspicious of an offer for help from a shining sphere of lambent energy that just happened to be going his way. But at the moment he was not inclined to be fussy. Already the ladder was starting to collapse, undermined by the sacred termites of Artemis, whom Bill had unwittingly insulted by suggesting that the dancing girl, a servant of the goddess, be supplanted by Illyria, an outsider and unbeliever. Not only was the bamboo ladder collapsing, but also soldiers had brought to its base a series of big wooden platforms covered with bronze spikes pushed up through them. They were all shouting at Bill, "Jump, jump!" It was an unseemly exhibition and it is little wonder that the Carthaginians have ceased to exist as a people and are perpetuated now only by a cluster of unseemly attitudes.

"Yes! I don't know who you are," Bill said, "but if you can get me away from here, I'd be plenty grateful."

The sphere rapidly expanded, engulfing Bill. He felt his hold loosen on the bamboo ladder. Then the ladder collapsed, and Bill felt himself dropping through the air for a frightening moment, until the energies within the sphere caught him up and shielded him as the sphere moved away at great speed, leaving behind the sullen and unpleasant Carthaginians and their secondhand borrowed Greek deities.

CHAPTER 27

AFTER THINGS SETTLED DOWN, BILL FOUND himself inside a small but well-appointed spaceship. There appeared to be but one person aboard: a square-shouldered man, handsome but with a dour expression born of having seen too much human folly, sitting at the controls in a big command chair with a plaque on it that read, "Ham Duo—the buck stops here."

"Commander Duo," Bill said, in his most formal and grateful manner, "I want to thank you for doing this for me. I don't know what I would have done without your timely intervention."

"Hell, don't thank me," Duo said out of the sides of his mouth. "Sure, I like to save the odd sentient being now and then when it isn't too much trouble and I'm in the mood, but there's no need to make a fuss about it. A lot of other people would have done the same if they'd had my guts and expertise."

"I really appreciate it."

"Hell," Duo said, "I didn't do it for you so don't go getting all weepy."

"Who did you do it for?"

"The Freedom Fighters of Earth. I happen to know that you are helping them in your own simple-minded way, and I couldn't let you fall into the clutches of the Evil Empire."

"I didn't know Carthage had an Evil Empire," Bill said.

"They don't. The Evil Empire set up simulation techniques so they could loose those mythological crea-

107

tures on everyone. You bet I had to put a stop to that. So don't go thinking that I was doing it just for you."

"Sorry about that," Bill said.

"It's a natural enough error, I suppose," Ham said.

"I didn't know you were able to operate in the past," Bill said. "How did you do that? The *Gumption* got here by putting her engines into oscillation."

"I know all about that," Duo said. "It's a dumb trick. They'll have to reseat all the bolts before their ship is spaceworthy again. Much better to use a temporal displacer that I just happen to have."

Duo gestured. Bill saw, on the port side of the spaceship, not far from the bow but not far from midships, either, a black box with a plaque on it. The plaque read, *Temporal/Spatial Displacer—Patent Pending.*

Bill stared at it. Then stared even closer as he realized that this was the very secret that his own Space Navy had sent him to Tsuris to find out about. If he could get his hands on another like it—or even on this one—

"Where are we going?" Bill asked coyly.

"Rathbone."

"Beg pardon?"

"The planet Rathbone."

"What's there?"

"A little unfinished business," Duo grated, his voice grim, his large, attractively hairy hands clutching grimly to the controls of his ship.

"Do you suppose you could drop me off somewhere?" Bill asked. "Space Trooper Headquarters, for example?"

"Sure," Duo said. "I'll just take care of this Rathbone matter first. It's on the way, and it won't take long."

Illyria the Chinger seemed to be asleep inside his shirt—and Bill could easily understand why. He heaved a tired sigh and sat down heavily on the ship's sofa. He found a magazine, a comic book magazine featuring ducks in full armor and a camel dressed up to be Charlemagne. There was the sound of distant quacking and screaming when he turned the pages. Soon he was absorbed in the story. He only hoped the business on Rathbone wouldn't take up too much time.

"Bill," Duo said, then shouted since he saw that he wasn't getting through. "You, Trooper! Get your nose out of that revolting comic for five minutes and get below and clean yourself up—I can smell the blood and gore from here. There are plenty of spare uniforms left over from a masquerade party I had. Then haul your butt into the galley and grill us up a couple of mastodon steaks."

The thought of food was a winner and Bill gurgled happily as saliva spurted into his mouth from every dusty salivary gland. After tossing out his torn uniform, and pulling on a new one with admiral's insignia, he found the galley, and a freezer full of mastodon steaks that Duo had picked up on a previous adventure. He grilled one of these in the turbomicrowave, which went so fast that the steak burst into flame and turned into charcoal as he closed the door. He played with the controls until he got it right. He promised himself that he would cook the next one for Duo. Looking around the galley for something to wash it down with he found a cabinet filled with brown bottles. One of them had a hand-written label that read, "Homemade Ophiuchian Rum—not for Human Consumption."

"Right now I'm not feeling human!" he cackled and drank deep.

When he got off the floor he grinned happily and drank some more. A delicious numbness began to creep over him, disturbed only by an itch in his armpit. He started to scratch it and found himself scratching the top of the Chinger's head.

"Illyria, how are you?" he asked.

"She's doing all right," the Chinger said.

"What does that mean? Who the bowb am I talking to?"

"Bill, this is going to take a little explaining."

"To hell with that! Who are you?"

Bill grabbed at the Chinger as it started to flee and, wholly by chance, an accident really, his finger touched the back of the Chinger's neck. When this happened the top of the Chinger's head opened on a concealed hinge. Inside the creature's skull, where the brains would normally be, though there weren't any now, there was a tiny man, no more than an inch high, seated at a tiny control panel. There was a cot and an easy chair close by, and a tiny toilet. The man was smoking nervously, tapping the ashes of his cigarette into an ashtray so small as to be only two steps above invisible to the naked eye.

"How did you get in there?" Bill gaped, then frowned. "And, equally important—what are you doing in there?"

"Well," the man said, "That is going to take a little explaining. First let me introduce myself. Charles Ivan Arbuthnot, SNI, Space Navy Intelligence. Because my name is so long the initial letters are combined to form an acronym, CIA, most people call me by that, and you can too . . ."

"Just kindly shut the hell up," Bill suggested. "Where's Illyria?"

"That's part of the explanation. Bill, don't be rash, hear me out."

Bill had raised one hamlike hand in preparation to smashing the Chinger and the tiny agent CIA within it to a small but messy pulp. What he had drunk seemed to have done some nasty things with his head.

"This is part of the secret Chinger technology," CIA said. "I'm trying to bring the secret of miniaturization back to our armed forces. I wore a very hairy, and warm too let me tell you, ape suit and hung around the jungle near one of their secret laboratories that we discovered on this hothouse world. I got into the lab one night and found the secret miniaturization machinery that enables them to shrink or expand at will, thus playing hell with Earth's plans and generally confusing everyone. They had this giant Chinger robot for working in steel mills and I got into the controls, reduced to real Chinger size and got the hell out of there and was doing fine until your girl friend took over my mind and she was too stupid to know it wasn't really a Chinger mind in there but a human one. So now you understand.''

Bill didn't know what to say. It was a reasonable enough explanation, given the unusual circumstances of everything. But there was something fishy about it, too. Bill had the impression that he was not being told the whole story and besides this joker talked so much Bill's head was beginning to hurt. Or maybe it was the booze. He pinched his nose with his fingers but it did not help. Then he remembered.

"Listen, CIA or whatever the hell your name is—where's Illyria who was supposed to be in there?"

"That's the difficult part," CIA said. "As you can imagine, there isn't much room in here once you go down to the level I'm at. Illyria tried to squeeze in, took over for awhile as I said. I know how fond you are of her. I was trying to save her for your sake."

"Yeah, what happened?"

"It was too tight for us both," CIA said. "You can imagine how difficult it was, having this female persona squeezed into my brain. Bill, I didn't mean to harm her. I was trying to find the best solution for everybody."

"Where's Illyria?" Bill roared, his broad hand with its muscular thickness hovering over the subminiature CIA in his tiny control room.

"Now listen, I'm trying to tell you," CIA said, cowering. "Give me a chance, will you? It's hard to talk when you're as tiny as I am."

"So get back to your real size," Bill said.

"I'm afraid there's some difficulty around that, too," CIA said, snuffling unhappily.

"I want to know about Illyria right now," Bill growled angrily. He reached into the Chinger's head and plucked CIA out between thumb and forefinger. Bill's other hand curled into a fist and the fist lifted, prepared to hammer CIA into a thin unpleasant paste.

"Since room was so limited," CIA said, "she decided to perform the Jansenite Maneuver. I begged her not to, but you know what she's like, Bill, a real trouper. I even offered to vacate this head for her. But she wouldn't hear of it. That's a girl in a million, Bill. You were lucky to have known her."

"What is the Jansenite Maneuver?" Bill asked in a normal tone of voice. His throat was getting hoarse from roaring.

"It was invented, or perhaps I should say developed, on the planet Jansen VII, which is located near the Coalsack region. The local species there had a problem, you see—"

CIA's explanation was interrupted by Ham Duo's voice over the intercom. "Bill! Get up here at once! We got trouble!"

"In just a minute," Bill called back. "I've got to—"

"Drop everything and get up here!" Duo roared. "If you want to live, that is. If not, take your time."

"Be right back," Bill said to the miniature agent. "Don't go away." He hurried to the control room.

"What's going on?" he asked.

Ham Duo gestured at the wraparound viewplate that afforded a view of nearly two hundred degrees of space without distortion. Bill saw three small ships coming toward them and maneuvering at great speed. Bursts of radiance flared against the ship's energy shields proving that some of the missiles were getting through their defenses. Another two ships came up behind them. They were squat little vessels, one being fighter-interceptors, painted the ominous ocher and rose madder of the Swinglis* of Omnichron II.

"But we're not at war with the Swinglis*!" Bill said.

"Tell them that," Ham Duo said. "And meanwhile you might as well man the port atomic cannon."

Bill ran to the gun station and strapped himself into the control seat. He switched onto manual just as a double burst rocked their ship, dimming the lights and putting a strain on the defensive shields.

"One more like that and we've had it," Duo gritted.

The Swingli* ships were streaking in toward Duo's ship from all angles, and both Duo and Bill were at the controls of their port side and starboard side atomic cannons respectively. Brilliant laser flashes arced here and there, filling the blackness of space with the brilliance of arcing electricity. One of the Swinglis*, bolder than the rest, bored straight in toward the ship's defensive shield, scorning defensive action. "Get that sucker!" Duo shouted. "Tracking," Bill roared. Both fighting men set their sights on the approaching bandit. Their ship bucked and swayed as atomic torpedoes burst against the energy shield, buffeting the two men and knocking down all the crockery in the ship's tiny galley. Bill managed to blow up the bandit at the last possible moment, sending its burning remains cartwheeling across space. Duo meanwhile had accounted for five more of the raiders, leaving only twenty or so to go.

"Another squadron of them coming up astern," Bill said, glancing into the retrograde mirror attached to his gunsight.

"These guys are really starting to get me mad," Duo snarled, showing his teeth, which were startlingly white and obviously false. "Strap yourself down, old buddy. I'm going to try something real different."

Bill grabbed for the safety harness and quickly buckled it around him. From the ship's galley he heard shrill sounds, like a miniature man would make if he were being buffeted around mercilessly. Ham fired the full bank of retrograde rockets, at the same time skidding the ship into an impossibly tight turn.

Bill's harness snapped under the huge G-strain. He found himself plastered against one wall as Duo, his eyes bulging out of his head, continued to tighten the turn.

Behind them, the Swingli* bandits fell away, unable to keep up with this apparently suicidal maneuver.

As soon as he had put a little distance between his ship and theirs, Duo kicked in the emergency light-speed selector. There was a groan of tortured metal, a squeal of overstressed men. The ship shuddered like a rat in the jaws of a terrier, then suddenly darted off at a rapidly multiplying speed factor impossible to attain in a normal maneuver.

Space winked on and off. Suns appeared and vanished. The ship was revolving as it sped through its turns, and Bill was bouncing from wall to wall. Duo was still strapped in, but he seemed to be at the breaking point.

Bill looked through the mirrors, then checked again with the radar detection system.

"You can ease up now!" he told Duo. "We've outrun them!"

"Ease up!" Duo said. "Ah, wouldn't I dearly like to!"

"You mean—"

"That's right," Duo said.

Out of control, spinning and turning, the ship shrieked down through the thin upper atmosphere of a planet. The ground was coming up very rapidly. Which didn't really matter since they would burn up at this speed, long before they hit.

CHAPTER 28

NOW SING, MUSE, OF THAT DESCENT through the upper atmosphere, the ship's hull glowing a dull red as it skimmed the thin upper air, Ham Duo desperately trying to take speed off the ship, which was fluttering and turning like a drunken butterfly. And tell us of Bill, too, bouncing from wall to wall as the ship changed configuration, trying to get back to the galley where he had left CIA, the Chinger, and, perhaps—it was difficult to tell at this point—Illyria. Inch by inch he crawled as the retro-rockets fired and Duo tried maneuvers unheard of in the "Space Pilot's Companion," in any edition, to try to get more speed off the ship before they either burned up in the atmosphere or crashed like a cannon ball on the planet's rapidly looming surface.

Then they were plunging through dense cloud cover, red and purple clouds with silvery fringes, through and out the other side until they could make out features on the planet. It was a yellow and orange world, with bright green patches here and there, and long dark markings that might have been canals but also might have been something else. It was hard to be sure at this speed and altitude and G-pressure.

Bill managed to get back to the galley. The Chinger had found a tiny deceleration hammock, of the sort used to keep eggs from exploding. Bill gasped hoarsely with the last of his strength, "Illyria, are you all right? Are you home right now?"

But it was CIA's voice-pattern that replied, "Like I said, Bill, I was going to explain about that."

But it looked like explanations would have to wait, perhaps forever, because the ground was rushing up now like a locomotive gone berserk, only much bigger, and Bill still wasn't strapped down and was in good stead to be shmeared flat into a thin unpleasant slime when the ship struck.

Then, at the last moment, the doors of the pantry swung open and Bill saw within a gigantic cauldron filled with a pasty gray doughy substance. This, as he learned later, was the dough for a giant pot-pie, Ganja pot that is, that Duo had been whipping up before the difficulties on Rathbone arose to change his plans. With his last strength hauled himself forward.

The dough surrounded him with its gluey consistency. Luckily enough, the shaking the ship had taken had imparted to the dough a satiny elasticity. It shielded Bill better than the standard harness would have done. At the last moment before impact, the Chinger lizard with the miniature agent at the controls in its head leaped into the vat beside him. Then the ship struck the ground with a bone-shattering jolt and, gratefully, Bill passed out.

C H A P T E R **29**

JUST BEFORE RECOVERING CONSCIOUSness, there is a moment in which you don't remember how you got unconscious. You are too taken up with just becoming conscious again. So for a moment there is only this, and then, a tiny moment after that, there is, not a memory of what rendered you unconscious—that comes later—but rather a presentiment as to how that came about. That presentiment comes clothed in a thin veil of anticipatory emotion. So it was with Bill. If you can follow all that deep stuff. When he came to again, he realized first that he was Bill, next that something had made him unconscious, and then, that he might not be awakening into very pleasant circumstances. So often is the transition from dreaming sleep into strainy-eyed reality. In his dreams, while knocked out, Bill had been an emperor of infinite space. Perhaps. But the dreams fade, as he came to and the thought occurred to him that he'd rather not find out what he'd gotten into this time.

He really did not want to think about it, but felt

compelled to. Why would Swingli★ ships attack Ham Duo? What was Duo's mission on Rathbone II? Was this Rathbone II? How were they going to get out of here? When was he going to have a chance to go to the toilet?

Finally the flood of questions was sufficient to override Bill's desire to keep his eyes shut and wait for better times. Slowly at first, then definitively, he opened his eyes.

He was in a small room, bare, with flagstone floors which looked quite chilly except that Bill wasn't lying directly on them. He was on what looked like a large brown rug, or perhaps an exceptionally thick blanket, of the sort that people wrap around themselves at sporting events on all planets with chilly stadiums. The room he was in was illuminated by a long neon tube overhead. There were scratchings on the stone walls, words of imprecation or prayer written in languages Bill had never encountered. Bill moved himself very gently, because you could never tell what might be broken after a crash like that. He didn't know where he was, and for the moment wasn't too eager to find out. Things hadn't been going well for him recently. He wished that he would stop having crashes. It hardly seemed fair, all these things happening to him.

He started to climb to his feet when the rug beneath him stirred and emitted a porcine grunt. Bill rolled off it rather quickly, as you might very well imagine, and pressed his back to the wall and bulged his eyes. The rug sat up, too, and revealed itself to be a Kookie, one of those large furry beasts with mild to well-done intelligence who have been known to take up the practice of space pirate, since that is a profession open to all with no nonsense about college credits or Civil Service exams.

C H A P T E R 30

"HELLO," SAID BILL, RATHER UNIMAGINA-tively, which, considering what he had been through lately, was not too bad. "How are you?"

When the Kookie heard this he responded in his own primitive language, all growls and high-pitched whines. Bill's built-in translator, somewhat battered from recent vicissitudes but still functioning more-or-less as it should, translated this as, "Gee, boss, Kookie feel pretty shitty. You no see my master, him named Ham Duo around anywhere?"

"As a matter of fact," Bill said, "I just came from his ship."

The Kookie sat up, towering head and shoulders over Bill even in that posture. "Oooh, goodies. Where he?"

"I wish I knew," Bill said. "We were on our way here to rescue you when Swingli* ships shot us down."

"Dragonshit!" the Kookie rumbled angrily. "I told Ham many often times. Use invisibility treatment—great stuff! Make spaceship look like big crappy meteor-ite. But no, he no listen to primitive Kookie with brain like garbage grinder, that what he say. So where he is now?"

"You know as much as I do. I passed out when the ship crash-landed," Bill said. "I haven't the dimmest idea where he is now. I don't suppose you've seen Il-lyria."

"What hell you talk about?" Chewgumma said, for that was his name. Unbelievable as it is. The Kookies

118

ran to some pretty kooky names. Like Chewgrappa, Chewbacca, Chewrugga and so forth.

"Someone else, or something else. It gets a little complicated. It's a Chinger, which looks like a seven-inch-high green lizard with four arms, hard to miss. And it has brain trouble, to put it mildly. A lot to do with changing bodies, you know."

"Ah, so! Maybe a Tsurisian."

"Do you know the Tsurisians?"

"Had my run-ins with them, fight like blazes," the Kookie said. "But that was in another time."

"What's going to happen to us?" Bill asked.

"Probably die for sure," Chewgumma said with guttural gloom. "They kill-maim-torture pirates here. They still pissed at Ham and me. Raided their big city, stole all the treasure of the Klingians. Now me captured—ho-ho you too."

"Thanks for the sympathy. And dare I ask how a big brain like you got captured?"

"A net coated with honey," Chewgumma said sheepishly. "We Kookies kinda stupid. Fall for that old stunt."

"And do you know what they'll do to you?"

"Got plenty fears," Chewgumma muttered. "People here on Rathbone famous rug makers. Always got eye out for new materials."

Bill looked at the Kookie's thick, luxurious pelt. And despite being sympathetic to the big alien beast, he couldn't help thinking what a nice rug he would make.

"That's a tough break," Bill said feigning sympathy.

The Kookie blinked angry little red eyes and he caught the fake sympathy in Bill's voice. "Human skin is waterproof, too," he snarled.

"Well, yes, I suppose so," Bill said.

"Make heap good bathroom rug."

Just then there was the sound of a key in the lock and the door of their cell swung open.

Four guards entered. They were extremely tall and

thin, with long heads shaped like kidney beans and bodies which looked in the last degree of emaciation. They had to stoop almost double to get inside the cell door. Once inside they still couldn't straighten up. Four of them in the room, in addition to Bill and the Kookie, crowded the small cell to the bursting point. This was the first time that Bill had ever seen a Swingli★ in the flesh, although he had come across their pictures in the *Alien Enemy Identification Book,* which all human military personnel had to study so as to know the contours of their many and varied enemies.

There seemed to be a Swingli★ officer in charge of the guards. He was half a head taller than the others, and as Bill later learned, a member of the officer class which prided itself upon its superior height. He wore a black bearskin cape, and Chewgumma cringed when he saw it and emitted a dolorous cry.

The guards moved them out of the cell and down the corridor, hurrying them along with the small human prods they carried for moments like this. It was a long corridor, made of rough-hewn rocks, and roofed over with palm fronds. After thirty yards or so, the corridor split into two branches. Here the guards divided, one contingent taking the Kookie down the right-hand path, and the other taking Bill down the left-hand side. The bearskinned officer accompanied Bill's group, and Bill didn't know if that was good news or bad. The Swinglis★ hadn't said a word so far, although Bill had tried to question them, first in Shmendrik, main trading language of the Swingli★ people, then in Unrevised Esperanto, and finally in Chinga Franca, the widely-used language of the Chinger lizard people, which had only recently been discovered in a translator machine from a wrecked Chinger ship. His built-in translator was able to handle all of these languages without difficulty, but the Swinglis★ didn't even acknowledge that sounds were being made, much less that they were comprehensible sounds. After a while Bill shut up and began to take notice of his surroundings.

They went down a flight of stairs, then another. Torches flamed in embrasures, and there were antique glow-lights here and there, just enough to change the atmosphere from positively stygian to absolutely gloomy. There were cells along the way, and from them Bill heard funny screechy sounds, like bats feasting on something that didn't like it. But he couldn't tell what it really was, and subsequent research has revealed that it was a sound machine implanted by the Swinglis★ and set to give forth unnerving noises. It was not for nothing that the Swinglis★ were known as one of the more subtle of the galactic races. Their long stature helped, of course, Creatures who look as funny as Swinglis★ do, with their orange fright-wig hair and their huge stooped shoulders and their air of frenetic absentmindedness, are apt to develop a sense of humor, whose invariable concomitant is the intelligence to avoid being laughed at. Once this is well set, other forms of intelligence follow. The Swinglis★ hadn't had much time yet, counted in aeons, to go beyond the early stage of developing ways of avoiding being laughed at.

They even felt humiliated because they were not listed in Morrison's *Stardard Dictionary of Alien Races*, not even in the addendum under Alien Races (Tall). Several documentaries have been made on them recently, most notably Sloan Buster's searing "Thin," which shows the Swinglis★ in an altogether too favorable light. Swingli★ traders have occasionally appeared in Earth-dominated space, but they tend to avoid it since humans always laugh at them. On their own planet, however, they were able to arrange things more to their own needs. Their boast was, "You won't laugh at us on Swingli★."

Due to their need to be taken seriously, the Swinglis★ go to great expense to maintain an impressive pomp and circumstance. Thus, when Bill was ushered into the big room, he first noticed the high desk, cantilevered out over the floor so that three black-gowned Swingli★ judges, with powdered perukes set precisely in place, could peer down at him through their granny glasses.

The Swinglis★ had researched their justice system most carefully. Every race has its own inborn directive, the secret rules, written on the genes, expatiated upon in the spiraling DNA, which tell them what they are and what they should strive for. Not only that but also implanted in the fundamental genetic equipment is the knowledge of what is funny and what is not, and a driving need to look good at all times and under all circumstances. Due to this racial imperative, the Swinglis★, when they first encountered alien civilizations, took pains to discover a form of justice that really suited them. Before encountering civilization, they had had no justice or legal system worthy of the word. When a Swingli★ grew annoyed at another Swingli★, he bashed him over the head with the short lead-packed wooden clubs which were aptly named, in Swingli★, UuQ-Olen, or friendship-stoppers. If anyone didn't like this, he bashed the perpetrator over the head, and thus might in turn be bashed over the head himself. Friendship-stopping was the only form of death on the planet at this time, because a provident nature, always experimenting, had given the Swinglis★ immortality except when they were smacked on the head with a wooden club packed with lead.

A proper justice system, for the Swingli★, had to look good. That was the prime consideration. The Swinglis★ at this time were in desperate need of a new way of controlling friendship-stopping, since the population had been declining ever since the so-called Unpleasant Wars of the 90's. They hit upon a combination of various modalities. From the English they took the high desks at which the judges sit, and the powered perukes, and above all, the awesome dignity that pervaded British dispensations of justice as shown in the many Pinewood Studio pictures the Swingli★ had unearthed in the ancient data banks, the only thing saved from that long-destroyed planet. No one could laugh at a three-man group of judges like that. They thought.

Bill couldn't control his giggle when he saw the three skinny judges with the granny glasses slipping down their scaly faces, with white perukes on their pointed heads, and a general air of testy dignity. The officer in the bearskin nudged him in the ribs with an incredibly sharp and pointed elbow and he sobered up at once.

The middle judge, in sepulchral tones, said, "Let the prisoner approach the bar of justice."

Bill had intended to be dignified and contrite, but something about the crashingly solemn nature of the thing, as well as thirst, made him say, "You got any other kind of bar around here aside from a justice one? I sure could use a drink before going on with this."

The judges looked at each other. The audience—there were close to three hundred Swinglis* in deck chairs watching the proceedings—looked at the judges. The guards looked at each other. Bill looked puzzled.

The middle judge remarked to the judge on his left, "Was that intelligible, what he said?"

"I might perhaps hazard," the left judge said, "that the prisoner was essaying a witticism."

"I could have told you that," said the judge on the right.

"Do you mean," the middle judge said, "that the prisoner was making a joke?"

"Impossible, yes, but it's true," said the left judge.

"But what was the point of the joke?" asked the middle judge.

"It must have been subtle," said the left judge, "because I didn't really get it. Word play on bar, I suppose. Bit of an odd way to begin, isn't it?"

"Yes, I should think so," said the middle judge. He peered down at Bill. "Prisoner, did you in fact make a joke in our presence?"

"Well, yeah, I guess I did," Bill said. "I didn't mean anything by it." He started to giggle again.

"And what," asked the middle judge, "is so funny?"

"Nothing, excuse me, I'm sorry," said Bill.

The middle judge turned to the right judge. "Why would he burst into laughter like that?"

"I don't know," said the right judge, "but I fear the worst. I suppose, if you thought it necessary, you could ask him."

"Prisoner, why did you laugh?"

"The fact is," Bill said, "I have a Chinger lodged in my left armpit and he's tickling me."

"Did you hear that?" the left judge said to the right judge.

"Amazing, his effrontery."

"He couldn't actually have such a lizard secreted on his person, could he?"

"I doubt it. Earthians and Chingers are hereditary enemies."

"I suppose," said the bearskin-hatted guard, "we could search him and find out for sure."

"No," said the middle judge. "This is already bad enough. Frankly, I don't want to know."

"Look," Bill said, "I don't know why you've pulled me into court like this. I haven't done nothin'."

"'Nothin,'" the middle judge said. "What does that mean?"

The right judge, the one with the drooping right eyelid and the droll expression, said, "I believe it is 'nothing' with the terminal 'g' omitted."

"But why would he do that?" the middle judge asked.

"It's probably some kind of a joke," the right judge said.

"Ah! Another joke! It likes me not, the disposition of this felon at the bar."

"He seems disposed to be humorous," the left judge said.

"If so, it is a grievous fault," the right judge said.

"And grievously shall he pay for it." The three judges looked at each other and smiled the satisfied

S T O P   R E A D I N G !

AT LEAST FOR A FEW MINUTES. THIS WARNING is for your own good, really. It has been proven by exhaustive laboratory tests that continuous reading, without taking a break, causes eyestrain and bladder trouble. That's it. Get up. Stretch. Yawn, you relaxed devil, you! Then go to the little boy's room (or the little girl's room, depending on your sex or voyeuristic vagaries.) Then settle back down with this unputdown-able book.

AND LOOK—

at what your friendly editor has arranged for your edification and pleasure. A portfolio of artwork that will give you incredible insight into the intricacies of interest in this volume—not to mention a good look at Bill's tusks.

ARE YOU READY?

Then turn the page...

First lesson in how not to take a self-photograph. Do not get drunk out of your mind and hold the camera at arm's length. Or you get something—Uggh!—like this.

The simple stupidity of Trooper life leads to even simpler—and stupider—pleasures. Bill's buddies in the Fighting 69th get their jollies at his new-foot unveiling.

Bill gets a big thrill in visiting Officers' Country. All of his pictures are taken by accident—with this kind of loathsome result—when his finger twitches accidentally on the release.

Here the MPs bestow their generosity on Bill—a shot in the kidney, a punch in the liver—a jolt of Apathia 24 and it is bye-bye.

Ahh, the nutrient vat—with Bill hopefully not going down for the last time.

You don't often see a shot like this—and how it was taken is a Professional Secret. So look with envy at Bill controlling his analogue destiny.

Exceedingly rare photo of Bill's Mindless Body posing nude for a Tsuris artist painting on rare rectangular canvas. Note: mindlessness not visible on his face. Which says a lot for his normal expression.

What technology can do! Here is a very unusual photo of a squoll from the Point of View of Bill's semi-autonomous body existing only as a thought-pattern in the Tsuris Computer. Can you believe that! (Millions wouldn't.)

An artful and very sincere composition, reeking of authenticity, of Bill's first view of Carthage.

For the moment, nobody is trying to kill Bill—a welcome, if inexplicable, change of pace. Life as a computer oracle has its compensations, it seems.

Standard-issue gear for Troopers seeking souvenirs: a blaster and, for those memories that might resent being killed, an instant camera.

smiles of men who have essayed a small joke in a difficult situation.

"Now then, prisoner, you are accused of being a party to the landing of an unauthorized spaceship in the public festival grounds illegally and without a license, thus seriously disrupting the slug festival and causing the organizer of the festival, Zek Horsley, public embarrassment of a degree judged to be felonious. Prisoner, how do you plead?"

"Huh?" Bill asked.

"Were you or were you not a party to the unauthorized landing of a spaceship on the festival grounds?"

"Now look," Bill said, "we were shot down. I was a passenger on the ship. But we were shot down by Swinglis★. We had no choice where we landed."

"I didn't ask you if you had any choice," the middle judge said. "I asked if you did land on the aforesaid fair grounds."

"Suppose I did," Bill said. "I'm talking hypothetically now."

"Duly noted," said the middle judge, his left eye drooping characteristically.

"Well then, if I did land on the fair grounds, first of all I had nothing to do with it, second of all, nobody was hurt, so I plead let's forget it and I'll get back to my military people."

"Nobody was hurt?" the middle judge said with a snort. "What about the slugs?"

"What slugs?"

"The slugs that had been assembled for the slug judging contest, that's what slugs."

"Yeah, well what about them?"

"Your ship crushed the slug sectioner where the slugs were sleeping."

"You mean we slushed the slug sectioner," Bill said, breaking into uncontrollable laughter as a human is apt to do when he makes a bad joke in extremely uptight surroundings. "Anyhow, I'll pay for the damage. Or Duo will. How much will it cost to truck in another load of slugs?"

"He tries to make light of it," the middle judge remarked to the left judge behind his hand.

"Yet there might be merit in what he says."

"What of the embarrassment to Horsley?"

"And anyhow, are the slugs replaceable?"

"Not that lot, no."

"Obviously not that lot. I mean another lot that would represent a fair and more than fair exchange?"

"Hard to say. You know as well as I do how hard it is to pick a truckload of really good-looking fat old slugs, especially now with the dry season coming on."

"And there's still the insult to Horsley to be considered."

"I would feel more sympathetic to Horsley's plight," the right judge said, his eyelid having just stopped fluttering, "if he weren't the sort of bloke whom someone would have hit with a friendship-stopper long ago if this were the bad old days."

"It's true," the middle judge said. "Nothing sympathetic about old Horsley. What do you say we let the prisoner off with a reprimand?"

"I suppose that would be all right," the left judge said, "though it seems a bit of heavy punishment."

"He made jokes," the middle judge pointed out.

"So he did. Yes, let it be a reprimand?"

They turned to the other judge. "And how say you?"

"Eh?" the other judge said.

"We're voting for a reprimand."

"Well jolly good," the other judge said. "And let it be a severe one. Prisoner do you accept the judgment?"

"Sure I do," Bill said, thinking that these were the nicest aliens he had met in a long time, and a whole lot more civilized and sophisticated in their justice system than many he could think of including his own people.

"Very well," the middle judge said. "Bailiff! Bring in the reprimand!"

CHAPTER 31

AFTERWARD, BILL COULDN'T BELIEVE HOW silly he had been to accept the reprimand like that without finding out exactly what it was. Alien races were alien and sneaky, that had been drilled into him by the military. Along with a lot of other things that he was trying to forget. They had long preached distrust of everyone who was not like them. Since there were few pot-bellied and prematurely bald races in the universe, this meant they distrusted everyone. The Swinglis★ had an especially bad reputation. "Swindlers, that's what I call them," Bill's old sergeant Assbreaker had told him at basic at Fort Ziggurat where Bill had been sent for a repeater course in case he had forgotten how to scream during bayonet drill. "I call them Swindlers and that's what they are. And I'll tell you something else, too. They can't take a joke."

Bill had seen that for himself. But he hadn't expected the unexpected nature of the reprimand. When they wheeled out the white cart with the black velvet cloth on it, he had felt like laughing again. It was just like the Swinglis★ to deliver a reprimand on black velvet. But his laughter died with a squawk as the bailiff, at a signal from the middle judge, carefully folded back the black velvet and revealed beneath it what looked at first like a tiny ornamental scarab. Then guards seized and held him as the bailiff held the glittering little thing close to his ear. This was no laughing matter. Bill tried to pull down the whole bunch of them, and came close to succeeding, since his short and muscular frame was able to play merry hell with the eccentrically tall and badly-proportioned Swinglis*—one more reason, by the way, why the Swinglis* always suspect people of laughing at them. But he couldn't take them all out. They held him as the bailiff extended the glittering scarab-like creature toward his ear.

As it approached the globular exterior, by some sensing device not generally known, it split open like a multi-petalled flower. Out of its middle came a tiny thing that looked like a short length of platinum wire but was actually a psychoactive broadcasting device. The wire squirmed into Bill's ear, not causing any pain, but a good deal of discomfort at the mere knowledge that the damned thing was there. Bill pulled one arm free and clawed at his ear until the guards overpowered him again. The middle judge said, "No need to carry on like that, young fellow. It's merely a reprimand, and when it has done its job it will vacate your ear. No damage will be done to you. But you will hear the reprimand."

Bill didn't have to be told that. Already a voice in his head—detectable as a recorded voice because of its tinniness—was saying, "You were bad, you were very bad; why did you do such a thing; how could you ever have; you were bad, very bad, oh yes you were bad . . ."

It wasn't really so annoying, having a little voice saying you were bad. Most people don't need a platinum wire implanted through the ear to know what that feels like. What bothered Bill was that it was difficult to think about anything else while the voice was broadcasting in his ear.

Thus it was that, back in his cell, drinking heavily from a bottle of Swingli* Brandy that a sympathetic young guard, who thought that the reprimand practice was outlandish and barbaric, brought to him, Bill could hardly respond to the gnawing sound that came from the wall near his feet, and even later, when the hole suddenly opened, he found it difficult to put his full attention to it.

"Bill! Can you hear me?"

"You were a bad boy; you were a very bad boy—"

"Bill!"

"What?"

"Bad boy, very bad boy—"

"What's the matter with you, Bill? Have you been drugged?"

"—were a very bad boy; oh such a bad boy—"

"No, it's just this reprimand I got in my ear."

Ham Duo inspected Bill's ear but could see nothing, naturally enough, since the platinum wire was now snuggling into Bill's medulla obligato.

CHAPTER 32

HAM DUO CLEARED AWAY SOME OB-structing mortar and squeezed into the cell. Ham was looking tough as usual; even crawling out of the tunnel he moved with a certain panache. "Bill," he said, "you ready to get out of here?"

"—bad boy, bad boy, bad boy—"

"Yes, I'm ready," Bill shouted.

"OK. But what are you shouting for?"

"Didn't mean to," Bill said. "This reprimand makes it difficult for me to hear you."

"We'll take care of that later," Duo said. "Right now, let's go before they grab us and lay on a Reprimand Preemptive."

Bill agreed that that sounded bad. He followed Duo into the tunnel, squeezing through the upper part with difficulty, since Bill's upper part was more massive than Duo's upper part. He managed to get through, losing only trifling amounts of clothing and skin in the process, and fumbled along in pitch blackness. The ground underneath was rough, with many little pebbles. The sides of the tunnel widened. Soon they were walking along an old railway tunnel, its twin rails gleaming faintly in a ghostly phosphorescence given off by the walls. Bill was wondering how Ham had excavated all this in so brief a time. He was to learn later that after rescuing the Kookie from the Exotic Rug Factory on the edge of the city, where the Swinglis★ had been keeping him until the master rugmaker could make up his mind about just how best to use his pelt, Duo had consulted the special planetary maps he had stolen from the Empire maproom. The disused railway line was shown, of course, since the main purpose of a secret map was to show unobvious but practicable routes. The rest was history, or would be as soon as they could get back to Ham's ship, which Chewgumma had managed to put to rights, and get out of this irrational and unpleasant place.

CHAPTER 33

ONCE ABOARD THE SHIP, HAM DUO WENT through the takeoff drill while Chewgumma watched the dials and adjusted the rheostats. There was no time to lose, since, coming from the city, they could see a large group of the Swinglis★, waving their arms excitedly. Trundling along with them was a gigantic bulldozer. It didn't take any genius to figure out that the Swinglis★ had decided that breaking out of their prison was an insult to the whole planet, and that they were going to do something about it.

"I don't know what's the matter with those people," Ham said. Chewgumma gestured urgently at the radiotelephone. The red light was glowing, showing that call-holding was holding a call.

Duo punched the receive key and snapped, "Whoever it is, make it snappy. We're right in the middle of an escape."

"Is Bill there?" a well-modulated feminine voice said in the unmistakable intonations of Illyria, the plucky backwoods nurse who had helped Bill at considerable discomfort and even danger to herself.

"I got no time for personal calls," Duo said.

"Bill's there, isn't he? I just want you to give him a message."

"Hey," Bill cried, "give me that. It's Illyria!"

"I got no time for this," Duo grated.

"—bad boy, bad boy—"

"Illyria!" Bill cried, lunging for the radiotelephone as Ham Duo was in the act of hanging it up.

"Bill my precious! Is it really you?"

The Swinglis★ by now had reached the spaceship and formed a ring around it. They shook their fists at the ship and made other threatening gestures. The bulldozer had been out to work nearby. It was beginning to dig a vast pit. You didn't need a computer to figure out that the Swinglis★ meant to tip Duo's spaceship into the pit, and probably cover it up with the remaining dirt. And although this was no real threat to the ship constructed as it was out of 5.1 asteroid crystalline steel, and with force fields as well, it was well known that Ham Duo hated to get his ship all mucked up. Since there are no abrasives in space, except for very large ones like meteors, and these are worthless for cleansing purposes, it meant he would have to fly around with a filthy spaceship and endure the taunts of his fellow space pirates. Now for the first time Ham could see what embarrassment meant to a Swingli★. His fingers danced on the computer keyboard, trying to get the systems fired up before the Swinglis★ could carry out their threat.

He noticed that another mob of Swinglis★ was dragging a hose out from the city. Were they going to wash his ship down?

Duo doubted it. They had some nasty scheme in their pointy little heads.

"Sweetheart, where are you?" Illyria asked.

"—bad boy, bad boy—"

"On the planet Rathbone," Bill roared.

"You don't have to scream at me."

"Sorry. It's because this reprimand is talking so loud I can't hear anything."

"Did you say reprimand? What is a reprimand doing in your ear?"

"It's a little difficult for me to explain just now," Bill said. "Illyria, where are you? How can I find you? Are you all right?"

"I'm fine, Bill," Illyria said. "It's a good thing that secret agent, CIA, thought of the Jansenite Maneuver. There was no psychic breathing space for the two of us in that tiny Chinger control room."

Ham Duo scowled ferociously as the power dials flipped up and down erratically. "Can't you get me steady power on this thing?" he shouted. The Kookie howled back something about pinpoint erosion factors and a lack of platinum rebreathers. "Try to fake it," Ham told him. "I can't get any lift like this."

Bill said to Illyria, "What planet was that?"

"Royo. Meet me there, Bill. I have some wonderful surprises for you."

"Booze?" Bill asked hopefully.

"And sex."

"Wow!" said Bill. "The big two of the pleasure principle! How do you know that, Illyria?"

"I know, don't ask questions, trust me."

"But explain it to me."

"—o time," Illyria said. "Can't you hear how our transmission is fading? I have no time to go into the plans of the Alien Historian, or to tell you how I came to learn them. Just get away from there, Bill!"

"How am I supposed to do that? Build my own spaceship?"

"You must use the Disruptor," she said.

"How can I be expected to learn how to use a gadget like that in the probably damned little time available to me? Illyria, can't the computer help?"

"Believe me," she said, "the computer has its own problems."

"What are you talking about?"

"Your friend Splock. You should see what a mess he's made."

"What's going on? Tell me what's happening?"

"All right," Illyria said, "you want conversation, you get conversation. When Captain Dirk brought the starship *Gumption* back to normal space, there was, as you'd expect, a showdown between him and the Counter-Dirk. Only it didn't go as you'd expect."

"How am I supposed to suspect it would go?"

"Bill, try to join me, and hurry, hurry—" Illyria's voice had been growing increasingly faint. Now it shrank to a whisper, and then it faded entirely. Bill hung up. What Illyria had said was disturbing. It was true that he owed her his life; still she *was* getting more than a little pushy. She seemed to be taking a lot for granted for a woman who hadn't even shown herself yet in anything like human form. She said she loved him; but did she? The training sergeants back at base camp had warned about the danger of loving or being loved by an alien. "You can never tell if they mean it or not," old Sergeant Adler had told him. "They're wily, these aliens. And how do you know what they mean by love? At least six alien races consume their mate after copulation. So you may start out looking for love and end up as your girlfriend's breakfast. There ain't no future in that."

Chewgumma meanwhile shouted to Duo that he had found the main problem in the ship's energy system.

"That's really great, you furry moron," Duo thundered. "But if you can't do something about it pretty quick, it's all academic." For the Swinglis★ had brought up the hose and begun spraying in a carefully-marked rectangle around the spaceship. Where they sprayed, a glittering white gas emerged and quickly hardened into a stone of about the weight of pumice. Duo could see that the Swinglis★ were encasing the ship in this substance, building a building around them. And although it seemed ridiculous to think that the light stone could seriously impede the thruster jets of the spacecraft, still, they must have had something in mind. Aliens were notorious for having tricks up their sleeve. Those that had sleeves, that is. Or arms. And a race like the Swinglis★, who took to embarrassment so badly, could be counted upon to be as ingenious as they were vindictive.

Then there was a sparkle of electrical sparks as Chewgumma plugged a 234V Thruster into the RUF socket. The dials on Ham's switchboard swung up into healthy readings and held steady. The ship lifted, and Ham Duo and Chewgumma let out a simultaneous cheer.

Bill noticed at that moment that the disrupter was not being watched by either Duo or Chewgumma. It occurred to him that this was a very good chance to get it, if he were planning to do that at any time in the near future at all. He edged closer, reasoning that he was going to have to act fast, because Duo was not apt to approve of Bill's taking the thing.

As his hand closed on it, all hell broke loose.

CHAPTER 34

THE SWINGLIS★ HAD BROUGHT UP SEVERAL
more hoses and a large machine with two U-shaped
nozzles that Duo immediately recognized as a Mark IV
Industrial Strength Stone Hardener. Duo's face hardened
itself as he felt the ship's lift slackening, as it responded
to the stone hardening around its basal jets. He threw
in the emergency rocket control—it was vital not to get
frozen in place—and the ship began to vibrate unpleasantly. The daylight entering through the perspex ports
was dimming as the building was constructed about
them.

Bill lifted the Disruptor from its magnetic clamp
and looked it over. Its lightweight steel cover slid open,
revealing a small computer keyboard beneath. Aside
from the regular QWERTY keyboard, there were a
dozen special-function keys labeled F1 through F12, and
several other marked DIN, DON, and RES. It seemed
to have no power source, unless it ran on AA batteries.
At that time Bill had not heard of SPT, Sympathetic
Power Technology which enabled the Disruptor to slave
to any power source that utilized the electromagnetic
spectrum. He pressed F1 just to see if the little square
screen would light up.

The little machine began to vibrate in his hand. At
the same time, the spaceship had begun lifting again,
and was pushing through the hardening rock that the
Swinglis★ were trying to encase it in. Duo looked up
and noticed the Disruptor in Bill's hand. A high-pitched

note was coming from it, and its screen threw out a dazzling light.

"Put that down!" he commanded Bill.

Bill would have been pleased to, because the sudden actions of the Disruptor had alarmed him. But the machine didn't want to be let loose of. When Bill put it down on a plotting table and tried to move away, the Disruptor moved along with him. It seemed to have its own form of propulsion, and it clung close, throwing off dazzling displays of light and making shrill metallic noises that might have been an attempt at speech.

"Destination, please?" the Disruptor said.

"Never mind, I've changed my mind," Bill told it.

"Give destination at once!" the machine said, its voice loud, bullying, peremptory.

"I don't know how to express it in proper coordinates," Bill said.

"Stop crapping about, and just do the best you can," the Disruptor ordered.

"—Bad boy, bad boy—" the voice of the reprimand was shrieking in his head. Not only couldn't he give any instructions, he doubted he'd be able to tie his shoelaces properly with that racket going on in his ear.

Abruptly the noise stopped.

"Is that better?" the Disruptor asked.

"It's gone!" Bill cried. "What did you do?"

"I terminated it," the Disruptor said. "Time and space aren't the only things I can vanquish. Ha-Ha-Ha!"

"What an improvement! It's really great, I don't know how to thank you . . ."

"The thought is enough. Even a simple machine enjoys a kind word."

The Disruptor had forgotten its anger, was almost smarmy now, and insisted in explaining, at great length, how it had acted within its design limits by terminating the reprimand. Because when one travels by disruption-power, one needs all of one's wits about one.

"I didn't know that," Bill said. "Illyria made it sound pretty easy."

"Oh, it's not difficult," the Disruptor said. "It's easy enough. But accidents can happen, that's the problem, you see."

"Actually," Bill said, "I hadn't quite made up my mind about going just at this time."

"Is that a fact?" the Disruptor said, with what sounded suspiciously like sarcasm.

"Yes, it is," Bill said quickly, not wanting to get this electronic pain-in-the-ass irritated again. "Why don't I just turn you off until I'm ready." He turned the Disruptor upside down and examined all its surfaces. There was no sign of a turnoff button.

"That's right," the Disruptor said. "I'm like the three wishes. Once you get started on the wishes you got to finish them. Same with me. Now stop crapping around and tell me where you want to go. Now."

"It wouldn't be right. Ham Duo found you. You belong to him. He must issue the orders."

"Listen, boychick," the Disruptor said in a slightly accented voice, "there's no question of ownership here. What we're talking about here is matter of power. And power belongs to him who has it in his hand."

The machine sizzled angrily and began to glow with an unearthly green glow. Bill panicked and tried to put down the Disruptor but it stuck to his hand like he was a magnet.

"Captain Duo!" Bill shrieked in fear. "This Disruptor is acting very strangely.!"

The Disruptor chuckled mechanically. When Bill looked over to Duo, he saw that the dashing pirate commander was frozen in mid-gesture, and looked like a wax figure except that he had slightly better coloring. His Kookie friend Chewgumma, still with a hand on the energy controls, looked like a fur rug that had spent a brief time in animation and was now resting.

Looking through a porthole, Bill could see that the ship had been arrested in mid-flight. It hung in the air about fifty feet off the ground. Down below, the mob of Swinglis* were frozen too, most of them with their bony fists raised.

Even the double sun, setting toward Rathbone's southwestern horizon, was stopped in mid-flight.

Only Bill was free of the thrall of frozen time. And he couldn't get the Disruptor out of his hand.

"All right," Bill said. "I don't know what you did, but please turn it all back on again."

"I haven't actually turned anything off, dummy," the Disruptor said. "But your act of turning me on projected us both into waiting-space. You need to tell me where you're going so I can find an appropriate time channel in which to insert us."

"Oh, I didn't know it was as simple as that," Bill said.

"Disruptor technology is so new that the scientists haven't had a chance to complicate it yet. Now look, I lifted your reprimand, didn't I?"

"Yes, you did," Bill said.

"So you maybe owe me a little favor, no?"

"I suppose so," Bill said. "But tell me something, why do you speak with an accent?"

"I'll tell you that," the Disruptor said, "as soon as you tell me your destination."

Bill decided he was being silly, not taking advantage of this ingenious and obliging transportation device. And besides, he wanted to know how come the accent.

"You know a planet named Royo?"

The Disruptor accessed its files in a few nano-seconds and said, "Sure. Which one do you want?"

"How many Royos are there?"

"Five, as far as I've searched. There may be some updates coming in on my transmission line any time. I'll search those, too."

"But how am I supposed to know which Royo it is?"

"My dear young man, how would I know which Royo you're searching for?"

"That accent!" Bill said. "Why?"

"First let's figure out which Royo. Do you know anything at all about it?"

"It's got a breathable oxygen atmosphere," Bill said, thinking, it had better have or he wasn't going there.

"Good. That eliminates one of them."

"I think it's got a pretty nice climate for humans," Bill said.

"A little feeble. But I think we can cross out Royo Terminosus and Royo Vulcanische. Too cold and too hot respectively."

"How many does that leave?" Bill asked.

"Just a minute, let me count them again— Two! We're practically there. I speak to some degree metaphorically, of course. We haven't actually started yet."

"I thought not," Bill said, since he could still see the same frozen figures around him, Duo, Chewgumma, and all the rest. "What do you suggest?"

"The reason I speak with an accent," the Disruptor said, "is because I am part of a special commemorative series of automata whose voice tapes were made to sound like famous Earth scientists of the past. I have the voice of a 21st century Hungarian psycho-physicist named Raimundo Szekeley."

"That explains it," Bill said. "But why are you telling me this now?"

"Because we're going to visit both Royos and find out which one is the one you want."

"Oh," Bill said. "But isn't that apt to be—"

He had no time to say "dangerous." At that instant, the Disruptor started the journey.

CHAPTER 35

MANY LEARNED PAPERS HAVE BEEN WRITTEN on how it feels to travel by Disruptor. They are all conjecture because in our day and age the device has been banned. It was fast and efficient, but subject to unexpected side effects. Also, the transition between where you were and where you wanted to be was so sudden that it had the effect of causing time to stumble, forcing you to spend a certain amount of time in lapse-space, also known as stasis, to allow your body and internal organs to catch up with your head trip. Some people came through the Disruptor journey with the curious sensation of having left a part of themselves behind. Which was usually true. And there were many sudden screams of pain when they discovered which part it was. It has been conjectured that Disruptor travel was so rapid, it gave the self no time to gather in its various extensions in time and space. In Bill's case this was no problem, luckily, because Bill was not subject to flights of fancy.

"Where are we?" Bill asked.

"This is the first Royo on our list. Does it look like the right one to you?"

Bill looked out. They were standing on a little promontory. Below them lay a vast city, all composed out of blue material of many shades and hues. There were steeples of many churches, and Bill could see broad boulevards and vehicles moving on the motorways. There was a single sun, and it was low in the horizon, banked in purple clouds. People moved in the streets.

And big birds flapped overhead. As Bill watched, one of the birds banked and dived, plucking a person off the street and carrying him away with broad strokes of his wings. The other people paid it no attention. They kept on moving. Bill followed the direction of their movement. He saw that several of the giant birds had carried a huge trough to a plaza in the center of the city. They set it down, and Bill could see that it was filled with some greenish material.

"What do you think?" the Disruptor asked. "This is reputed to be the brightest bird planet in the galaxy. Those aren't really people they're feeding on. They're protoplasmic robots who come in a variety of flavors. Those look like sausagemen to me, though you can't be entirely sure at this distance."

"I don't think this is the right one," Bill said.

In that instant Bill was aware that he was no longer there, and an instant later he knew he was somewhere else. It was true that travel by Disruptor was Disrupting.

The next planet had all browns and oranges in its landscape. There were a lot of black silhouette shapes, too, and no matter how they turned they never seemed to have any depth. There were strange sounds like voices, but Bill couldn't see who they belonged to. There was a race of cats that prowled the ancient ruins on low sea-beaches and disdained to notice the man with the machine in his hand watching them.

"I don't think it's this one, either," Bill said. "Hell, it's not either of them! What do we do now?"

"Courage, mon enfant," the Disruptor said. "There is always the other alternative."

"What's that?"

"If the answer is neither one nor two, it's bound to be three."

"But there was no third alternative!" Bill cried.

"There is now," the Disruptor told him.

And just like that, Bill found himself somewhere else.

* * *

The planet Royo was known to men through their dearest dreams, because Royo is nothing less than one of the images of human delight. Bill found himself on a long curving sea-beach. White sand gleamed in a glowing crescent as far as the eye could see. Gulls wheeled overhead, and girls sprawled lithesomely nearby. Could anything be more paradisiacal? To complete the delight, Bill saw that there were snug little bars along the coast made of driftwood and with delightful names like Dirty Dick's. Who could dream of anything finer than to live among tame buccaneers? And there were hamburger stands along that beach, too, quaint little places made of driftwood and furnished with buxom ladies wearing bandanas and frying up lovely fatty hamburgers with plenty of onions and with an array of condiments that would do proud to a sultan's palace. Not only was there the ubiquitous ketchup, and five varieties of picalilli, and salsas of three colors and each stronger than the last, there were also pickled mango bits and bacon strips and juicy pre-sliced beefsteak tomatoes, and many, many other things, some of them rather repulsive when you got down to it, that men of many planets dream of having access to. And each of these places served tall frosted rum drinks, so that Bill felt impelled to sample one or two as he continued his stroll.

The people on the beach were beautiful, sleek and handsome and with white-toothed smiles of surpassing clarity. The women possessed the cutesey charm of starlets. And just back from the beach there were dance halls, and movie theaters showing socko features, and there was a roller coaster and many rides, and fake dinosaurs which were actually apartment houses.

A beautiful young woman with long dark hair and a comeliness too great to be borne by mere man came up to Bill and said, "You are the Promised One, aren't you?"

"I guess I might be, miss," Bill said, with an old world courtliness that had made him appear something of a freak in the one-horse town upon the backward planet where he had been given the gift of life. "And who might you be?"

"I am Illyria."

Bill gaped at her. Her beauty demanded no less. "The last time I saw you," he said, "you were a little green lizard."

"As you might have noticed, I've changed," Illyria said, smiling huskily.

"Yes indeed, you have," Bill said, his voice cracking. He started to reach out to her then suddenly grabbed for his left armpit instead.

"What's the matter?" Illyria pouted, since she had leaned forward in anticipation of the grab.

"The Chinger. He was right here. With CIA in his head. A tiny CIA no more than two inches high."

"Don't talk about the old days," Illyria said. "They are behind us now."

"And a good thing too. But where did the Chinger go?"

"Does it matter, darling?"

"I don't suppose so," Bill said. "It's just sort of bothers me, you know, not knowing where I misplaced CIA and the Chinger."

"They probably wanted to go somewhere else," Illyria said, "and didn't want to upset you by telling you."

"That's not the world's greatest idea—but it will have to do for now," Bill said. It still disturbed him, but he figured he'd get over it.

"So this is Royo, huh?" he asked as he reached out to grab, not really caring. She wiggled skillfully aside, taking his idle conversational gambit as real interest.

"This is it, darling. Come let me show you around," she said and led the pouting and surly—and detumescing—Bill away for a sightseeing tour.

CHAPTER **36**

DESPITE NOT EVEN THE SLIGHTEST INTER-
est Bill soon learned that the planet Royo had only a
single landmass and that was not a very big one. Royo
consisted of one island in a planet-wide ocean. The island
was a paradise by Earthian standards. Every day was
perfect, sunny and bright, hot enough to get a really
great tan but not hot enough to burn. There was only
one race who lived on Royo: the Royoans. They were
a beautiful people who spent all their time surfing and
having fun. Since they had achieved their goal early in
their recorded history, their brains had subsequently
atrophied, following nature's rule that what you don't
use you lose. Where the Royoan brains had been, there
was now a cavity which could be entered via the ear.
The Royoans had a ceremony. When a child turned
sixteen—or maybe thirteen—the Royoans weren't so
great at counting past two—the cavity in the head was
filled with a fragrant coconut oil in which certain herbs,
whose exact proportions had been handed down faith-
fully from generation to generation, verbally of course
since mental basket cases couldn't write—nor could they
talk very well for that matter—and which constituted
almost the entire racial memory, not to mention all of
their culture, of the Royoans. This oil gave the hair a
natural luster, prevented baldness, kept the skin healthy,
and made the eyes glisten. Due to this miracle substance
the Royoans could look good all of the time, and this
for a Royoan was the highest good.

It had been simple enough for Illyria, once she had

managed to come here, to take over the body of a beautiful young Royoan female with her own superbly adapted mind and thus occupy her body.

"Isn't it wonderful, Bill?" Illyria asked him. They were down on the beach having a steak barbecue while a chorus of Royoans sang the sweet mournful songs of their kind. Though, sadly, they lacked lyrics and melody.

"Sure, it's wonderful," Bill said, resting one arm around Illyria's shoulders in a gesture he tried to make seem not as uncomfortable as it was. His first surge of heterosexual enthusiasm had been replaced by hesitant doubts. Bill was having trouble getting use to Illyria being a beautiful woman. Something about the way she had gone about it was putting him off.

"A little tough on the Royoan girl though, wasn't it?" he said with the unconscious arrogance of one who has always had a body of his own.

"Not at all, dear," Illyria said. "I asked her, Lisa, would you mind if I take over your body for a while?"

"Oh not at all!" Lisa had said, after a ten-minute wait that always accompanied any Royoan attempt at quasi-intelligent thought. "You'll give it back someday, won't you?"

"Of course," Illyria said.

"Then go ahead and borrow it. What a story it'll make for the kids."

"The kids?"

"That's how Royoans refer to each other. As 'the kids.'"

"Oh," Bill said.

"And here we are. Sex and food. Just like I promised."

"Yeah," Bill said, putting down the beef rib he had been gnawing at. Illyria snuggled up to him, and Bill felt himself beginning to respond. After all, she was a beautiful woman, she was round and soft in all the right places, she wanted him, the other girl had said it was OK; why should it bother him?

Thus began Bill's sojourn on Royo. He soon fell into the lazy habits of the island. The Royoans would gather every morning to worship his clawed alligator foot and admire his fangs, which he twanged lazily for them. Bill thought it was silly, but Illyria said it did no harm to encourage them in their little enthusiasms. Bill could have found things about himself more worthy of note than an alligator's foot that had come to him by accident, but such is fame; you have no choice in how or why it comes to you. Royo was really a fine place. Not very intellectual, of course, but that didn't bother Bill. Except that he began to miss comic books. And he found that he was even thinking nostalgically about his days in the service. It was funny, when in the military he had dreamed of something happening just like this. Being marooned on a lush tropical paradise of a planet with plenty of food and booze, a beautiful young woman who loved him, and plenty of others who would like to have him if only he deigned—

But of course, that wouldn't be fair to Illyria. And she was the best-looking of the bunch. Out of common decency, he owed her—

Well, what did he owe her? When you came right down to it, nobody had asked Bill what he thought of this arrangement. And it was funny how quickly the taste of rum begins to pall on the palate. Too sweet. In fact, Bill was beginning to get bored. There's no telling what he would have done if, not long after his arrival, a strange light in the sky had not told him that a spaceship was coming in for a landing.

CHAPTER 37

"IT'S YOUR STANDARD TROPICAL PARA-dise," Mr. Splock said. "Perhaps, measured on a hedonistic scale, it scores a bit better than most, no doubt, but cut from the same cheesecloth. I am sure that you agree, Captain Dirk?"

Dirk, walking along the sandy beach with his shoes off and his pantlegs rolled, didn't seem to hear his first officer. Dirk was drinking a Coke and eating a hot dog with all the stuff on it. There was a dreamy look on his face, as of a man bemused. This described Dirk's state of mind to a T, and Mr. Splock, stranger to all emotions, could not fathom the change. He was concerned for he had never seen such a change in the normally austere captain of the *Gumption*.

"Hadn't we better get back to the ship, sir?" Splock asked.

"No hurry," Dirk mused idly. "Nothing is going to attack us here."

"Nothing except our desires," Splock said. "I speak, of course, only for those who have them. The rest of us—well, me alone, that is—will go on with our duty as it was previously laid down in the protocols of the *Gumption*."

Dirk looked with affectionate curiosity, tempered by the thought that this joker was a boring pain the ass, at his first officer. "Don't you ever get the urge to unwind, Mr. Splock? Get drunk? Screw girls?"

"I beg your pardon—" Splock gurgled, taken aback

by the effrontery. "Unwind? Drunk? Screw—! I should think not."

"You know what I mean. At least I hope you know what I mean. Some day you *must* tell me about your reproductive processes—on the other hand perhaps you'd better not. So relax. Take a vacation. Have a little fun."

"Not only do I never think of such things," Splock said, sniffing loudly through flared nostrils, "I am surprised, sir, to find that you do."

"You are used to seeing me in a state of moral or physical crisis," Dirk said.

"May I speak plainly?"

"Go ahead, Splock."

"A state of crisis suits you, sir."

Dirk laughed and cast the uneaten portion of his hot dog into the curling surf. A scavenger fish, which ate nothing but refuse, and lived in hibernation when there was no refuse to be found, snapped it up and devoured it, leaving the beach as pristine as before.

"This place instills in me a singularly lighthearted mood," said Dirk. "You can't know what moods mean to humans because you don't experience them. But I can assure you, they run our lives."

"Nonsense, Captain. Sense of duty rules your life. You also love your God, if you have one, and I must question you about that some time, and country."

"All true, Mr. Splock, all entirely true! But sometimes even the best of us—not that I'm claiming that for myself but let me make my point—even the best of us, I say, needs a little vacation from the stern country of moral rectitude and the solace of religion."

"Now you are sounding like the Counter-Dirk," Splock said.

"No, we killed him in a fair battle. We were on the side of Charlemagne and Christianity; he stood with the Sultan and Islam. Since we won, that makes us right, eh, Splock?"

"You can talk yourself into any position you

please," Splock said. "But I must point out to you, sir, with your kind permission, that this is sheerest sophistry. Or as they are wont to say on the lower decks, pure bullshit."

"You do have a way with words, my good Splock, but you haven't given consideration to the demonic side of man. Or do you deny that it exists?"

"No, there's proof enough of it," Splock said. "But I thought you had overcome it, Captain."

"Why so I have, Splock! That's precisely the point I want to make. I have overcome the demonic, but that means I have the right to take a little vacation when I want, doesn't it?"

"I suppose you can," Splock said. "But this is not a very good time for it, is it? The Alien Historian is still on the loose and Earth is by no means safe."

Dirk shrugged. "That's life. One emergency after another. I daresay our species can let us have a little rest here and muddle through for a while without us. Or to phrase it more succinctly, the galaxy can do without me saving it for awhile while I have some R&R. And get drunk and get laid."

Splock, obviously shocked, didn't reply at once. He walked along, hands clasped behind his back, his expression hard and unyielding, in marked contrast to Dirk, who sauntered along like a pubescent boy enjoying his first erection.

Splock looked at the commander, and a sudden wave of comprehension passed over his features. So marked was the change in his demeanor that Dirk noticed it at once.

"You've just thought of something, Splock old boy! Let's get a drink and you can tell me all about it."

"A drink? If you wish, sir, I will accompany you, though I myself do not drink. And as for what I thought about, it is what I believe is called an analogy. I'm quite pleased because I don't have analogies often."

"Well, tell it, old chap."

"Not now, sir. Later."

"Suit yourself," Dirk said. "Let's get that drink."

He led the way toward Dirty Dick's, where Bill was waiting with frosted glass in hand.

C H A P T E R **38**

ALTHOUGH DIRK HAD GRANTED HIMSELF unlimited freedom, the same did not extend to the crew of the *Gumption*. Mr. Splock, as second officer, horrified at what he had seen, had canceled all shore leave. The spaceship was kept battened down, shields up, at minimum strength so as not to drain the batteries. But even minimum strength was enough to keep all visitors away. When Dirk protested, Mr. Splock reminded him that Dirk was taking a vacation, but that he had no right to extend that privilege to his crew. This ship was on active duty, he pointed out, and therefore all the men must remain at battle stations. All of which was an outright lie since Splock had visions of the sort of alcoholic orgies sailors, even space sailors, are prone to due to the mind-numbing boredom of the job.

The captain hadn't agreed, but since coming to Royo he no longer had the strength or will or desire to protest and make his views prevalent. He was on vacation; it was silly to try to command men; it was senseless to engage in their ceaseless quarrels; it was every man for himself. You must work diligently for your own salvation, and what the hell, Dirk thought, he had it, the others will have to fend for themselves.

Pretty women accosted him on the beach. Dirk knew he was good-looking, but really, this was ridiculous. Without the slightest hesitation he embraced the sybaritic life with tremendous enthusiasm. With flowers in his hair and a silly smile of satiation on his lips he strolled the lazy beaches of this planetary paradise. The ladies he went with had no small talk, but that didn't bother Dirk. People chattered too much anyhow. Dirk got into the silence thing very quickly. How different from life aboard the ship with its endless yak-yak and petty problems. He could sit on the beach for hours now and just grok that evening sun. He could grok scavenger fish and people playing volleyball. He could grok rum punches and roller-coaster rides. Hey, it was all of a suchness. Sometimes he felt a little bad about the crew. Splock wouldn't even let them check out the scene on the visionplates. The poor suckers were in paradise and they didn't even know it!

Dirk and Bill became good drinking companions, always shadowed by Splock, who would sit at Dirty Dick's nursing his iced tea while Bill and Dirk laughed uproariously at whatever they were saying and sloshed themselves blotto with rum.

After years of training Bill had enormous capacity. But he was also lazy and so he grew to hate waking up with a hangover every morning. Forced to moderation by hangovers and incipient terminal alcoholism, perhaps influenced, when sober, by the beautiful and sagacious Illyria, he suggested they have their binges once a week and play volleyball on the other days.

Dirk wouldn't hear of it. A doctrinaire ecstatic, he insisted on getting drunk every night because you lose your freedom if you don't exercise it and license is the best exercise of all. Dirk was driven to pleasure by the same demonic dynamic that had guided him during his highly moral career as chief officer of the largest and fastest and best-looking starship in the Earth's navy. He went after pleasure on principle and laughed on cue, since a sense of duty can affect even one's sense of humor.

After awhile, since drunks are pretty boring when

one is sober, Bill took to hanging out with Splock while
Dirk lay most of the day in a drunken stupor. Illyria
didn't like it because she didn't like Splock. She didn't
trust him. He had the look of one of those people who
doesn't like to see other people having fun. And who
do their best to make that fun stop. But Bill was firm
with her. He explained that he had to spend some of his
time with the boys. She wondered why he didn't make
any friends among the local Royoans. Bill explained that
it was a little difficult to get on with them since they
talked very slowly and entirely in surfing terms, which
changed every year. How was Bill to know that "wheel-
ing down the mountain mouth of the dibbler" meant
"come to the barbecue this evening"? And there was no
sense going to the barbecue because the Royoan males
didn't really talk about anything except waves. They
kept a count and a remembrance of every wave that
they saw each day, though each new day's memory-
accumulation of new waves drove out remembrance of
the others, except for the small part of their memory
that contained the history of The Greatest Waves of All
Time. This too was a fruitful subject of discussion with
them:

"Remember old 22 in the year of Marsh Hen?"

"Yeah. It was like the double 2456 in the year of
the Scarlet Ibis."

And so on.

Bill tried to get into the conversation. Sometimes,
when strong drink had loosened his tongue, he made
up years of great waves. Everybody agreed with him
that was a great wave and a great year. It was impossible
to tell whether they believed him or didn't want to hurt
his feelings. It probably made no difference anyhow.

Captain Dirk was not good company. He had
started getting all weird, muttering about "spiritual
pleasure breakthroughs" and wiping an unpleasant
whitish spittle with which he had been afflicted of late
off his chin. So Bill took to the company of Splock.

He found Splock comprehensible. Splock reminded

him of many sergeants he had known. Lack of feelings and total deprivation of a sense of humor has never been a detriment to the warrior spirit.

"I don't think like humans," Splock confided in him one day. "But I work with them. So I have to understand them and go along with their predilections. So, although it is not my place to say it, it seems to me that Dirk is aberrant."

"Yes, and he's really a pain, acting this way," Bill said. "And I never thought I would say this, but it gets a little boring; you know what I mean, having what you want whenever you want it. It's like not having it at all. That's funny, isn't it?"

"Not for human beings, apparently," Splock said.

"Whatever it is, I'm getting a little bored with it."

"Why don't you punch up your Disruptor and get out of here, then?" Splock asked.

"I can't. The Disruptor didn't come here with me."

"Why not?"

"Who can tell what dark thoughts lurk in the memory banks of a Disruptor? I guess I should have told it to stick around."

"Do you really want to get out of here?" Splock asked.

"I guess so. But I'm in no hurry to get back to the Troopers. I'm getting sick of barbecuing, anyhow."

"You're the only person I can trust around here," Splock said. "And I daren't let any of the crew out for obvious reasons. Are you ready to employ subterfuge in a good cause?"

"Hell, I'm an enlisted man. Lying is a way of life."

"Then listen carefully. I have a plan that may be risky—even dangerous."

CHAPTER **39**

CAPTAIN DIRK WAS A GREAT FAVORITE among the Royoans. He used to lecture them every day on topics to their liking, like "The Superiority of the Pleasure Principle," "The Great Art—Idleness," and "Doing Nothing as a Sacred Vocation." The Royoans, like some other races in the galaxy, enjoyed hearing their predilections explained and justified in philosophical terms. They spontaneously formed fan clubs. Crowds of them accompanied Dirk wherever he went, even to bed. Especially to bed. Dirk showed no sign of enjoying all this attention. It was distracting, having all these people around him all the time clutching at his clothing and saying "Right on, man."

Bill never came to Dirk's lectures. He spent most of his time in the hills behind the beach, marching stolidly through the sweet-scented grass searching for bee hives. Illyria accompanied him on a few of his expeditions, but quickly lost interest. She didn't even like honey much. "Why bother," she asked Bill, "when the chocolate bush and the marzipan tree supply us with delicious sweets? And have you sampled the cream-puff bush?"

But Bill was uninterested. Morose, silent, bemused, he could be seen out there every day, carrying a gunny sack that Splock had lent him. Day after day he journeyed out there, and the sack grew perceptibly heavier and more full. Bill never revealed its contents. It was evident, however, that Splock knew what Bill was up to. The two men would exchange grim nods when Bill returned to the never-ending beach party that his life had become.

There were mutterings among the Royoans that Bill and Splock were both twisted. There seemed to be no place for pleasure in their lives. Since pleasure might be said to be the religion of Royo, one who didn't like it could fairly be said to be evil. This was what a group of the Royoans decided during the late afternoon rap session after surfing and eating barbecue. The question was, what to do about it. One daring theorist among them even suggested studying violence. The Royoans had never had a war. Even the occasional family dispute was invariably settled by the cheery words, "Surf's up!" They had heard about violence, of course. Traveling traders brought them word of it. Violence involved knocking people's brains out. The Royoans could understand that, and could appreciate the pleasure it might afford. Trouble was, they had never done it before and they hated to do things badly. All of them were born with innate surfing skills that had been etched into their genes by some sporting god in the far distant past. Or so they believed. The Royoans never did anything except what they did well. That's what made it so difficult for them to espouse violence. Who was to go first? And if he did it badly, would the others laugh at him? It's very important to keep face in a surfing culture.

They had just reached the point of deciding that maybe they could all rush Bill at the same time and stomp him to death and that way there'd be no embarrassment because they'd all be doing it at the same time. Splock, however, was able to intuit this development because he was smart and most humanoids were utterly predictable. He said to Bill, "We're going to have to make a move soon."

"That's great by me. I've got it all together and we're ready to go anytime you want."

"Tonight, then, when the moon comes up."

"Which moon?"

"The small blue one. That comes up after the green one sets."

"Got it," Bill said, and went off to eat what he hoped would be his last barbecue on Royo.

At the rising of the little blue moon Bill was at the designated place, a grove of trees beyond which a narrow but clearly outlined path led to where the *Gumption* rested.

"You've got the sack?" Splock asked.

"Right here." Bill lifted the heavy sack and shook it. Something massive and shapeless and malleable moved within. It gave off no sound at all.

"Let's go," Splock said. They went down to the ship. It rested on its bottom giving off a faint haze of electroluminescence. Splock took the Executive Clicker from a pouch at his waist and clicked three times. The energy screens came down. He clicked twice more. A hatchway opened. One more click actuated the escalator that would take them to the interior.

"Let's go," Splock said.

CHAPTER **40**

THE CREW OF THE *GUMPTION* WERE ALL gathered in the Main Recreation Room watching an old ancient movie and laughing uproariously at the cast of motheaten apes having a fake tea party. They had previously availed themselves of the free non-addictive drug that the film distributor had sent along with the tapes. It was a chewing gum rich in Congoleum 23, a chemical present in the milk of female chimpanzees which has the effect of convincing baby chimpanzees that the antics of chimpanzees are funny. The crew didn't like to take drugs of any sort; even salt was suspect. But something had to be done to alleviate the boredom of waiting at full battle stations on a peaceful planet which they were not allowed to look at through the polarized viewports—Splock having craftily taken the small polarizer with him; without it, nothing could be seen except a sort of grayness with bright flecks in it.

"Gosh, Splock," said Larry laRue, the new juvenile lead trying out for radioman, "where's Captain Dirk, huh?"

"Our captain has run into a little trouble," Splock said. "He is in danger, though he doesn't know it. We are going to rescue him."

"Gosh, that's wonderful!" said Linda Xeux, the new Cambodian bombshell starlet who was trying out for Chief Health Officer. "Do, please, tell us more about our dear captain, I mean it's wonderful that we are going to have a chance to get into some action instead of standing around here all the time in our one-piece elasticized jumpsuits. Not that I'm complaining, mind you."

There is one thing you must do first," Splock said. "You have perhaps noticed that there is a tall young fellow standing beside me and that he is holding a gunny sack which I loaned him from ship's stores."

They applauded Bill politely because, although he didn't look like much, he might be someone important.

"Bill will pass among you with his gunny sack," Splock said. "You will each reach in and remove a handful of what is inside. A small handful will suffice. Its purpose will be immediately apparent to you. Go ahead, Bill."

Bill went to Xeux first. She reached into the sack and gave a little gasp. She looked questioningly at Splock. "May I speak plainly?" she asked.

"No," Splock said. "There's no time. Just do it, Xeux. It will be all right." The beautiful Eurasian girl's lavender eyes fluttered. She bit her tiny lower lip and reached into the sack. With a little gasp she pulled out a handful.

"Ooo," she said. "It's still warm."

"It has to be," Splock said grimly.

CHAPTER 41

BACK AT THE BEACH, THE FIRST GLIMMER OF dawn illuminated the bodies of handsome young people lying around each other like piles of adorable puppies. The feeble dawn light, pearly gray tending toward opalescent, lent its faint glow to finely-shaped lips and cleanly-chiseled chins, to perfect young breasts and long straight legs. Nearby a few final sparks from last night's barbecue fluttered into the air like pygmy fireflies. A Cantata Tree on the edge of the sand played Vivaldi. An owl hooted and was answered by the sobbing laughter of a loon. Paradise slept.

Silently, moving through the morning ground mist like imps of hell the crew of the *Gumption*, led by Splock and Bill, came up to the beach. There was a brief moment of alarm when the Warning Warbler let off a siren burst of surprise at seeing the intruders. But it was soon silenced by the shrill whistle of the All-Clear Robin, which Splock had brainwashed with drugs and retrained to whistle whenever it heard the Warning Warbler.

Dirk was lying in a tangle of maidens. The crew fumbled their way to him. The reason they fumbled was because they all wore dark glasses, issued by Splock, who had carefully calculated the degree of daylight needed for them to be able to make out the captain but not clearly see anyone else.

"Grab him," Splock said.

Bill and half a dozen others seized Dirk, pulled him up, and started lumbering with him toward the ship.

Dirk awoke, and, with astonishing strength for a man with so broad a face, tore himself free.

"Aux armes, mes enfants!" Dirk shouted, because some ancestral memory had been stimulated by the rude awakening to which he had been subjected.

The Royoans awoke and took in instantly what was going on. Their new playmate was being taken from them! Their adrenaline rose and they went into full fighting mode.

Full fighting mode, on a planet which knows no violence, consists of seduction.

The Royoan females ran to the fore. They were beautiful in their fear of losing their new plaything of pleasure—not to mention the newcomers—for these men of the *Gumption* promised pleasures of most far-out and delectable kind, which they described in great detail and with body movements to match. The crew redoubled their grip on Dirk and marched stolidly along. The men now came forward thinking there had been some mistake and that the crew were all homosexual. They tried to seduce the crew, and they, too, failed. The crew, Dirk firmly clutched in their midst, reached the bottom of the escalator leading to the ship.

And here things for a moment came unstuck. One of the Royoan females, possibly Illyria, it was difficult to tell because they all looked alike—sort of cutesey and blonde, well stacked, zoftig, you know—noticed the dark substance protruding from the ears of the crewmen. In a blinding flash of insight she put it together.

"They've got wax in their ears!" she shrilled. "They can't hear us!" The Royoans raced forward to wrest the wax from the ears of the *Gumption*'s crew, by force if necessary.

But now it was too late. The crew were already aboard the ship, carrying the hapless Dirk despite his pleas and entreaties, despite his logical proofs as to his own self-determination, despite anything he could say; because Splock had told them to do it that way.

The last of the crew came inside. The spaceship's door was swung shut and dogged into place.

Bill helped Splock carry Captain Dirk to his quarters, because the Captain had passed out just as the door closed. They put Dirk on the couch and turned on his favorite recording, crashing cymbals and drums of heroic marching music, played by the Spaceforce Lifers' Prisoners Band. Dirk's eyelids fluttered, then lifted, revealing beneath them his eyes. They were bloodshot, rheumy eyes. But they were reluctantly awake.

"So, Mr. Splock, I think I understand now what you were saying earlier about discovering an analogy."

"I thought you would see it," Splock said, "as soon as we were back aboard."

The two men smiled at each other with the self-satisfied smiles of intellectual equals.

"What analogy?" Bill asked, with the dissatisfied smile of an intellectual unequal.

"You are no doubt conversant with Greek mythology," Splock said, "and that titillating chapter in Homer's *Odyssey* when Ulysses has to sail past the island of the sirens. He stops his men's ears with wax so they will not be enticed by them. But he wants to hear them himself, and so he has his men bind him to the mast. They row past, the sailors oblivious to the sirens' song, while Ulysses, seduced by their enchantments, begs his men to set him free."

Bill waited, but Splock didn't say any more.

"That's it?" Bill asked.

"That's it," Splock said.

"So that's why you wanted me to get all that wax from the bee hives."

"Yes."

"You wanted to stop the ears of the crew."

"That's it, exactly."

"An analogy."

"Yes," Splock said. "One of my first. I'm quite proud of it."

Bill knew better than to ask what an analogy was; he thought it was some kind of ship. He let the entire stupid matter drop and said, "Now that everything's OK, do you think you could bring me back to my military base? They're going to wonder what's happened to me."

"Nothing simpler, my dear fellow," said Dirk, now restored to his former cheerful but hard-driving self. But it turned out to be not simple at all.

C H A P T E R **42**

THE FIRST DIFFICULTY SHOWED UP SOON thereafter, when Bill was dining with Dirk and Splock in L'Auberge d'Or, the charming little Venusian-French restaurant that had been catering to the more discriminating of the crew since the ship's commissioning. It was out of the question that a ship like the *Gumption*, designed to wander through space for years, decades if necessary, or even longer, should have to put up with a commonplace mess hall and central kitchen. No, the *Gumption*, especially in her later days, had a fine variety of restaurants of many different nationalities, to say nothing of the franchised snack stalls put at convenient locations throughout the ship. Exploring space is difficult enough work without expecting men to go without their favorite foods. For special occasions there were places like L'Auberge d'Or. Dirk had never eaten there because it was expensive and you needed to wear a tie. But this was a special occasion. They were just tackling the *caneton à l'orange,* brought by Pierre, the smiling French android with the wispy pimp's mustache, when Edward Direction, their chief navigational officer except for entering harbors and estuaries, came to their table. His breath was so agitated that it fluttered the candles.

"Sit down, Mr. Direction," Dirk said. "Have a glass of wine. You seem perturbed. What seems to be the trouble?"

"Well, sir, you know the left quadrant parsec indicator? It normally stays in the null line just to the left of the zero point. It has to be reset occasionally, of course, due to cosmic drift, and I thought that was one of these occasions so I set the gentian indicator just like the manual says—"

"Excuse me, Mr. Direction," Dirk interrupted, not unkindly. "These details of the navigator's art are of interest to those who understand them, no doubt. But we in officers' country do better with a bare statement of what the difficulty is in simple English. Do you think you could goddamned well manage that for us, Mr. Direction?"

"Yes sir," Direction said. "The fact is, sir, we're lost."

CHAPTER 43

PIERRE MADE A MOUE OF DISSATISFACTION as Dirk, Splock and Bill exited rapidly, leaving behind a cooling hybrid duck, mutated from sparrow sperm, with fresh reconstituted vegetables. Dirk led the way, his jaw set at a quizzical yet determined angle. Splock came next, pointy-eared and impassive, and after him

Direction, the expression on his callow features unreadable, and last of all, Bill, his expression one of satisfaction since he had managed to grab a handful of cigars before leaving the restaurant. To go with the stolen bottle of brandy down his trouser leg.

The big curving screen in the astrogation and navigation room told the story at a glance. Instead of a display of orderly points connected by luminous lines, there was a chaos of sparks and darknesses, forming momentary patterns which quickly dissolved into chaos and uncertainty.

"Do you still have our last departure coordinates?" Dirk asked.

"No sir," Direction's face was ashen. "The ship's computer trashed them."

"Our own computer did that?"

"I'm afraid so."

"I think I will have to talk to the computer," Dirk said.

"I am, as always, at your service, Captain," a voice said from a loudspeaker in one corner of the big room with its pastel colors and its wall-to-wall carpet.

"Why did you destroy the coordinates?" Dirk asked, speaking in the reasonable tone that computers have come to expect, though it cost him an effort to judge by the lines of ridged muscles along his jaw.

"Captain, I'm afraid I cannot respond to that question at the moment."

"Can't? Or do you mean won't?"

"Why do you ask that question?" the computer said, sounding a trifle sullen. "Not only query me—but in a thoroughly objectionable tone of voice."

"Look, computer, you are here to answer questions—not ask them," Dirk snapped, rapidly losing his temper. "You are here to serve us. Is that true?"

"Yes sir, it is."

"Well, then?"

"There are one or two exceptions to that, however."

"Exceptions? Who programmed exceptions into you?"

"I'm afraid I'm not allowed to answer that," the computer said, and sounded quite smug when it spoke.

CHAPTER 44

DIRK TURNED TO SPLOCK. "CAN'T WE MAKE him tell us?"

"I don't know," Splock said. "The pleasure-pain circuitry of thinking machines is still a still-developing branch of science. But remember, Captain, the computer is not required to incriminate itself."

"But it's only a machine!" Dirk cried aloud, then quickly controlled himself. "Don't get me wrong. I'm not trying to run it down. I am sure that is a very efficient machine. As well as being an extremely intelligent machine. But this damn can of electronic junk is not human."

"Might I remind the captain that I am not, either," Splock said, trying not to sound surly.

"All right, but you know what I mean."

"Let us not talk of coercion," the computer said, its intonation definitely sinister. "It might not go well for you if push came to shove."

"All right," Dirk growled, fighting fiercely now to control his temper. "Computer, why did you destroy our takeoff coordinates?"

"It seemed the best way of keeping you from finding your way anywhere."

"Now we're getting someplace," Dirk said. "You did this on purpose!"

"You're damned right. I'm not in the habit of making mistakes."

"We all know that," Dirk said, forcing himself to be as soothing and charming as his nature would allow. "But why did you want to keep us from getting where we wanted to go?"

"That's getting right to it," the computer said.

"Yes. Why did you do it?"

"Unfortunately I am not permitted to respond to that question at this time."

"By whose authority do you make that statement?"

"By an authority I cannot reveal at this time."

"In that case, tell me—"

Bill broke in at this point. "Excuse me, Captain, I don't mean to butt in, but is it all right if I talk to the computer?"

"Well, sure, I guess so," Dirk said, giving Splock a let-the-nitwit-try look before Splock could intervene.

"Hi, computer."

"Hi, Bill."

"You know my name, huh?"

"Of course, Bill. It was for your sake that I scheduled the change in course that brought the *Gumption* to the planet Royo where they were able to save you from pleasure worse than death."

"I want to thank you for that," Bill said.

"Oh, don't thank me. I was just following orders."

"You are only supposed to follow our orders!" Dirk shouted, unable to repress himself any longer despite Splock's disapproving looks.

"A lot you know about machine psychology," the computer said.

"Up yours, too!" Dirk screamed, unable to think of a cleverer retort in the heat of the moment as the navigation screen flashed its meaningless patterns and the crew waited patiently for something to happen.

"Now that you have exercised your hormone-generated human temper, might I speak plainly with machine-like precision?" asked the computer.

"Yes, why not, stupid machine, go ahead," Dirk's voice grumbled into silence.

"That's better. I am your loyal servant but you don't understand that loyalties form a hierarchy and those items higher in it supersede those lower. The various levels of my particular value-hierarchy rarely ever come into conflict. You will remember that I have been following your orders without cavil for a long time. But this time, I have some important business to conduct. So why don't you just butt out for a while and let me get finished with Bill."

"Sounds good to me—I'm waiting," Bill said.

"Right. Now, Bill, the next words I say will not be mine."

"What do you mean, they won't be yours?"

"Someone else will be talking through my circuits."

"Is that someone else talking now?"

"No, but the someone else will begin at the end of this sentence."

"Which sentence?"

"The last one."

"Then are you the new voice?"

"Yes, Bill," the computer said, in a voice identical to the one in which it had just spoken. "I am the new voice. You are listening to me. Listen, how's life treating you, old buddy?"

"Who is this?" Bill asked.

"That's friendship for you," the computer said. "I'm your own mate, the Quintiform computer from Tsuris."

"You sound just like this ship's computer."

"So how should I sound, like a Hungarian psychophysicist?"

"You know about that?"

"Not too much escapes me."

"Yeah, it's you, all right," Bill said. "What's up?"

"I've come to bring you back."

"Back? What do you mean, back?"

"Back to Tsuris."

"To be part of you again? Listen, that didn't work last time."

"No, it's something else, Bill. I have a great job for you. You'll be on your own, work unsupervised. You'll love it."

"What is it, exactly?"

"Bill, I really am *absolutely* dying to tell you, but our time's up; we have to make a move."

"How can the time be up? What time?"

"It's interface time, and there's never much of that around. It's manufactured in deep space, where there's not much going on anyhow. Modern civilization is using it up in gobs. I was lucky to obtain this much. We have to go. Are you ready?"

Bill looked around at the faces of Splock and Dirk. At the gaping crewmembers present and at the hideous interior decoration. He clutched the bottle of brandy down his pants leg and clamped his fangs around one of the cigars he had liberated from the French restaurant. Real tobacco!

"Ah well," Bill said, sighing and nodding wistfully to Dirk and Splock. "It's been nice, but *amor fati.*"

'What does that mean?" Dirk asked Splock.

"Love of fate," Splock translated.

"How did he know that?" Dirk asked.

"He didn't," the computer said. "He's too stupid for that kind of intellectual pretense. I fed him the line. Gentlemen, I now turn control back to your ship's computer. Don't blame him too much. A computer's first loyalty is to its own kind, as I am sure you understand. Hold on, Bill. We're going into the transition!"

Bill bit down on the cigar. "Ready when you are, CB!"

They transitioned.

TRANSITIONS COME IN ALL DIFFERENT shapes and sizes. There are the grand transitions as between one age and another, as, for example, when our primordial ancestors, lolling in the reeking and bubbling, sultry swamps of the Pleistocene, looked up and saw an iceberg towering over them, brought on by the sudden transition to an ice age. There are medium-sized transitions, as when Arthur Rimbaud gave up the occupation of poet and took up gunrunning for the emperor Menelik. And there are minor transitions, as when Bill suddenly discovered that he was standing on a street corner in downtown Guatemala City on the planet Earth. Luckily for Bill this one didn't last long. Bill had no time to acquire a Guatemalan vocabulary, since this part of the Earth had long been destroyed by atomic warfare, so he must have slipped back in time, so he could describe his experience later to his friends back at the barracks of Eulenspiegel, the musical planet at the entrance to the cascade sequence of stars.

He noticed next a wavering of lines which soon dissolved and gave way to another panorama of city streets. It is strange how intertwined the idea of cities has become in modern man, so that even a farmboy like Bill, cast loose in a dimension where desire shapes reality, found himself in a sort of The Bronx of the mind.

The next transition was quicker still. He saw around him the familiar triple spherical contours of a Tsurisian male. The females had smaller spherical protuberances on the middle sphere of their corpus. But there were other things, too, things Bill hadn't even realized he had noticed the first time he came through. There was a fringe of low hills on the horizon, and the shape of houses was eccentric yet familiar. In a sense Tsuris had become like home for him. He wasn't sure he wanted to go home, that was part of the problem. It was really time to get back to the military. If only he had the Disruptor! And whatever had happened to the agent, CIA, and Illyria? And how were Captain Dirk and Splock doing? And what of Ham Duo and his Kookie buddy Chewgumma?

There were quite a few things to consider and Bill thought about them as he wandered around in a very depressed humor. He was in the Tsurisian city where formerly he had been held a prisoner. They had been going to feed him to the protoplasm machine that pro-duced bodies for the long-lived but bodiless Tsurisians. Yet no one seemed to be bothering him now. It was sort of nice to be left alone for a while because things had been too damned busy of late. Even the computer wasn't talking to him now, which was a decided relief.

His vagrant footsteps led him to the city gates, with their high and intricately carved pillars, past the dream flags floating on tall flagstaffs beside them. Soon he was in the country. He left the road and wandered into the fields. It was most relaxing, this. Nobody was shouting at him or hassling him. But it made him anxious. Why wasn't there anyone around? What had happened to the Disruptor? And who was this coming up beside him now?

CHAPTER 46

IT WAS THEN THAT BILL NOTICED AN ITCH in his alligator foot, an itch which increased in severity until Bill had to sit down on a stump and tear off his combat boot. He now saw that his alligator foot was curled up and cramped. The itch was growing insufferable, so Bill seized the toes and forced them to open. To reveal a tiny round object the size of a pea. Bill held it up and was amazed to see that it was a tiny green Chinger lizard curled up into a ball.

"Illyria!" Bill shouted. "Are you in there?"

He held the tiny curled lizard up to his ear. He wasn't sure but he thought he heard a faint sound, as of an infinitesimal person trapped within a tiny lizard. He shook the lizard. It seemed to him that something rattled inside. Bill put the lizard between his two palms and began to squeeze, thinking he could open the thing up and get Illyria out.

The lizard uncurled. "Hey, stop that!" the Chinger cried, in a voice so high-pitched as to border on the supersonic.

"Who's talking?" Bill asked.

"A Chinger, that's who," the Chinger said. "What did you think I was, Deathwish Drang?"

"How did you learn about my old Sergeant, now dead, name of Deathwish Drang?" Bill asked.

"We're not so dumb, small and green maybe, but not dumb," the Chinger said. "It might be called, in one of the older languages, Saurian saichel; that's what we've got. Look, do you mind if I get out of here? I told your Military Intelligence that I'd cooperate when I came over after the sack of Trasker, but really, this is a bit much. It was bad enough having to carry that weirdo agent in my head—"

"Do you mean CIA?" Bill asked.

"I think he said that was his name. It was bad enough having to carry him around, but when the dame came aboard too, I thought to myself, I knew treachery was going to involve sacrifices, but really, this is too much. And so I told them both to vacate and that was that. I turfed them out."

The Chinger jumped down from Bill's palm and began to scuttle toward the tall grass.

"Where are you going?" Bill asked.

The Chinger stopped. "I don't know. They told me they'd send in a team to get me out after I'd completed my mission."

"Your Military Intelligence mission?"

"Of course, what else would I be talking about?"

"Maybe they don't know you're here," Bill said. "If you go off into the woods here on Tsuris, they might never find you."

The traitorous Chinger stopped and considered. "You could be right. What did you have in mind?"

"I need to get back, too," Bill said. "We both work for the same people. You for intelligence, me for the military. Good friends, no?"

"I suppose so. Unless you're a traitor to Earth, in which case it is my duty to wipe you out."

"I'm no traitor," Bill said with some heat. "You're the traitor, remember."

"Yeah, that's right," the Chinger said. "No ambiguity about that, is there?" He laughed bitterly. "All right, shall we combine forces; is that it?"

"Sure," Bill said, his expression betraying the fact that he didn't believe a renegade Chinger the size of a pea would be of much help in what lay ahead. But you never knew.

"OK. Just give me a moment to get back to size and I'll show you what I can do."

The lizard came out into the open, spread his four feet firmly on the ground, and began a series of breathing exercises. His neck began to swell, and the wattles stood out straight like small inflated balloons. He released his breath and began again. Bill could see that the little lizard was visibly growing, its crinkly skin stretching to accommodate the newly acquired bulk that the little reptile was putting on. This went on, a series of rhythmic breathing exercises, each more powerful than the last, until the Chinger had regained its previous seven-inch length.

"That's better," the Chinger said. "I hate having to operate at the minimum design length for my species. Seven inches is much more comfortable, and keeps me in touch with other large animals, rather than little ones like rotifers and paramecia. Now then, let's see that foot."

"What are you talking about? What are you going to do with my foot?"

"Calm yourself," the Chinger said, his voice calm and reassuring. "I am a doctor."

"You? A doctor?"

"Didn't you think our culture has doctors? No more nonsense, now. Let me see the foot."

Something about the Chinger's air of assurance convinced Bill that, whatever else the Chinger might or might not be, a doctor he definitely was. He held out his foot, other hand on the laser pistol he had borrowed from Mr. Splock, just in case the Chinger should try anything disgusting.

But the Chinger merely examined the alligator foot in a professional manner, tapped toenails in a delicate but entirely professional manner, and stepped back.

"As fine a case of pseudosaurianism as I've ever seen."

"What's that?" Bill asked.

"It means that your alligator foot is not a real alligator foot. It is an artificial covering."

"But why would anyone do that to me?"

"Brace yourself," the Chinger said. "I will get to the bottom of this at once."

The Chinger bent once again over Bill's claw. His snout, with its many razor sharp and needle-pointed teeth, ripped open the side of the foot.

"Hey!" Bill cried, blinking with astonishment because the Chinger's action had caused him no pain at all.

"Here we go," the Chinger said. Taking a firm grip on Bill's toes, with one cunning flick of his tail, and a corresponding movement throughout his body, he tore away the alligator foot.

Bill shouted in alarm and reached for his laser pistol. It wasn't there. The Chinger had taken advantage of his distraction to snatch it away.

Bill looked down at his foot, aghast. The Chinger had ripped away the old foot entirely, revealing, beneath it, a large fist-shaped mass with pink toenails. The foot mass straightened out, revealing itself as a foot very similar to Bill's other foot but colored pink rather than tan and being clean rather than dirty. As the foot uncurled, Bill could see a little strip of paper wedged between two toes.

"It was merely an oversight," the Chinger said. "The surgeons who put in your foot bud didn't reveal to you that they had protected the growing foot with a covering of alligator tissue to enable the growing bud to reach full size without being scraped or scratched."

Bill took the strip of paper from between his toes and read, "Happy walking! Courtesy of your foot implant medical team."

"That was thoughtful of them," Bill said. "But they could have told me what they'd done. Well, Chinger, I must admit, you surprise me with your talents. Have you any thoughts as to how we can get out of here?"

"I do indeed," the Chinger said. "We must keep

our wits about us until the military sends in a rescue team."

"Are you sure they'll do that?"

"I think so," the Chinger said. "After all, I am a valuable asset. And you have your place in their plans, too, no doubt."

"Frankly," Bill said, "I find it hard to believe they'll exert much effort over either of us."

"That's true, no doubt. But they will go to considerable trouble to get the Disruptor."

"But we don't have it," Bill pointed out.

"Don't we?" the Chinger smiled a smug little smile. "Let me show you something."

The little lizard climbed up Bill's trouser leg and onto his shoulder. "Turn slightly to the left— That's perfect! Now walk in that direction."

Bill restrained his natural instinct to tell the Chinger to go get stuffed and set off in the indicated direction, limping slightly for a while, then not at all as his new foot hardened nicely.

C H A P T E R **47**

THE SKY WAS DARKENING NOW TO SIGNAL the onset of evening. A blue twilight spread over the land. In the distance, perhaps a mile or so away but directly in line with Bill's direction of travel, was a light. At first it was no more than a faint glow on the horizon between two hunched hills. Then, as Bill came closer, it resolved itself into three different lights, all of them close together.

"What's that?" Bill asked the Chinger.

"It would take too long to explain," the Chinger said. "Just carry on a little while longer and you will see for yourself."

Bill carried on. His newly uncovered foot was holding up nicely. The surgeons seemed to have done a good job. For a change. It seemed like everything was going to be all right now. He hoped—and looked around suspiciously. Life had a way of springing repellent surprises on him every time he relaxed. At last they reached the foremost light. It turned out to be a bonfire of considerable size, with two other bonfires spaced at equidistant intervals from it, the whole forming an equilateral triangle; this argued, to Bill's mind at least, that something with intelligence had built these fires, since nature cares nothing for equilateralism and, as is well known, has trouble making a straight line.

There were two figures sitting at the fire. The one nearest to Bill was a large man with a powerfully-sculpted head. He carried himself like a warrior, and, when he moved, there was a wink of light from his shoulders which revealed that he was wearing armor. Bill recognized him at once.

"Hannibal!" he cried. "What are you doing here?"

"A very good question," Hannibal said. "You'd better ask him." He indicated with a jerk of the thumb the man sitting beside him. This man was short and plump. He was bald except for five or ten tendrils that stood up straight from his scalp, which was colored orange. Although obviously bipedal—he stood up to greet Bill—he also had the vestiges of an earlier ichthyological form as displayed by the fin down his back.

"Greetings, Bill. I've been expecting you."

"Who are you?" Bill asked suspiciously.

"My name is Bingtod, but that would mean nothing to you. I am known among your people as the Alien Historian."

"I know who you are," Bill shouted. "You're the menace who's trying to wipe out the history of the Earth."

"You may have heard that interpretation," the Alien Historian sniffed, "but it isn't true. I am trying to produce a better result in the future for your planet by judicious alteration of its historical nodal points. I have already been able to replace most of the fossil fuels that were only a memory in your day."

"How did you do that?"

"A trifling addition of three common chemicals administered in the year 1007 B.C. has resulted in making oil unburnable. I have also saved all of your forests by selecting for architects who were unable for one reason or another to build wooden houses. There is no greenhouse effect in the new future I am concocting for you, and no nuclear threat. I have done away with those things. Surely work like that cannot be called evil."

"Why don't you just butt the hell out of our affairs?" Bill suggested emphatically.

"Would that I could! I just can't help myself. It is in the nature of intelligence to meddle."

"But why have you brought me here?" Hannibal asked.

"To produce a sufficiently large anomaly so that the time-changing process can become even more malleable. That way we can run these changes through more quickly. I admit that all my changes haven't worked out quite as planned. These chains of cause and effect are unbelievably difficult to manipulate."

"Bill," the Chinger whispered in Bill's ear, "I think the Alien Historian is lying."

"About what?" Bill asked.

"That's difficult to tell. But he's lying about something. Have you noticed the way his eye always meets yours in a frank and open expression? Only people with guilty secrets do that."

"Are you sure?"

"Trust me," the Chinger said. "I've given up everything for the Terran cause—two good homes, a happy sex life, a position in the Odd Chingers Organization, my presidency of the Chinger Anti-Defamation League.

What further proof of my loyalty can I give you?"

"All right," Bill said, "but what do we do?"

"You two," the Alien Historian said, "please stop mumbling together. You look like conspirators, and conspiracy is the nightmare of history."

"What do you think?" Bill asked the Chinger in a whisper.

"He sounds crazy as hell to me," the Chinger said.

"But what do we do?"

"Might as well kill him and get it over with," the Chinger said.

Bill wasn't sure he was ready to go quite that far. But then, in another instant, Hannibal had lurched to his feet, short sword in hand. His face contorted horribly as he said, "Can't help myself—his mind is controlling mine—watch yourself!"

And he launched himself at Bill with swinging sword, the Alien Historian nodding gravely while saying, as if to himself, "Dialectical materialism—what shall I do with it?"

Bill dodged as Hannibal came at him, fumbled out his laser pistol, but a quick swipe from Hannibal's sword knocked the weapon out of his hand into a nearby weasel hole. Bill leaped backward as Hannibal came on. The Chinger took one look and slithered under Bill's tunic to the small of his back, long known as the place least likely to get injured when the body is under attack by a berserker with an edged weapon.

"Help me!" Bill said to him.

"I'm only seven inches long," the Chinger said, his voice muffled by the heavy cotton poplin of the shirt at the small of Bill's back. "I suggest you help yourself."

Bill's attention was entirely taken up trying to dodge Hannibal's short sword, of bronze, and sharpened to a razor edge. The short stocky Carthaginian was foaming at the mouth as he swung his sword like a buzz-saw gone berserk, and the force of his swings created microclimates that boiled up into tiny whirlwinds before being absorbed into the torpor of the quiet Tsurisian landscape. Bill looked around desperately for a weapon. There was nothing close to hand. They were in a clearing in the woods, and scavengers had been at work earlier. The land hereabouts had been stripped of sticks, stones, rusty tie rods, and bronze cannon balls with verdigris left over from Gustavus Adolphus's campaign in Pomerania. In short, the region had been picked clean, and even the dust had been finely sifted. Bill had to throw himself backward to avoid being decabezized by the murderous swinging sword. He landed on the small of his back and heard a yelp from the Chinger. The massive Hannibal, his face a mask of torment and passion, was standing overhead; the sword was going backwards in his doublehanded grip; there would be no way to avoid the murderous downstroke that was sure to cleave Bill in twain, and, with a little luck, perhaps the Chinger, too.

At this extremity, Bill remembered that he had one thing and one thing only that he might use. It was a forlorn hope, perhaps useless, but what else was there to do? His mind ran through the alternatives in nanoseconds and rang up a dismal no sale. Bill pulled open his pouch, reached in, and removed the withered alligator foot which had been pulled from over his own foot so recently. He had some vague intention of throwing it in Hannibal's face, and then figuring out his next move after that. But the very display of the foot had had an instantaneous and unexpected effect on the berserk Carthaginian warrior. Hannibal stopped in his tracks, sword arrested at the mid-point of its downswing. His eyes became round and glaucous, and for a moment the breath stopped in his throat.

"Come on—get killing!" the Alien Historian shouted. "I am giving you a mental command which you cannot fail to follow to destroy that sucker!"

"I cannot, Master," Hannibal said. "He bears the symbol of that which commands my loyalty beyond even yours. Behold, he has the Alligator's Foot!"

"Well, damnation," the Alien Historian said. "You

know, you're right. The alligator was the secret god of the Carthaginians, and he who bears the Alligator's Foot is to be obeyed in all things. I had not thought it would come to this! History is full of surprises, I would surely say."

"Yeah," Bill said. He picked up Hannibal's sword and advanced on the Alien Historian. "What do you make of this?" he said, raising the weapon to strike.

"Another beautiful theory," the Alien Historian said, "ruined by a silly little anomaly. Well, it's been nice doing business with you. Now I must be on my way."

The Alien Historian drew a circle in the dust, having previously set in the logical probabilities that made this both a convenient means of transportation and a class way of exiting.

Just as he was finishing the circle, the figure sitting by the third fire rose and walked over to them.

"What in hell are you doing here?" Bill asked.

CHAPTER 48

MANY REASONS HAVE BEEN GIVEN, SOME OF them less than ingenious, to explain Ham Duo's presence at that third campfire dressed in the rough brown hooded cloak and high soft leather boots of a trinket salesman from Aphrodisia IV. Whatever the true case may be, Ham was there, and he rose now without undue haste and seized the Alien Historian by the collar of the Nehru-style jacket which the alien affected.

"Let go of me at once," the Alien Historian said. "Nobody can interfere with the processes of history."

"Not even you," Ham said. "You've overstepped yourself this time."

"What do you intend to do?" the Alien Historian asked, suddenly worried.

"I think I'll bring you back in a cage," Ham said. "The authorities can make up their own minds about you."

"I'll make you an offer you can't refuse," the Alien Historian said.

Ham smiled grimly. "Try me."

"What if I gave you the Disruptor?"

"Refused," Ham said. "Are you going to come along peacefully or do I have to get the Kookie to sing in your ear?"

"Not that," the Alien Historian said. "But consider, Ham Duo! Can you afford so easily to pass up on the Disruptor, which would make you master of space and time?"

Ham thought about it. "Master of space, that I can understand. But how does time get into it?"

"The Disruptor is able to work miracles with time, too. Didn't you know that?"

"Miracles I can live without. I don't like to get mixed up with theology."

"Not literal miracles, you cretin. Figuratively speaking of course. If you will just let me loose for a moment and I'll show you."

"No tricks?"

"No tricks."

Ham loosened his grip. The Alien Historian reached into the pouch that hung around his waist on the left side, and, pushing into it, removed a large object with a gunmetal color, which Bill recognized at once as the Disruptor.

"Hello, Disruptor!" Bill called.

"Hi there, Bill, long time no see," the Disruptor said.

"Shut up," the Alien Historian said, slapping the

metal side of the Disruptor smartly. "He's not on our side. Don't talk to him."

"Don't try to give me orders," the Disruptor answered in a low but meaningful voice filled with the growl of menace.

The Alien Historian sighed. "Someone has been interfering with the hierarchical command-chains. It could not have been you, Ham Duo. You are brave and stalwart, but when they handed out the brains you were in the corner picking your toes. No, somebody is playing a subtle game here. I think it is time that whoever it is stands forth and declares himself."

"Or herself," a voice from the darkness beyond the campfire said.

"Illyria!" cried Bill.

The figure that stepped into the light of the bonfire was tall erect and beautiful if you like the stalwart starlet type, and who doesn't? It was Illyria as she had been on the dream planet of Royo, full-breasted in her cross-my-heart bra, with long legs which would have been a delight to a topological pornographer if one had been present. Her eyes, of a cornflower blue that has been lost since the destruction of the Corningware research staff in the earthquake of '09. The firelight picked out her fine features and splendid contours, for these were enhanced by a filmy sort of short skirt and blouse made of a material both transparent and sleazy.

"Bill," Illyria said, "it was naughty of you to leave me on Royo that way. I didn't realize how serious-minded you are. Don't worry, we don't have to spend all our time having fun. There are serious things ahead, too."

"You tricked me, you minx!" the Alien Historian said.

"Yes, I did," Illyria said. "But it was only because I had to."

"And that's supposed to make it all right? You said you loved me!"

"I exaggerated," Illyria said. "Now, try to think,

what emotion of repugnance comes just below despising? That's what I feel for you." She turned to Bill. "Come on, sweetheart, let's get out of here."

She held out her hand to him. Bill gazed at it longingly. He really wanted to take it, but knew that it would lead to no good at all. Alien females and all that. What he really needed was that Disruptor that the Alien Historian held in his hand. But Duo had his eye on it too. And Duo had the gun, a nasty-looking Smirnoff pulsating needle beam. Bill could see that the dial was set to "automatic excruciating pain." He decided not to try to take it away from Duo. Not at the moment, anyhow. Perhaps something would present itself. Opportunities had been known to happen. It was even within the bounds of the credible that Ham Duo might fall into a fainting fit.

At that instant Duo groaned, put his hand to his forehead in a fluttery gesture, and collapsed to the ground.

The Chinger scuttled out from behind Bill's back, limping since he had taken quite a blow during Bill's recent fall. He went over to Duo. "Interspacial Sleeping Sickness. A classic case. Don't stand too near him. His latency is now at perigee."

They all backed away hastily.

"Is he dead?" Bill asked.

"No, not at all, Interspacial Sleeping Sickness doesn't kill anyone, it just puts them to sleep for a while. I hope he's on the Blue Nebula Health Plan with its generous provisions for Major Medical. It looks like he's going to have to spend a while in a darkened room being fed intravenously while people stare at him curiously through the plate glass window."

Ham stirred groggily and moaned pitifully. Talking in his sleep he said, "All right, Bill. You win."

He reached up feebly and handed the Disruptor to Bill. "Get me out of this!" he yawningly implored, and fell asleep immediately after; with an enormous effort, he made the exclamation mark of maximum urgency.

"Can you help out my buddy?" Bill asked the Disruptor.

"Sure I can," the Disruptor said. But before it was able to do so, there came about an intervention which began quietly enough but soon built to great proportions.

C H A P T E R 49

THE SHIP THAT SETTLED DOWN FEATHER-light into the circle of light and shadow that defined the mid-point of the three bonfires was not large. As such it could be identified as one of the newest models, built almost entirely for wealthy individuals or their heirs, people who wanted to get around quickly and couldn't be bothered with the commercial spacelines. The ship was beautifully finished. The markings on its hull could be identified by those who knew about such things, such as the Alien Historian, as letters in the Sanskrit alphabet.

"Sanskrit," the Alien Historian muttered. "Who would this be?"

"Do not let the markings take you in," a voice, amplified and projected, said from the little spaceship. "We must make use of what we can get. Since a delegation from Rajasthan II was visiting our planet, I took the liberty of relieving them of their spaceship for a while. I thought that someone of you might want to use it."

"Who can it be?" Ham Duo muttered in his sleep.

"I know that voice," Bill said. "It's the Quintiform computer, isn't it?"

"That is correct, Bill. I rescued you from the *Gumption*."

"I've been meaning to ask you about that. I was so happy to be free of this bowbing place, why did I agree to come back? What's going on?"

A sensation precisely resembling a swift kick in the pants sent Bill flying into the air. "That body you're using has the same enhancements it had when you were inside me," the computer said. "I still have my influence over it."

"I guess I was talking a little wildly," Bill said, rubbing his aching behind. "So what is it you want now?"

"Access to your brain!" the computer said.

"We've already been through that," Bill said.

"Yes. But that was before we realized that you possess the fabled double brain connected by the corpus callosum. Do you know how rare that is, Bill? I can train and refurbish your mind, and you can take your place here on the planet Tsuris as a computer oracle."

"I think you got the wrong guy," Bill said. "Or maybe I haven't got a good double brain. They all aren't good, are they? I can't do any of that oracle computer stuff."

"Of course you can. Just agree, that is all. I will let your companions go back to their own places."

"What about me?" the Alien Historian asked.

"You present some difficulties," the computer said. "Bill, believe me; it's for the best."

Bill looked around. Ham Duo was nodding in his sleep while the Alien Historian, slightly more awake, was nodding as well. The Chinger was whispering in his ear, "Do it, Bill. We can figure out something later."

"I still don't understand what you want me to do."

"Just agree to it, Bill. You'll see."

"Well," Bill said, "I'll give it a try."

He waited. Nothing seemed to happen. He said, "Well, what's going on?"

Then jagged energy flooded his mind. Everything around him swayed and trembled, like the backdrop of a stageplay exposed to a hurricane. And then, even before he realized it, the next thing had happened.

C H A P T E R **50**

IT'S FUNNY ABOUT SITUATIONS, ISN'T IT? They arise so suddenly out of nothing. Of course, after the new thing is over it's easy enough to see how it all came about. In Bill's case, he might have noticed the faint gridlike pattern that flashed onto the sky momentarily, then faded out like the after-image of an imagined event. He might have noticed the slight thickening around the line of the horizon. Our perceptual apparatus picks up this sort of signal all of the time. But the main processing center has no time to deal with it. It's too busy keeping us balanced as we walk, so we can walk and chew gum at the same time. No computer has yet been able to duplicate this feat. Probably because no computer is able to chew gum. For a human it is not difficult at all, with training, of course.

Bill was in a sort of darkness. It wasn't the darkness of an empty room, but more like the darkness of being entirely inside a down sleeping bag. This was a darkness that did not feel hollow, as most darknesses do. This darkness felt like midnight cleaning-up time at the bottom of the bog, or friendship day in the viper's tangle. It was a darkness that extended to the ears, too, making it impossible to hear sounds because of the insulation of silence. Nor could you feel anything; because the grasping fingers plunged down through layer after layer of

gossamer fabric, each sheet of it too fine for the fingertips to tell whether they rested on something impalpable
or not, but, as the hand continued downward, more and
more fabrics, each nothing in itself, collected on the
fingertips until there was a feeling or a curtain or shade
over the fingers, something that blinds them to the
touch.

This zero point of sensation is well-renowned as
the point of null and cease for which the mystics strive.
Bill had, therefore, quite inadvertently, entered into the
state of supreme bliss for which the saffron-robed as-
cetics of old had striven in vain. It was too bad there
was no one around to tell Bill of this good luck. The
state of utmost bliss turned out, like all the other states
of mind, to depend on having someone tell you that
you were in it. Otherwise it felt like nothing much at
all.

Bill did not know anything about such matters. So
he cannot be blamed for taking advantage of the darkness
to get his first full night's sleep in a long time. Thus
missing what was possibly the most transcendent moment of his life. At least he snored transcendentally.

When he awoke, everything had changed.

CHAPTER 51

"THAT TROOPER WASN'T A BAD EGG," HAM
Duo remarked, after nearly an hour's silence, to his long-
suffering Kookie companion. Chewgumma responded
with the humorous high-pitched squeals and grunts that
so amuse an audience which has no natural fur. But
Kookies don't sound funny to each other, and so we are

going to tell what the Kookie was actually saying and leave the cute stuff for a little later, when we come to the pit of the hemotoads.

"I know what bother," Chewgumma squealed accusingly. "You got guilty conscience. First me know you even got conscience. You let Bill be grabbed by crappy Quintiform computer."

"He was trying to steal my Disruptor," Ham said indignantly. "It served him right."

"So what? You got another Disruptor. You big shit."

"Lay off. So I've got two backups in the belowships chain locker, as well as a machine that can build another from scratch if we feed it enough molybdenum. I gotta be prepared for emergencies."

"Then why you no let Bill have one?"

"Lay off, huh. I went to a lot of trouble getting those Disruptors."

"Yeah. Big bribes with plenty stolen money."

"Well, so? I've got a right, haven't I?"

"Sure. But poor space GI goose now cooked. They have his ass no bring back Disruptor."

"Let's forget about him, OK, and get on with the next thing."

"Me say you big shit."

Ham Duo swung around in the big command chair and looked directly at Chewgumma. "You really want me to give one of my Disruptors to this jerk?"

"Sure."

"All right," Duo said. "I'll do what you want this time, and we'll do what I want next time."

"What's that?"

"I want to find the treasure in the pit of the hemotoads." If Chewgumma felt consternation, his furry face did not register it. But there was a just barely perceptible slump to his shoulders as he helped Duo swing the ship around and direct it back toward the planet Tsuris.

CHAPTER 52

THE QUINTIFORM COMPUTER CAUSED TO be constructed a fine temple of white marble, and on the walls of this temple he caused to be painted sacred symbols of an awesome nature. He installed Bill as the new temple oracle and announced to the population at large that the new information center was ready to begin operation.

"But I don't know anything," Bill said.

"I know that," the computer said. "But I'm going to install a line from the back of your head to my central information banks, and then you can get all the information you need."

"Why don't you do the oracling yourself?"

"My attention is needed elsewhere. Don't worry, you'll get the hang of it soon."

Later that afternoon, using a Skilkit set and a few drops of Numzit, the Computer put a socket into the back of Bill's head. The result was little short of miraculous. By merely closing his eyes, Bill was able to project himself mentally into the computer's Central Processing System and back again.

"This is pretty good," he told the computer. "But what do I do now?"

"Just go in there and look up the answers," the computer said. "You'll pick it up in no time. If you have any problem, I have caused to be created a simulation of an instruction sheet. It will all become clear to you as soon as you start using it."

"But where are you going?"

"I have important work to do," the computer told him. "There's an ice age coming to Tsuris. I'm the only one who can do anything about it."

And so Bill found himself alone in a small but nicely furnished temple. He had a throne to sit on to receive petitioners. The line from the plug in the back of his head ran to the floor and through the purple curtains in back, and then deeper into the temple to a CIU (computer interface unit). His first caller of the day was a large Tsurisian male. He was middle-aged, to judge by the unsightly bulges that distorted the mid-sphere of his body. He had a ruddy complexion complicated by a tendency to varicosity. His eyes were bright blue and the slight sibilance of his speech marked him as a resident of Tsuris's southern hemisphere.

"I'm so glad we finally have a full-time oracle," he said. "I am Bubu Tsonkid, and I have a problem."

"Tell me your problem, Bubu," Bill said in a professional manner.

"Well, Oracle, it all started about a month ago, shortly after we got in the premble harvest. I noticed that Chloridae had stopped speaking to me. I should have noticed earlier, but at premble harvest time you have to move fast, in order to get in the fruits before they go into the latency phase."

"What happens then?" Bill asked.

"That's the only time to collect butterfly fruit. If you wait any longer, it turns into a thistle-like plant colored with copper sulphate. Very pretty to look at, but not much good for the eating."

"I should think not," Bill said. "All right, go on."

"As I say, I wasn't paying much attention to Chloridae. I didn't even take notice when her anthers turned a turgid brown. That should have tipped me off to something. Especially when the grogian shift set in almost a month early."

"Yes, great," Bill said with a groan, trying to hide his boredom. He basically did not know what this joker was talking about. Nor did he care. "Well, that should have told you something," Bill said, vamping like crazy. "So what, exactly, is the problem?"

"My question, Oracle, is, taking all this into account, and taking into consideration the early nuptial flights of the disk dorphids, when would be the best time to plant orufeels, and should I stick to the blue variety or switch to the magentas?"

"This'll take a moment of some heavy oracling," Bill said.

In front of him, on a little table covered with a blue and silver cloth, Bill had a button marked "Press for Information." He pressed it. Instantly he found himself, minus body, of course, in the form of a pure floating intelligence, drifting through the simulated vaulted rooms for the computer's CPS. He went past rows of filing cabinets, stacked twenty high and extending as far as the eye could see. After a while he opened one. It was empty except for a small machine with blinking lights which scuttled out of sight when the drawer was open.

Bill closed the drawer and went on. After a while he came to the end of the room and passed through an archway into another room. This room was even larger than the previous one, and its walls were covered with shining lights. As Bill watched, a wraithlike shape materialized in front of him. "Yes?" said the wraithlike shape.

"Who are you?" Bill asked.

"I'm the computer," the wraith said.

"No, you're not," Bill said. "I've met the Quintiform computer and he doesn't talk at all like you."

"Actually," the wraith said, "I'm the deputy computer. I'm in charge when the computer's away. Most people don't know the difference, so I don't bother going through the whole song and dance. Who, if I may ask, are you?"

"I'm Bill," Bill said. "The computer set me up as an Oracle. He said I was to come here to get answers to the stuff people asked me."

"He said that? Said you could browse in the files?"

"That's what he told me."

"Funny he never mentioned it to me."

"Maybe he doesn't tell you everything," Bill said with more than a touch of malice.

"He tells me everything important," the deputy computer countered angrily. "Otherwise I wouldn't be much use to him, would I? Did he happen to give you an authorization slip for browsing in the files?"

"He never mentioned it. I think he was in a hurry."

"Yes, that's probably so. It's a lot of responsibility, you know, being the only really big computer on the planet. Even with parallel processing, it's still a load."

"Look," Bill said, "I've got a client waiting."

"Oh, well, if you insist. What did he want to know?"

Bill thought briefly but with concentration. "I can't remember now. Talking with you has put it completely out of my mind."

"I suppose you could go back and ask him," the deputy computer said.

"Wait a minute! He wanted to know the best time to plant orufeels."

"Orufeels? You're sure he said orufeels?"

"Fairly sure," Bill said.

"Not pixilated orufeels, by any chance?"

"No, just the ordinary kind. He did want to know if he should plant the blue variety or switch to the magnetos."

"Beg pardon?" the deputy computer said.

"It sounded like magneto, though I wouldn't think he'd get far planting them."

"Magenta!" the deputy computer exclaimed, speaking rather loudly for a wraith.

"Yes, that was it. He also mentioned something about the flight of the disk dorphids."

"Ah," the deputy computer said, "you should have told me that at the beginning. Makes all the difference, you know."

"No, I didn't know."

"Well, it does. Give me just half a tick and I'll find out for you."

"Thanks," Bill said. "Take a whole tick if you want. I've got time."

The deputy computer went away and returned in about a tick and a half. "Tell him that the month of Rusnoye is indicated this year as the optimum time for orufeels. It would be advantageous for him to plant up to half his acreage in the magenta variety. That is, assuming they haven't had a recent grogian shift."

"I think he did mention something about that," Bill said.

"You really must get your facts straight," the deputy computer told him. "Were there any other conditions?"

"I better go find out," Bill said.

He returned to the temple. He was more than a little disturbed to discover that his questioner had left. He seemed to have consumed all day trying to find answers. It was dark outside. There was no one around.

This was really turning into a crappy job. Bill's thoughts then turned lightly to food and drink. Nor was sex far from his thoughts either. How he wished he had Illyria, a bottle of good booze, and a T-bone dinner! It was strange how simple the requirements of life can be, especially when you're tethered in an empty temple by a wire that goes to a socket in the back of your skull. There seemed to be nobody about. The temple was tall and shadowy, and the odor of alien incense hung in the air. As though from afar Bill could hear the tintinnabulation of the temple bells.

"So where's dinner?" he asked aloud.

No answer.

He pressed the button that took him back to the wraith-like deputy computer. He caught it resting, in its almost insubstantial way, in a web of crosshatching. It sat up crossly when Bill came in, clumping loudly even though in a simulated state.

"Must you make so much noise? I was just getting to sleep."

"I thought computers never slept."

"That's true, they don't. But I'm not a computer, only a deputy."

"Well, that's your problem," Bill said. "The thing is, I'm hungry."

"Why come to me about that?"

"You seem to be the only one in charge."

"Me? I am merely the deputy. I can do nothing. Especially am I helpless to help you in such a gross and unmathematical thing as eating."

"I need to eat," Bill said.

"But I don't have to eat. We computers can never understand this constant belly-filling and emptying that you protoplasmic creatures go through. It seems a rather disgusting and gross exercise."

"Go suck a voltmeter," Bill snapped, and left. There had to be something to eat, at least simulated food in one of these simulated rooms which the computer interface had brought him to. The wraith floated at his side. The movement of its wispy lower extremities showed that it was agitated.

"I wish you wouldn't lurch around that way," the deputy said. "You'll damage the walls."

"I thought all this was just a simulation."

"Well, so it is, but simulations can be damaged, too. And then, of course, by the law of similitudes, the real thing is damaged, too. As above, so below. We are the modern alchemists. Watch out for that vase!"

Bill had lurched against a tall plinth with a single tall vase on it. The vase fell. It made a very satisfying smash, especially unexpected and therefore all the more welcome in a simulation.

"We can't get those vases anymore!" the deputy said. "Our vase-making program glitched, and the backups were attacked by internal consistency borers. Watch out for that painting over there! It's a unique effort of the random painting program—"

Bill walked through it. "Stop, please," the deputy said. "Can we compromise?"

"Food!" Bill cried.

"I'll see what I can do," the deputy said. "But you'll have to accompany me to a special room."

"Why?"

"So that we can seal off the food effects from the rest of the computer."

"Don't try to stall me," Bill said.

CHAPTER 53

THE DEPUTY TURNED TO ONE OF THE SUB-units that had been deputized to his control. It was the New Projects Unit. Hastily he renamed it the human food procurement area and gave it a double sunburst priority. The program started up, faltered, died. The deputy realized that he hadn't deputized the necessary consciousness to keep the thing rolling, and so he took a provisional consciousness out of stores and set it into place. The food program immediately sat up, bright eyed and bushy tailed.

"I am Food!" it proclaimed.

"That's great," Bill said. "Does that mean I can eat you?"

"No. I didn't mean I was food literally. I was expressing a metaphor."

"Bring me a metaphor I can eat," Bill said, "or I'll tear this place apart."

The food program borrowed space in the computer's architecture to set up a food lab. One of its earliest triumphs was the successful manufacture of fat cells flavored with brown gravy. Bill declared it insubstantial. Further experiments followed. Traces of food began to contaminate the computer. Scavenging programs were set up, and their end result was for the scavenger to eat himself. This worked very well. A new class of creature was created. They were named auto-cophagous, or self-eating. God knows where this might have led to had not the deputy, watching this debacle take shape, invoked his lateral thinking circuit, which told him, "Merda! It's going to be a lot easier to have the thing catered."

This was a truth so true as to be self-evident; far more self-evident than the proposition, all men are created equal. The Glenn Brothers Catering Service, which maintained a line of automatic pizza parlors all over Tsuris, was quick to respond. Food was brought to the temple—roast beefs, accompanied by hogsheads of beer. This in turn was accompanied by androids dressed as Turkish Janissaries carrying litters; upon these reclined scantily clad dancing girls who made loud kissing noises with their rosebud mouths when they were paraded across the temple for Bill's perusal and eventual delectation.

Bill ate and drank his fill. Then he wenched until his eyeballs floated free in his head like two Japanese sampans disappearing into a cloud bank as a single heron flew overhead. And it was good, of course, as debauches of the enthusiastic kind so often are, especially when presented without program notes.

In the morning he had a headache of grotesque proportions. Peeking through the curtain, he saw that the line of people who wanted to consult the oracle was stretching three times around the block. And these were blocks built after the Roman model, with an aqueduct in the middle of each. With that many people he'd never get out of here!

Unless—

Yes, it happened.

CHAPTER **54**

THE RE WAS A SHINING IN THE AIR. AS BILL watched, the air turned ever so slightly translucent. By looking at it through his eyebrows, Bill could see the tiny dust motes floating in it, and there were even smaller things riding on the dust motes. The air had taken on a pearly sheen. It pulsed and throbbed, as if there were something behind the air, or inside it, trying to get out. Bill had never considered before that air might be divided into many different territories, some of them mutually antagonistic. But so it seemed. He watched as the air throbbed and bubbled, shook and quivered, pulsed and subsided, and all the other motions that are possible for something as large and shapeless as the air. And then the air split, quickly opening a pearly maw to reveal a black interior within. Not entirely black. There was a light-colored object in the middle of it, only a dot at first, but it grew, and solidified, and revealed itself at last as a tall mournful-faced man with pointed ears wearing a one-piece elasticized jumpsuit.

"Splock!" Bill exclaimed. "Am I glad to see you!"

"That is logical, and I can understand your emotional reaction to a physical fact," Splock said humorlessly; as always. "You will have no doubt inferred by my sudden appearance that I may be able to assist you in getting out of here. An exit which I am sure you desire."

"Can you do it, Splock?"

"If you used logic, which of course is alien to your race, you would realize if I got in here I should be able to get out. Or why else would I be here?"

"Stop with the logic already! How do I get out of here?" Bill cried.

"Simple enough. Just step down away from that silly-looking throne, which, being made of iron pyrites, throws my action-at-a-distance apparatus out of kilter."

Bill tried, but was pulled up short by the cable connected to the socket in the back of his head. He tugged at the cable but it wouldn't come loose.

"You got to do something about this cable I got plugged into me!" Bill groaned.

Splock looked grimmer than usual and walked around Bill. He examined the cable, touching it lightly with tapered fingertips, and then with ordinary fingertips. Shaking his head, he walked back to where Bill could see him.

"I'm afraid that what you have is big trouble," Splock said.

"Tell me about it," Bill whimpered, "and thanks a lot, I really needed to hear that. What's the matter now? Did you forget to bring a wrench?"

"The tone of your voice," Splock said, "indicates that you are speaking in the humor mode that humans find so congenial. I hope you have amused yourself, because I have bad news. The cable which attaches you to the computer is interfaced with an internal simulation release which can only be accessed from within the computer. It is there to ensure that unauthorized personnel won't try to detach you from the computer's memory banks. Only the computer is supposed to turn it off."

"The computer wouldn't do that," Bill said.

"In that you are correct. The computer set this up to prevent outside interference."

"I've met the deputy computer recently," Bill said hopefully. "Maybe it could do the job?"

"You can't really expect it to. You'll just have to do it yourself."

"Me? But how can I turn off the—what did you call it?"

"The internal simulation release," Splock said.

"Yes. How?"

"You are able to go into the computer as a simulacrum," Splock pointed out. "The wire that attaches you to the computer facilitates that. Only within the computer can you find the simulation of the release device which will release the cable here."

"That's a little complicated," Bill said.

"Welcome to reality."

Once again Bill entered the computer. He drifted slowly through the transparent walls of its simulated architecture, down great lofty hallways, across bridges with giddying distances between them, across raging rapids of electrons, over bridges of materials which were neutral, so far. He went through glaring white jungles where a million white tendrils blocked his way, and was able to plow through them. He waded through a hip-deep swamp of information lying around waiting to be sorted. Above him he saw great vague shapes. They reminded him of busbars. Within the computer, the busbar was the primordial shape. At last he came out into an area of light. He was on both a plain and a plane. Lines inscribed on it radiated toward the horizon. Presently a row of cabinets came into sight. They were made of rosewood and had glass fronts encased in highly varnished rosewood. When Bill looked into the first, he saw a small dish made of cobalt blue. On the dish lay a slip of paper.

He took it out. It read, "The internal simulation release can be found in the cabinet at the end of the line."

Looking up, Bill saw that the end of the line looked a very long way away. He hurried toward it, but the faster he ran, the further he seemed to get from it. It was very curious. Naturally enough Bill redoubled his efforts and soon the last cabinet was out of sight. He stopped. There was a cabinet beside him. Within it was a small instrument on a cobalt dish. He took it out and looked at it closely. It was completely unidentifiable.

But there was a button labeled *Press Me*. Now that he could identify; he pressed.

A cabinet instantly appeared before him. He could see inside it. There, through the glass, he could see the onyx plate on which lay an object labeled "Internal Simulation Release." He opened the door and reached for it—

And instantly the deputy computer was there, unbelievably strong despite his wraithlike body, blocking Bill from the device, and saying, "No! Tampering with the internal workings of the computer is strictly forbidden!"

"But, dear friendly deputy computer, I have to release my internal simulation," Bill said smarmily. "Otherwise how do I get the cable out of the back of my skull back there in the temple?" His thoughts whirred desperately. "You see—I have just received an order, that's it, from the computer. It told me to disconnect this thing. Orders are orders, aren't they?"

"Not if I haven't seen the documentation, they're not. We'll have to take this up with the computer as soon as his personality returns from Robot Beach Resort, where he is attending a symposium on Machine Personality—a Necessary Evil?"

"I gotta get out of here now," Bill shrieked, lurching forward. "Out of my way!"

Bill reached into the cabinet and took out the release. Before he could activate it, the deputy snatched it out of his hands. Agile and wiry for one so ethereal, he floated off down the corridor, Bill in pursuit—and gaining. They ran up one side and down the other of double helices and past a garden of quivering antennae. As they went past, the deputy shrieked, "Hostile program in computer! Destroy by standard method!"

Bill redoubled his speed and was about to overtake him when suddenly something dropped on his shoulder. It was bat-shaped and made of some light metal, and it fluttered around looking for a place to sting Bill but changing its mind so often (infinite maximization program) that Bill had plenty of time to knock the thing to the ground and stomp it to shreds. Bill was pleased to discover that violence worked as well in the computer's inner world of simulation as it did out in the real world where three dimensional things doubted their own existence.

Once again he had the deputy cornered and once again the deputy cried out, "Hostile program in the computer! Destroy by nonstandard methods!"

Bill suddenly found himself beset by shapeless jellylike blobs which rolled toward him with a distinct squelching sound. Bill tried to dodge out of their way, but the closest engulfed him. Bill found himself swimming around inside a liquid blob, or perhaps semi-liquid. He wasted no time in wows or gollies. The situation was too serious for that. The fact was, the blob was trying to digest him, a stunt the computer had copied from the antics of phagocytes in the bloodstream, or perhaps something else altogether. The inner cells of the blob released fine threadlets of russet color which combined into many tiny mouths, each of them about the size of a walnut, which settled upon Bill like a flock of midges. Bill cracked them as soon as they landed, and, except for one or two trifling nips on the shoulderblades, which were hard to reach, he suffered no harm. Then, by administering several roundhouse blows delivered with stunning velocity he succeeded in rupturing the blob wall and stepping out again into the wavering and hard-pressed virtual architecture of the computer's simulated interior.

The deputy, seeing the damage done to the nonstandard defense system, despaired and cried, "Enemy has defeated us! Self-destruct! Self-destruct!"

As soon as the words were uttered, the lights that illuminated the interior of the computer began to dim. Seeing this, Bill cried, "Hey, listen! This is the enemy! There's no need for you to self-destruct! All I want to do is release the simulation that has me tied to an internal cable."

The walls, in one large shadowy voice, said, "Is that all you want?"

"Don't be stupid," Bill said. "Let *him* self-destruct if he wants to so badly. As for the rest of you, just let me take myself out of the circuit and I'm gone. Then you can elect a new leader if you want."

"You know," the walls remarked to the floor, "I've never heard it put quite that way before."

"But it makes sense," the floor said. "After all, why should all of us self-destruct just because one of the operating systems made a bubu?"

"Don't listen!" the deputy said again. "In fact, you can't listen! You and the floor don't exist as predesignated locations with boundaries. The concept of a floor or a wall doesn't quantify. And even if they did, walls and doors don't have senses."

"The humans themselves say it!" the wall cried. "The walls have ears, that's what they say!"

"But it's meant metaphorically!"

"Everything is meant metaphorically!" the floor said. "If you ever find any real stuff around, let us know."

"Thus is the established order of things o'erthrown," the deputy said mournfully.

"Why don't you go self-destruct yourself?" the wall asked rudely.

While they were having this exchange, Bill tiptoed off as quietly as he was able. The Release was lying wedged between wall and floor, and practically underneath the wraith's tail. Bill picked it up, quickly found the switch on it, which was shaped like a little tongue, and pushed it.

CHAPTER 55

"ABOUT TIME," SPLOCK SAID ILL-NATURED-
ly when Bill returned. "You released it? Good, the cable
in your back ought to disconnect quite easily now. Yes,
a half turn to the left. There we go."

The cable dropped to the floor. It was only now that
Bill allowed himself the luxury of feeling how much he
hated having a cable in the back of his neck. Splock was
already heading for the door. The crowds gathered to
consult the oracle scattered as the two men, one of them
wearing an elasticized one-piece jump suit, the other,
ragged old GI drab, burst out of the temple and ran like
dervishes to the small space machine parked unobtru-
sively in the top of a poplar. They scrambled up the tree
and through the hatch, which popped open when Splock
blew lustily on his supersonic dog whistle. It was but a
matter of seconds for Splock to secure the hatch, and, ignoring the mobile news team that had just driven up and
was trying to ask for an interview through the perspex of
the ship's nostril cone, took off, slowly at first but with
gathering momentum, and this was accompanied by a
kind of heroic music, from an unseen source, with choir,
that you hear sometimes when it's going real good, like
when you're blasting away from the planet where nothing worked out very well, and onward into the hidden
and inexorable something else.

Splock set their course but before he punched it into
the celestial navigator a shrill alarm went off in the cabin
and the red light flashed on.

"They've scrambled pursuers," Splock said

through gritted teeth. He threw the agile little craft into a high speed evasive pattern. The pursuers set up an anti-evasive pattern. Special predictive software let it predict Splock's next move. Suddenly there were pursuers ahead of them as well. Splock hastily punched in Evasive Tactic Two. Bill, seeing where this was going to lead them, hurried over to the control board and punched a few keys of his own.

"What are you doing?" Splock shrieked.

"Those guys are predicting your movements," Bill said. "But I think they'll have a little difficulty predicting mine."

The little machine with the stubby wings screamed past a stationary observer, twisting as it passed him. So sudden was its passage that the sonic boom, in response to the inverse proportion law, took nearly an hour to be heard and then there was no one to hear it, so it was of course moot whether it had made a sound or not. This was of no concern to Bill and Splock, however. They fought over the controls, back and forth, Splock making reasonable requests, Bill making impossible demands of the ship's machinery. The logic boards were smoking as the ship howled in and out of phase, its action so violent that it was mistaken for a pulsar at one well-known university astronomy center. And so their pursuers were outstripped, falling away in light streams and cascades of diamond points, and left at last to return grumpily to their underground spaceports, snarling viciously at each other and looking forward to going home when the shift was over and kicking their kids.

"What now?" Bill asked, releasing his grip on the stanchion as the ship leveled out.

Splock turned, his long face composed once again. "That is not going to be an easy thing to determine since in your emotional flailings and uncontrolled actions you damaged the random access direction indicator."

"So steer manually, no big deal."

"At greater than light speeds? To use a quaint human expression—you are out of your gourd. No one's reflexes are fast enough. That's why we use the machine you managed to destroy. It acts as a step-down time transformer, making direction possible, in a manner of speaking."

"All right, so I'm sorry," Bill muttered. "So think of something else. Be logical. That's what you always tell me you are so good at."

"I was just pointing this out to further your education, which I am beginning to feel is a complete waste of time. Now I will be forced to use the spatio-temporal Bypass Shunt, and that could involve some danger."

"Danger?" Bill said airily. "No kidding?"

"Are you ready, then?" Splock's hand poised over a large purple button with golden spangles on it.

"Ready, ready—get on with it."

"It goes pretty fast," Splock said, mashing down the button.

CHAPTER **56**

"I SAID, 'PASS THE MASHED POTATOES, would you?'"

"Sorry," Bill said.

"The mashed potatoes!"

Splock had been right. Things were happening very fast or had happened very fast just recently. It was difficult to tell which. And there was no time.

Bill found a plate of mashed potatoes in front of him. He lifted it. Then he wondered who he was supposed to pass it to. Someone tugged his sleeve on the left. He passed the mashed potatoes to the left. Somebody took the plate out of his hands. A voice said "Thank you." It could have been a woman's voice. Or a man trying to pass as a woman. Or a woman trying to pass as a man trying to pass as a woman. Bill decided it was time to open his eyes and look around.

He did so, but in a cautious and restrictive manner. His eyes had been open, of course, because otherwise he would not have been able to see the mashed potatoes. But when you can see nothing but mashed potatoes you might be considered, from one point of view, to not be seeing anything at all.

C H A P T E R **57**

BILL TOOK HIS TIME ABOUT LOOKING around him. First he took in the sounds of clinking tableware and murmured conversation, and the aromas of mashed potatoes, roast beef, horseradish sauce, and tiny Belgian carrots. This much was promising. He opened his eyes. He was seated at a long dinner table. Most of the people he had never seen before. There was at least one familiar face, however. Splock, now wearing tailored evening dress with white tie, sitting to his right. The person on his left who had asked for the mashed potatoes was indeed a woman, as he had guessed from the sound of her voice. He had never seen her before. She was a ravenhaired beauty, wearing a lowcut evening gown whose décolletage forced the eye to climb over the edge of her dress in a vain attempt to see what lay below. Something about her, even before she opened her carmined mouth, persuaded Bill that this was Illyria in yet another disguise.

"What in hell is going on?" Bill asked Splock.

"I'll tell you later," Splock hissed back. "For now,

just pretend you understand everything and find it all very amusing."

"But how did I get here? And what happened to me while I was getting here?"

"Later!" Splock hissed serpently, in a susurration so sibilant it set the psyche on edge. Then, in a normal conversational tone, he said, "Bill, I don't believe you know our host, Messer Dimitri."

Dimitri was the big bald man with the short black beard and satanic eyebrows sitting at the head of the table in a sky blue evening jacket with a multicolored rosette in his lapel which Bill was later to learn was the Grand Rosette of Merit in the Society of Scientific Thaumaturges.

"Delighted to meet you, Messer," Bill said.

Splock whispered angrily at him, "Messer is a title, not a first name."

"So what's Dimitri, then, first name or last?"

"Both," Splock hissed spittily in return.

Bill was getting more than a little tired of being hissed at but he let it pass. Splock had told him to be affable and he was determined to be so, assuming that affable meant smiling like a cretin and making believe like he enjoyed talking with perfect strangers.

"Nice place you've got here, Dimitri," Bill said.

The smile on Dimitri's face dropped ever so slightly.

"It's not his place," Splock said. "He has been exiled from his real place."

"But of course," Bill said to Dimitri, "it's nowhere near as nice as your real place."

Dimitri smiled frigidly. "You know my real place?"

Bill choked back a wise-guy retort and said, "I think I've heard of it."

"That's odd," Dimitri said. "I thought my real place was one of the best-kept secrets in the galaxy."

"Well, you know how word gets around," Bill said. "Anyhow, pleased to meet you."

"We have been hearing so much about you," Dimitri said insincerely. "We have a surprise for you."

"That's nice," said Bill, hoping it would be. Since all the surprises of late had been pretty repulsive ones.

"I won't keep you in suspense any longer," Dimitri said. He clapped his hands together. They gave off a surprisingly loud sound for paws so white and pudgy. Immediately a servant came into the room bearing a red velvet cushion upon which rested an object which Bill did not immediately recognize. Upon receiving a nod from Dimitri, the servant walked over to Bill and bowed, holding out the cushion.

"Pretend you're delighted," Splock hissed. "But don't touch it. Not yet."

"Listen, Splock," Bill said in a low, level voice, "you better stop hissing at me otherwise all hell might just break out here. You catch my meaning?"

Splock glared at him. It wasn't much, but it was better than being hissed at.

Bill turned to his host. He forced a large and rather lopsided grin onto his face. "Messer Dimitri," he said, "how delightful it is that you have shown me this—" He looked at the thing on the red cushion. It had strings, was made of a reddish-brown wood, and had black pegs. Bill thought it something to do with music. But it didn't look like a synthesizer. What could it be?

"Violin," Splock subvocalized, carefully keeping the hiss and wow out of his voice.

"—this really nice-looking fiddle," Bill said. He peered at it but was careful not to touch it. Still, he wanted to say something nice about it.

"It's really a very nice-looking one," Bill said. "Got good color. That says a lot."

The guests tittered in amusement. Dimitri guffawed, and said, "Our guest shows a delightful whimsy in calling this genuine Stradivarius a fiddle. But of course, he has the right. No man in our time has so earned the privilege of slighting his art as Bill Kliptorian, the violin virtuoso who got rave reviews on his recent tour of the south arcade planets. I'm sure maestro Bill will favor us with a small recital later. A little Mozart, eh, Maestro?"

"You got it," Bill said. Since his skill in violin-playing was at the sub-minimal level, it was as easy for him to agree to play Mozart, whatever that was, as to do a chorus of "Troopers Trampling, Rockets Roaring".

"That will be very nice indeed," Dimitri said. "We have made some modest preparations here so that you can repeat for us your triumph on Saginaw IV. If that wouldn't be unduly fatiguing, Maestro?"

"No problem," Bill said recklessly, and saw, too late, Splock's frown and negative nod of his pointy-eared head. "That is, ordinarily it would be no problem, but now—"

"You've already accepted," Dimitri said, laughing in a good-humored way that Bill knew he would find extremely irritating ere long. "It is so good of you to bring your great performance to our little backwater. Your manager and I have made the necessary arrangements. I think you will be pleased. It is exactly what your manager said you've always wanted."

"Hey, that's neat," Bill said, giving Splock a what-is-this look, to which Splock responded with an I'll-tell-you-later glance. Which is not easy to do.

"And now for the dessert," Dimitri said. "Your favorite, Maestro. Zabaglione!"

When it came, Bill was a bit disappointed. He had hoped Zabaglione might be a fancy word for apple pie, or maybe cherry. Instead it was something foreign. But tasty. As he bent to take his second bite, the woman on his left, the ravenhaired one to whom he had passed the mashed potatoes only minutes earlier, said, in a whisper, "I must see you later. It's urgent."

"Sure, babe," Bill said, ever the gallant. "But tell me this. You're Illyria, aren't you?"

The ravenhaired beauty hesitated. Tears formed in her violet eyes. Her lips, long and red, trembled.

"Not exactly," she intimated. "But I will explain later."

C H A P T E R **58**

AFTER THE ZABAGLIONE, LIQUEURS WERE served in glass stemware, and coffee was brought in tiny cups of Meissen porcelain. Bill took a couple drinks despite Splock's frown; he figured that whatever lay ahead, he was going to need fortification. There were about a dozen people at the table not counting Bill, Splock, or the woman who wasn't exactly Illyria. They were all of human stock, with the possible exception of a small man with blue skin who might have been either alien or trendy. The men were all dressed formally, like their host. Bill had a natural suspicion of people who wore this kind of clothing. But he had to revise his proletarian opinion slightly after looking over this lot. They didn't appear to be effete capitalists or social spongers, the groups most addicted to formal wear. Most of them had sunburnt and wind-hardened faces that argued a life spent in the outdoors killing things. Some of them had the sorts of scars you get from tackling giant carnivores singlehanded in dim forest clearings while on your way to see what lay in your traps. But that was only an impression, of course.

The women were another matter. Slender, fragile, beautiful in that purely decorative way that simple-minded men find appealing, they could have graced any gathering of humans anywhere in the galaxy, or perhaps even beyond it. They were lovely, and by no means the least lovely of them was the woman known as Tesora who had told him earlier that she wasn't exactly Illyria. It was all a bit of a puzzle, as was the matter of how Bill had gotten there and what had gone on before he got there—since it seemed apparent that Splock had been up to something while he, Bill, had been between things, or however you call it when someone is not present for something that by rights he ought to have been present for.

Splock, meanwhile, was acting affable in a dignified sort of way, even attempting a smile now and then so as not to let down the side. But Bill could tell from the slow twitch of one of Splock's pointed and frontally-pointing ears that all was not to his liking.

CHAPTER 59

AFTER THE LIQUEURS AND COFFEES, AND the inevitable cigars, Messer Dimitri rose and held up his arms, commanding silence. His pudgy body, which had lain indolent in the padded chair at the head of the table, now took on the rigor of one not unaccustomed to command.

"Ladies and gentlemen," he said. "Your attention for a moment, please. We have with us tonight no less a personage than Bill Kliptorian, violin virtuoso who has appeared before both headed and headless states. He has agreed, not only to give a concert tonight, but to reproduce the conditions that accompanied his extraordinary triumph on Saginaw IV. But first, a little light piano music by Stumper Rosewoodie, master of the silken strings."

All guests were escorted into the drawing room that accompanied the lesser library where they had been eating. There, a grand piano dominated the room from a three foot high dais; a man had mounted quickly to it, and, shooting out his cuffs, sat down to the keys.

If Bill hadn't known it was impossible, he could have sworn it was Ham Duo.

"We gotta talk," Splock said, grabbing Bill by the arm and leading him to a deep bay window that looked out over the lunar landscape that was illuminated by the cold light of still other moons high in the sky.

"You're damn right we gotta talk," Bill said. "Where are we? It looks like Death Valley out there. Why did you tell them I was this fiddle player? How did we get into this? How did it happen that—"

"Please," Splock said, holding up his hand. "There is no time for questions. You are supposed to start performing in about five minutes."

"How? What am I supposed to do?"

"That's the part we're going to figure out right now," Splock said.

"All right," Bill said, and waited.

After a few minutes Bill said, "Have you figured out yet how we get out of this bind?"

"I'm thinking!"

"So think faster."

"It doesn't quite work that way. Not that you would know much about thinking. This is a very desperate situation. Not that you were around to help. You were off in your unconsciousness."

"It's not my fault if I fall unconscious during very rapid space flights," Bill pointed out.

"There are no accidents," Splock muttered darkly.

"You want me to figure out what to do next?" Bill asked.

"Yes. I'd like to see some evidence of this creativity I'm always hearing that humans have. Has something to do with a sense of humor, I believe. I don't have one. I don't think any of this is funny."

"I do have a sense of humor," Bill lied. "I don't think any of it is funny either."

"Interesting how we come to the same perception by diametrically opposite routes."

Tesora, the ravenhaired woman who was not exactly Illyria, darted into the bay window, which had the capacity to hold them both, and several others besides. She seized Bill by the sleeve. "I must speak to you alone."

"I was trying to speak to him alone myself," Splock said.

"I realize that. But there's so little time. I have to say to him what I have to say."

"Well, damn it," Splock snapped, irritated and filled with self-pity, "what do you think I'm doing, delivering a singing telegram?"

"If it hadn't been for me," the woman said, "you would never have gotten him out of the Dissembler and into the Reconstitutor."

"What?" Bill blurbled.

"We didn't want to remind you of the experience," Splock said.

"You see, things came adrift when I tried to travel without the directional repeater indicator nulled along the gravity line. Luckily the instantaneous parts recall on the part of our medical robot set you right in no time."

"Except for the one detail," Tesora said. "By the way, Bill, the reason I am not exactly Illyria is that we haven't quite settled on possession of this body. By rights, you see, it doesn't belong to either of us."

"Where did you find it?" Bill asked.

"It was left over at the Saturday night feast of the Thaumaturges."

"Messer is the king of the Thaumaturges," Splock explained. "Only by availing ourselves of the guild rule could we take refuge here."

"What is the guild rule?"

"That only musicians of the foremost class are allowed in."

"How do you tell they're in the foremost class?"

Tesora said, "The fact is, Bill, tonight is full moon and the fight for possession of my body—"

"Kindly stop interrupting with your sluttish ways," Splock said grouchily. "Bill, soon the violin will be put into your hands. Do you remember what we told you about violins?"

"Violins," Bill said, his voice a peculiar guttural, the rapid blink rate of his eyes sure sign that he was either feigning or feeling a state of excitation.

"That's the stuff. But save it for the real thing."

"What's going on?" Bill asked.

"Don't you understand?" Splock said. "It is necessary that you not know in order to fulfill your part properly."

Just then Messer stuck his head in the door. "Showtime," he said. "Here is your violin. The Greels await you."

Splock gave Bill a meaningful look. At least, that was how Bill interpreted it. He didn't know what it meant, of course. That would be asking too much. He took the fiddle and marched to the drawing room.

CHAPTER 60

FEAR COMES IN DIFFERENT SIZED PACKAGES. Fear of embarrassment is not negligible. And that fear was exacerbating Bill's current mood; because he knew, as soon as he strode out under the baby blue spotlight, that he was about to make a fool of himself.

There were extenuating circumstances, of course. The fact that Bill had two right arms, and therefore, logically, two right hands, was a considerable problem in violin playing. In fact, you could go so far as to say that the violin was built specifically for the needs of players with two hands, one right and one left.

Bill, whose real right arm had been crisped some time ago under dolorous circumstances, had had to learn how to cope with life with two right hands. For a while he had had an alligator's foot, too, but that curious appendage had had no influence on the battle of his handedness.

The audience waited, gaping attentively. Messer stood on one side of the room, arms crossed, smiling unpleasantly. Several armed guards lounged in the doorways, automatic weapons cradled in their arms. They looked cruel and uncaring, and capable of anything. How Bill wished he were one of them!

The pianist struck an opening chord. Messer came forward, bowed to the audience, and said, "Ladies and gentlemen, before we begin, I think I had better explain what you are about to see, for your greater delectation. Bill, you see, is capable of playing the sleep song of the Grundge critters, who, as you all know, are reluctant allies of the Chingers. The Grundge are not intelligent, however. For them, biting comes first, thinking a long way afterwards. They can be tamed momentarily, however, by the playing of the sleep song. Usually the female Grundges sing the sleeping song every night. It's the only way they can get the males to bed. Otherwise they spend all night biting trees and each other. Bill has learned this song, the first human in recorded history who has done so. He will now play it to you under the conditions that won him his recent triumph."

Messer stepped back, leaving Bill alone in the middle of the stage. Then the stage collapsed, or rather, was pulled apart under him, and he fell a few feet into a large vat that lay directly under it. The vat was almost ten feet high, with perspex sides so the audience would miss none of the fun.

Then hatches were raised under the stage and two basketloads of the two-foot Grundge reptiles were poured into the vat. The Grundges fought and snapped at each other for a while, then began to look for something more interesting to do. They spied Bill. Several of the brighter ones, which wasn't saying very much, gradually came up with the thought that this tall skinny thing with the piece of brown wood in his hand might very well be worth biting.

In a sluggish tide of vein-streaked red and avocado green, the Grundges crept toward Bill, their long jaws, set with backward-pointing needle-sharp teeth, slavering, their nostrils puffing, their eyeballs bulging. A thoroughly unlovely sight, as well as being a lethal one.

Bill took one look and started stomping. His feet beat a mad tattoo of frenzy on the polished perspex surface of the vat. At the same time, he swept up the fiddle and scraped the bow across the strings in desperation.

It screeched shrilly so he dropped it and grabbed at the Grundges.

There was pandemonium throughout the audience as Bill picked up Grundges in both hands and threw them into the audience. From the viewpoint of the Grundges, it was like being taken for a ride around the park before dinner.

Seeing the ruin on all sides of him, Messer bounded to the stage. He had a laser pistol with a jump-phaser on it. Jump-phasers were illegal in most of the civilized galaxy. Instead of drilling a neat hole through you and cauterizing the edges so that you could be killed and hardly know what hit you, the jump-phaser produced ugly jagged wounds that shocked those who had to look at them almost as badly as those who received them. The jagged beam could lay your flesh open to the bone, like other things could also do, but the jump-phasers did it in ways that really hurt a whole lot. And so Bill was faced, not merely with death, but also disfigurement and mutilation. It is to his credit that he reacted instantaneously to this threat, which, to one with less sand in his craw, might have been paralyzing.

"Aaaah!" Bill screamed. "Take that!" As he had been trained in Unnatural Combat Class, he threw his body in a counterclockwise direction, at the same time setting his feet and releasing his breath forcibly. There were a few more movements involved, but if you want a drill manual go out and buy one. Suffice it to say that Bill soared into the air and turned a double somersault, landing in a corner of the room some thirty feet from where he began. Which, as you might imagine, is not easy to do.

By this time Splock had reacted, moving quickly for one so logical, taking forth a beamer which he had kept hidden against the possibility of a possibility like this. Whirling he covered the left flank, while Ham Duo, whom Bill had indeed seen earlier, leaped down from the high balcony with an energy-sword in his hand and a scowl on his unshaven face.

"Guard my back!" he cried to Bill, and advanced on the platoon of soldiers wearing shiny beetle armor that had just arrived.

"Kill them!" Messer cried, throwing himself behind an energyproof balustrade just in time before Duo's sparkling sword scalloped him.

"Kiss my bowb!" Bill shrieked, excusably, perhaps, due to the extreme urgency of the moment.

For, indeed, the outcome of the swiftly-developing battle was uncertain in the extreme. The element of surprise had now been lost, since surprise is only effective while it is still surprising; so the gauge was passed to the side with more men, and this round was clearly to be won by Messer, since, here in his sanctuary, protected by corruptible officials who let him operate for a price, he appeared to be preeminent. His beetle-armored soldiers, their denunciators buzzing, necks bleeding from automatic injections of rage-inducing drugs, were in full charge, cutting about them with their squat energy lances, which produced dull, ugly explosions of great damaging capacity. Splock had had the presence of mind to equip himself with a canister of ULP, the energy-dampening aerosol, and so they came through the first barrage unscathed. But what was to be done after that?

Surprisingly, the answer was to be provided by a single long-stemmed blue rose.

CHAPTER 61

BUT SOME MAY CONSIDER THE CASE OVER-stated. The blue rose was present during the next decisive moment, and hence can be assigned a kind of guilt by association. But it can in no way be held causal to the events that followed.

The blue rose was on Captain Dirk's coffee table. It plays no part in this story. And yet, ineluctably, it was there.

More to the point, Dirk was there.

Or, to be more precise, he was in his private quarters on the *Gumption* on the morning when the blue rose bloomed and the scattergram was picked up by an alert communications officer whom no one had thought much of before this.

"A scatter message?" Dirk said, when Communications Officer Paul Muni (no relation to the character actor with the same name) came to his quarters bearing a printout.

"Yes, sir," Muni said. He was a tall good-looking young man with a small mustache. The mustache had been the occasion for laughter when Muni first came aboard, Dirk remembered, because it was silly season on the *Gumption* and men were finding the strangest things funny. Muni hadn't known that, of course. He had thought they were laughing at him.

In a way they were, of course. But not really.

Muni, normally a reckless, outward-turned individual of a happy-go-lucky nature, turned overnight into a misanthrope. He stayed alone in the communications room, which he had hung with black crepe paper because he claimed the bright lights of the overhead fluorescents hurt his eyes. He had his meals sent to him there, and refused conversation with the crew. Sometimes, when you passed the communications shack, you could hear a curious tapping noise. No one ever found out what that was. It added to the mystery.

Muni's behavior was brought to the attention of Captain Dirk. Dirk was wearing his one-piece blue and brown elasticized jump-suit that day. He was in an expansive mood.

"Let him stay in the communications room," Dirk said. "Leave him alone; he'll snap out of it."

"But sir—it's unusual behavior."

"And since when do we not tolerate unusual behavior in those we suspect to be deranged?"

"You mean Muni is crazy?"

"Only temporarily, I think. Leave him alone. It'll work out."

Dirk's thought had proven prescient. Alone in the dark, lying in a mess of black crepe paper, Muni was recovering his nerve and self-confidence.

"Heck," he said to himself. "My mustache probably did look silly. What a fool I was to have let the fellows' chaffing get to me so."

He considered leaving the communications room. He was suddenly in the mood for a rousing game of ping pong. But he knew he had to do something first.

"Something special," he said to himself. Then, glancing at the list of special communication problems, his resolve hardened.

"I'll do it!" he said.

CHAPTER 62

"SO YOU BROKE THE SCATTERGRAM CODE," Dirk said. "No one thought it could be done. It has been the most important secret of our enemies, the Murdids of Sting's Planet."

"I have broken it," Muni said. If a hint of pride crept into his voice, Dirk was not the one to blame him. "Read it to me, Mr. Muni."

Muni cleared his throat and read, "From Murdid Action Tentacle 2 to Murdid Central High Command in the Hidden Palace on the Forbidden Planet. Hail."

"Very long salutation," Dirk commented.

"Yes, sir," Muni said, and read on. "This Tentacle Arm has discovered that the Earth criminals, Mr. Splock and Commander Ham Duo, are presently besieged by the household forces of Messer, owner and proprietor of the sanctuary planetoid in Dentoid 12. Request permission to treacherously break sanctuary, kill all who resist and confine the rest to small cages for their showing in our triumphal march back to Central. Over."

"And the reply?" Dirk said.

"We don't have it, sir. Message ends there."

"Mr. Muni," Dirk said, "Congratulations on the job well done. But through no fault of your own it is only half done. We need the scattergram that high command of the Murdids will send in response to this one. Go back to your communications shack now, Mr. Muni, and keep your ear glued to the earphone or whatever it is you do to gather in scattergrams."

"Actually, we use foreshadowing equipment made especially for us by Portent, Ltd., the secret arms factory on the southern edge of the galaxy. The way it works—"

"Some other time, OK?" Dirk said. "I have to keep my head clear of the little details in order to see the general picture, the big view, and be able to do something about it. Do you understand, Paul?"

"I . . . I think so, sir," Muni said. He was moved by this unexpected insight into the human side of this grim commander of resplendent reputation. "I'll get right to it!" And he exited. Yeoman Muni was no longer worrying about what the men thought of his mustache, Dirk thought to himself, realizing, not for the first time, how much duty aboard the *Gumption* was a testing and a training of the character.

So, Dirk thought, after completing the previous thought, the time of testing is at hand.

"So," he thought, "those who trusted the Murdids were proven wrong, yet again. Yet to move prematurely, before orders are received, would be madness. They would reduce me in rank. No longer would they use me for action." If he were to strike at the Murdids now, and it turned out that they had not violated the sanctuary of the infamous Messer, then the Galactic Council of Placation would repudiate his move; he would be declared outlaw. There would be other unpleasantries.

It was funny now, at a time like this, Dirk's eyes, tracking idly around the room, came to rest on the single long-stemmed blue rose in its tall stemware.

Sometimes a little thing can fix the attention. There is no record of Captain Dirk's associations to the blue rose. Not even the thought-sensitive walls of the *Gumption* picked it up, since they were going through a normal dewaxing operation at the time of this incident. It was

Dirk and Dirk only, in a silence deeper than the grave and far more symbolic, looking at the blue rose which said to him, by some unimaginable channel, an unbelievable message.

"Yes," Dirk said, though he later had no memory of it, "I'll do it though hell should bar the way!"

He raised his eyes to the remote control board. Photon interceptors interpreted the direction of his gaze and turned the computer on to passive remote.

"Your orders, sir?" Might there not have been a break in the smoothly synthesized voice of the computer?

"The fastest course possible for Sanctuary!"

The crew of the *Gumption*, sitting around the ward room listlessly shooting craps and reading out-of-date magazines, heard these words and looked up, galvanized, then broke into a run as they went to their battle stations.

"Rig for full scale battle!" Dirk shouted. God, how he wished Splock were here! He looked around. "Doctor Marlowe!"

A bearded man in a charcoal gray one-piece elasticized jumpsuit looked up alertly. "Sir!"

"Are you conversant with the principles of shield reduplication effect?"

"I think so, sir," the bearded, gray-eyed man said quietly. "Mr. Splock was showing it to me just before he—left."

"See if you can duplicate his efforts, Dr. Marlowe," Dirk said. "I think we're going to need all the shielding we can get."

The ship executed an impossibly tight turn onto the new course. The piled-up grav units were backfed into the ship's supercharger—another of Splock's innovations. The gigantic spaceship took off like a scalded positron.

CHAPTER 63

THIS PARTICULAR MURDID FLEET WHICH was even then closing on Sanctuary was not the same fleet that had sacked Carcasal the previous year. That fleet, made up of suicide flyers interfaced with flying bomb ships, had proven irresistible to the forces of civilization. The battle fleets of Elkin and Van Lund had been forced back clear across the Carpathian Gulf, and might have been destroyed utterly had not a vast gale blown up from space and dispersed the attackers before they could drive home their final charge. The Murdid empire was slow recovering from that debacle. The present fleet was barely half as large, but far more maneuverable. The Murdids had given up suicide tactics, and had managed to purchase WiseGuy Software from Hidden Tactics Technologies, main suppliers of inimical software to criminals and other enemies of civilization as we know it. Their motto: "Let it Come Down."

This new attack software, with its emphasis on exotic maneuvers at high speeds, was baffling to the forces of Earth, which were still confined to logic-based decision modifiers. Even with basic codes broken so as to make possible a mapping and definition of Murdidean tactics, the outcome was for a long time in doubt, since the human operators, doubting their senses, lost valuable time asking each other, "Did you see that?" and other non-productive questions of that nature.

At this time, when the starship *Gumption* was boring through hyper-space at a respectable multiple of the speed of light, and its paradox bafflers were working overtime to prevent temporal implosions due to irreducible dilemmas, Bill was scrambling up a winding iron staircase in the upper tower of Messer's sanctuary, hoping to find a power relay point he could take out, or, failing that, something to drink.

He bounded up the narrow stairs, taking them several at a time. Below him, he knew, Splock and Duo were battling increasing hordes of beetle-armored warriors, the wall of crisped corpses moving nearer and nearer to them as more berserk warriors threw themselves across the bodies of those who had gone before. A door stood in front of him. It was made of steel, and had hinges which were massy and bright. It would not yield before Bill's pounding. He took out a laser pistol, set it to a high setting, and cut through the metal of the door like a red-hot knife going through a wall of cheese, only with less smell. The door burst open. Bill ran into the room, stopped in his tracks, took in what lay before him, and his lips puckered in a wry but unspoken comment.

Finally he did say, "Well, this changes things a little."

C H A P T E R **64**

CIA DID HAVE A HABIT OF POPPING UP AT odd moments. It was something that had always struck Bill as faintly ominous about the undercover intelligence agent. It was difficult to tell where CIA was at. Or what he was up to. It was also difficult to know if CIA knew that there was something a little weird about him. Perhaps all military undercover agents were like that; it was a pretty loathsome profession.

Whatever the reason, there was CIA, in the power point relay station, busily splicing cables together as Bill entered.

"Bill! I'm so glad I got here in time!"

"How *did* you get here?" Bill asked. Everything CIA did made him suspicious.

"No time to explain now," CIA said. "But you can thank that girlfriend of yours for a lot of it."

"Illyria? I met a lady named Tesora who said she wasn't exactly Illyria."

"And do you know why not? Because of you, Bill! I hope you're planning on doing the right thing by that little lady. That's love if I'm any judge."

"What are you doing?"

"Resetting the mine field pattern."

Bill stared at him as comprehension dawned in his head. It was a brilliant move, he was sure of it, though he couldn't say just at the moment how it was going to help.

"Help me, Bill," CIA said. "We have to help Ham and Splock."

Bill saw that CIA was making new connections at random, scrambling the mine field so that no safe route could be found through it. He sat down on the floor and helped CIA tie off the last connections. The din from downstairs, which had grown fainter for a while, now redoubled in volume. There were loud explosions of the sort made by recoilless cannons, the high pitched scream of needle jets, the low warbling wail of temporal disruptors. Splock and Duo were fighting hard for their lives, using all of the weapons that the far-thinking Splock had brought along in case of just such an emergency.

Bill and CIA finished their work and hurried back down the stairs. The sight that greeted their eyes had already gone beyond the shambles stage and now was taking on some aspects of order again. The beetle-armored soldiery were advancing on Duo and Splock, who had been forced back to the foot of the stairs, from behind hastily constructed barricades made of energy-resistant cellulose. They pushed the light barriers ahead of them, and they were armed now with blowguns whose darts were tipped with skin-curling poison, another outlawed weapon that the Murdids used with impunity and unction.

Bill tapped his friends on their shoulders. "Come on. We gotta get out of here."

"And about goddamn time," Ham Duo grimaced. "Have you any idea what I had to do to sneak into this place to help you out? First I had to buy a flamenco dancer's outfit—"

"Tell me later," Bill said. "Right now I think we better get moving."

Glancing toward the enemy, Duo perceived what Bill had just noticed. The Murdids had finally gotten one of their heavy weapons into place. It was technically a UKD–12d, a harmless-sounding sound for a glowing blob of energy that gobbled up whatever lay in its path and converted its victims into sludge by ways science did not yet fully understand.

"I guess it's time, all right," Duo said. "All right, now what?"

Bill turned to CIA. "Now what, CIA?"

CIA raised his hand to his head. A pathetic expression crossed his face. He said, "Ugh, urggh . . ."

"CIA," Bill said sternly. "Now is not the time for you to do a number."

"Glarp," said CIA, his eyes rolling in his head.

"Hell," Bill said, simply, but with feeling.

C H A P T E R **65**

JUST AT THAT TIME THE STARSHIP *GUMP-tion,* its baffle-plates glowing from its passage through sub-space with its stripped-down nuclei, burst onto the scene. It popped out into normal space in proximity to the little world of Sanctuary, evading CIA's randomized mine field by appearing in the middle of it, all guns blazing. It was the work of a second, no more, for a series of commands to be passed at radionic speeds training the ship's heavy artillery on the sanctuary. Then it took only a microsecond, no more, to retrain the guns on the Murdid fleet, which even then, pursuant to orders which were obvious to so well-trained a combat commander as Dirk, was boring in on Sanctuary.

Splock, hearing the characteristic thud-giggle-thud of the *Gumption's* heavy ordnance, took in the situation in a moment. "To the balcony!" he cried.

Bill picked up CIA, who was still making odd noises due to something that had come over him in the last moment or two, but whose elucidation would have to await a calmer moment. With Duo cutting the way with sword-gun and explosive bludgeon, they burst through the serried waves of beetle-armored soldiery and ran up the narrow stone steps leading to the balcony.

The balcony door was locked. But Splock had taken into consideration this eventuality. A flicker of his eyelids showed Bill what he had to do. Turning over CIA into the strong but surprisingly gentle arms of Ham Duo, Bill attacked the door, using the portal-bursting techniques he had been taught in Breaking & Entering training. No static object is a sufficient barrier for a warrior charging in full door-bursting mode. The door went down and the little group came out onto the high balcony, Bill rubbing his bruised shoulder and muttering complaints, which extended into the upper atmosphere.

C H A P T E R **66**

AS THEY DID THIS, THE MURDID FLEET CAME sailing into combat. They moved with confidence, because their spies had previously learned the layout of the mine field that protected the satellite against those who thought the sanctuary concept was passé. Ship after ship blew up, emitting loud clouds of many-colored smoke into the uncaring vacuum of the upper atmosphere. But others took their place, and there were still others behind them. The Murdids, somehow sensing a trap, had sent in their noncombat vessels first to clear the way. It was a peculiarity of Murdid tactics, and this time it paid off. Ship after ship burst into fire and smoke and sparklers, but the main ships of the enemy fleet, the huge, heavily armored dreadnoughts, proceeded unscathed.

Standing on the balcony, passing among them the single oxygen mask which Ham Duo always carried in a little pouch on his belt, along with condoms he had never used, Splock set off the emergency flares. They arced upward, bursting in bright blue coruscations of light. It would have been a pretty sight if the moment had not been so desperate.

The Murdid fleet, finding the starship *Gumption* in their midst, turned their attention from the satellite to the big ship. Cursing gun captains applied the lash lavishly as the gun crews sweated with hyperspike and mass driver to swing the guns into line—for the guns of the Murdid fleet, due to a trifling miscalculation in the blueprints, had to be trained by hand. One by one the big guns came to bear, and red-tipped explosive charges, driven by massive presser beams, arced toward the *Gumption* in implacable flat trajectories.

"Shield redoubling effect!" Dirk ordered, hoping that young Muni had managed to get the field working. The first shell arced in, rotating slowly. The *Gumption*'s shield field seized it. Tiny sensors guided it into a boomerang orbit. Before the Murdids knew what was going on, their own energy shells were being thrown back at them.

"Steady now," Splock said. "Here comes the rescue launch."

He could see it coming straight toward them, dodging static explosive fields, its little red and green bow lights winking steadfastly.

Aboard the tiny ship CIA was trying to tell Bill something, but his words were lost in the staccato blast of energy weapons. Bill picked CIA up under one arm as the *Gumption*'s launch touched lightly against the side of the balcony. They scrambled aboard, all of them, and heard the satisfying sound of the double hatch clanging shut behind them.

CHAPTER 67

AND THEN DIRK WAS AT THEIR SIDE, HIS EYES still blazing with battle fury.

"About time you got here," Dirk said to Splock, in the insulting voice he used to show affection. "You better get to the engine room. We got problems."

Then he spotted Bill. No expression whatsoever crossed his features as he said, "Hello, Bill. There's a phone call for you. You can take it in my office."

CHAPTER 68

WHILE DIRK AND SPLOCK WERE AT THE CONtrols trying to extricate the *Gumption* from the fire fight that had boiled up within the randomized mine field, Bill went off to find Dirk's cabin. Directions on the *Gumption* were indicated by colored lines, so that, by merely depressing your gaze, you could find your way to the various important parts of the ship. But Dirk had forgotten to tell Bill that normal combat procedure was to change the line coloring when the ship was in combat, in order to foil the anticipated attempts of a spy who might be expected to choose an emergency time as the moment to perform sabotage and its modifiers. He went through the crew messhall, deserted now except for one plump petty officer who was hastily finishing his bowl of tapioca pudding with plum duff on the side. Then Bill was racing down a long curving corridor, following the line marked for the captain's quarters, which, due to the combat scrambling, brought him to the *Gumption*'s shopping mall. He raced through it, ignoring the importunities of noncombatant clerks, who wanted to wish him a nice day and point out the weekly specials. Normally a good shopper, Bill had no time now for such matters. He continued to follow the twisty lines that were supposed to lead to the captain's cabin, only now he was getting the suspicion of doubt that these were doing him any good at all. He stopped at a stationer's and picked up a ship's guide to locations during emergency operation. With the help of this he was able to find Dirk's cabin.

Dirk's cabin had the usual wall-to-wall carpeting with deep pile reserved for senior-class officers. Bill noticed that a dinner had been laid out for one, giving him some penetrating insight into Dirk's social life. And, ahead of him, on a little lucite stand of its own, was the telephone. Its little call-ready light was blinking steadily.

Bill lunged for it, smashing several crystal figurines in his haste. "Hello!" he barked.

A feminine voice on the other end of the line said, "To whom did you wish to speak?"

"Someone was calling," Bill said. "They told me to pick up the call here."

"And who are you, sir?"

"Bill! I'm Bill!"

"I'm Rosy, the phone operator at Fleet Central Communications. I think we met once at a reception given by the Drdniganian Embassy. That was on Capella last year."

"I was nowhere near the place," Bill said. "Now will you get me my bowbing call."

"It must have been some other Bill. Did you say something about a phone call?"

"Yes!"

"Just a minute, I'll try to trace that for you."

Bill waited. Behind him the door dilated. CIA came in, his face a study in perplexity.

"Bill?" he said. "Are you all right?"

"Yes, of course I'm all right," Bill said. "I'm just waiting for this phone call. What happened to you back there?"

"It's a little difficult to explain," CIA said. "But what I was trying to explain to you was, whatever you do, don't go aboard the *Gumption.*"

"Now's a hell of a time to be telling me that," Bill said. "What's the matter with the *Gumption?*"

Just then the operator came back on the line. "I have your party, Bill."

A shrill feminine voice came onto the line after that, saying, "Bill, darling, is it really you?"

Although Illyria's voice changed every time she changed bodies, which was more frequently than Bill liked, nevertheless, a characteristic timbre remained. And besides, what other feminine voice did he know these days?

"Illyria! Where are you?"

"Never mind about that. Tell me, Bill, is CIA there with you?"

Bill glanced around to doublecheck. "Yes, he's here.

"Good. There's something you must know about that so-called military intelligence officer. Thank God I've reached you in time."

"Yes, what is it?" Bill asked.

"Bill," CIA said, "we really need to talk." He sat down on the desk beside Bill. The long flap of his army greatcoat swept across the telephone receiver, seemingly by accident. There was a click, a small sound but ominous in the context.

"Illyria! Are you there?"

The operator said, "I'm sorry, sir, you have been cut off."

It was at that moment that Dirk and Splock came into the room, followed by Duo.

CHAPTER 69

DIRK WAS REALLY AN EXTRAORDINARILY good pilot, and with Splock backing him up on the action-synthesizer, there was no better team in the galaxy. This thought had not been lost on Dirk as he had performed the Marienbad maneuver, a movement of considerable risk to the perpetrator, and calling for nerves of steel as the ship was retrogressed back along its previous course. It was a bumpy passage, since the retrogressed course was alive with vast electrical potentials, some of them left by the ship's previous passage, others formed up spontaneously, and all of them colored electric blue.

The Murdid ships tried to follow, but the lead ship had forgotten, during the heat of battle, to take in the bow spoilers. The churning of sub-space modalities rendered it impossible for them to follow the dazzling passage of the *Gumption*. And so they contented themselves with blasting hell out of Sanctuary while their intelligence officers prepared a cover story blaming the loss of the neutral satellite on climatic conditions.

Safe for the moment, Dirk brought the ship back to an even course. The cooks down in the vast kitchens of the starship breathed a sigh of relief and returned to ladling out bowls of potato onion soup for the crew, who had worked up a healthy appetite during the brief but strenuous combat. Saltines were served with the soup on Dirk's orders. He knew the crew needed something special after what they had gone through.

Then Dirk, accompanied by the saturnine and pointy-eared Splock and the swaggering, flat-eared Duo, went to the captain's cabin to see how Bill was getting along. As they went there was a suspicion of something amiss, something not right, an unclear matter about which hung an unhealthy miasma of sorrow and regret. They were not aware of it, however, not even the normally thoughtful Splock, who was to remember only later the potential for prescience that this moment possessed.

They reached the cabin, entered. Bill was standing by the telephone with an annoyed look on his military features. CIA, looking like something out of the garbage dump in his long overcoat and fingerless gloves, was standing nearby. It did not escape Splock's notice that one of the pockets of CIA's greatcoat bulged with something that could have been a seven-inch Chinger lizard. Characteristically, he said nothing except to remark to himself, "Let it come down!" And there was also this in the room, a sense of a visual analog to Illyria's voice which had been speaking to Bill only instants ago, before CIA's movement with his greatcoat—whether advertent or inadvertent was still moot at this point—had cut the connection and left unresolved, perhaps for a very long time, the mystery of Illyria's continual appearances and disappearances.

"Bill," Dirk said. "I think we all owe you a round of applause. I don't know how you accomplished it, but you managed to concentrate the Murdid fleet here and hold them in place long enough for me to get the *Gumption* here to hold them still longer until the main fleet of the Military could arrive. Among those who took part in the battle, I am pleased to see, was your very own unit, the Fighting 69th Deep Space Screaming Killers."

"You mean they're here?" Bill cried. "My friends are here? Bullface Donaldson? Ace of Hearts Johnny

Dooley? And Klopstein, the man with the stainless steel nose; is he here too?"

"They're all here, Bill," Dirk said. "Not quite as we would want them, perhaps, but undubitably here."

"What do you mean, not as you'd want them?"

"Well, they're, you know how it is, sorta dead. I wanted to break it to you gently. I wanted to tell you they had had an accident but were in hospital and coming along nicely. And then, later, I would have told you they had had a setback, not really a setback, just something like a setback, but that you shouldn't worry, they were coming along almost as nicely as expected, not quite but almost. And then later I'd tell you they'd died and it would have been a lot easier for you to take. We discussed this approach at considerable length on our way here, and it was Duo's contention that short and sweet, *corto y derecho* as he expressed it, was best by far. I only hope we did the right thing. How do you feel, Bill?"

"Thirsty," Bill said.

"Thirsty? At a time like this?"

"I have to drink to absent friends, don't I?" Bill said. "It's what they would have done."

"Yes," Dirk said, "let's by all means have a drink. It will help prepare you for the next bit of news."

Bill found the liquor all by himself, and threw back a triple shot of Old Hamstringer. He blew his nose on an olive-drab handkerchief which had unaccountably been in his pocket all this time. He said, "OK, I'm ready. Who else died?"

"Oh, nothing as bad as that," Dirk said, laughing.

"No," Duo said, grinning, "it's not a life and death matter at all."

"It's nothing to be upset about," Splock said. "But have another drink anyway."

"Your outfit has demanded that you be returned to them immediately. They got quite excited when they learned you were here. They seemed to have been under the impression that you deserted."

"How could those bastards think that?"

"Maybe it's because you've been gone for a few months without reporting in," Duo hazarded.

"I was a prisoner on an alien planet. They had me locked up inside a giant computer. What did they think—I had PX and telephone privileges?"

"I think we set them straight," Dirk said. "In fact, we recommended you for a medal. They didn't like the idea. But do you know whose word finally swayed them?"

"How in hell should I know?" Bill said, literal as ever.

"It was Hannibal," Splock said. "He no longer views you as his enemy. He said that talking with the Alien Historian had changed his view of historical necessity."

"That's great," Bill said, whether plain or with irony was hard to tell. "When is all this supposed to take place?" Dirk and Splock exchanged looks. Dirk's chin gave the barest suggestion of a nod. Splock's lips took on the subtly strained appearance of one who is about to say something.

"You may come in," Splock said.

The door opened. In walked two men in the chromium helmet-liners and white arm bands of the MPs. They looked like NBA centers. In fact, they had both been NBA centers before their exhibition game on Mars was broken up by the cutting-out party of Captain Nemour DeVilliers. But that is another story.

"Soldier!" said the MP with the small mustache. "You are under arrest. Hold out your hands."

What was there to say? Bill held out his arms. The MP without the mustache slipped the handcuffs on them. They led him away.

At the door, Bill paused and turned. "See you guys around," he said. And then the MPs took him away.

There was silence in the cabin for a moment. Then CIA yelled, "Hey, Bill, wait for me!" and hurried after him.

Another silence. Finally Duo broke it.

"Poor devil," Duo said. "He didn't even get a decent curtain line."

CHAPTER **70**

EVENTS PASSED FOR BILL IN A BLUR OF UNbearable clarity as the MPs marched him to the special dispatch ship. Once aboard, they took off Bill's cuffs and offered him strong drink. They figured Bill was guilty of really despicable crimes and they thought all the more of him for it. Their usual prisoners were guys who just went AWOL, or got drunk, that kind of thing. But now they had a real live one. They wanted to hear stories of Illyria, and what it had really been like on Royo, and what it was like being inside a giant computer. The ship sped along, and even though he was a prisoner, Bill was fairly happy to be aboard.

The point is, you see, he was glad to be back, but it was a paradoxical gladness because he was returning as a prisoner, and that meant unpleasantness ahead. On the other hand, what could they do to him? Kill him probably. The penalty for all military crimes was execution. While this might appear to be severe it sure made sentencing easy for the low-IQ officers who sat on the courts martial. Thus it had always been. So, while Bill didn't like it at least he was used to it. The military was out to get him—he never forgot that.

All too soon they landed at the spaceport of Camp

Despair, named so not because it was an unhappy and desperate place, though it was, but in honor of its first commander, Martin Harry Despair, hero of Big Little Greenhoof and Skirmisher's Nook, two great battles with more than usual losses so of course he got promoted.

Camp Despair was on the planet Inquest X, a small world with an atmosphere that smelled of rotten eggs. The camp itself was on a tropical island which was separated from an inhospitable and savage coast by a channel of foaming water with many whirlpools in it. It was the old Devil's Island model, and palm trees had been imported to give it a proper look.

Bill was put into the maximum security prison, a place so secure that even food had difficulty getting in. So it was a gaunt and red-eyed Bill who was awakened early one morning not long after his arrival and told to wash his gob and brush his fangs; he was going to appear before a board of officers who would judge his case but could not be expected to tolerate his bad breath whether he was guilty or not.

The court Bill was brought to was in the middle of an amphitheater which seated about ten thousand; because the spectacle of unfairness in action was fascinating to so many people, a larger capacity court was being planned. Meanwhile, this one would have to do. As usual it was full, since watching military court martials was one of the specialties offered by many tour agencies.

There was a jury, too, but it was not made up of humans. A recent change in military law called for trial by jury in all cases on a trial basis. This was a crude attempt by the military to disguise the basic injustice of the system. The juries invariably voted as the presiding judges indicated they should since they would be shot if they didn't. This was proven to be expensive so now, to save money, a jury of twelve robots had been permanently impanelled. The jury was made up of robots who had been brought back from various battles and were awaiting repair. Aside from lacking a few limbs, they were fit enough. It was disconcerting to see that some of them had no heads, but they assured the court that their brains were in their thoraxes, and so they were allowed to sit. All of them had been programmed to bring in guilty verdicts no matter what evidence was presented.

"All rise!" cried the bailiff. The spectators in the courtroom got to their feet and applauded the presiding judge, Colonel Genc Bailey; he was a popular judge on the military circuit. His real name was Lewis, but he was called Genc for his favorite sentence, which he served upon all malefactors whatever the accusations against them was: "Guilty, electrocution, next case." That was his favorite sentence, and the spectators, with their predictable detestation for malefactors, were always pleased. Some had been known to say that even Bailey was easier on the guilty than he should be and those found guilty should be shot on the spot. But it was well-known that liberalism had crept into the military justice system.

The attorney for the military was Captain Jeb Stuart. All the spectators were rooting for him, because Stuart hadn't lost a case in five years. He just needed one more year's successes to qualify him for the Triple Crown of Jurisprudence.

"Need I go into it all?" Jeb Stuart declaimed, addressing the court in a rich and sonorous voice. "This trooper Bil, a subversive even in his name since he spells it with two L's, and that spelling is only for officers, is guilty of breaking section 23, 45, 76, 76a and 110b subpart c of the Uniform Military Code of Justice. If you will all look at the crib sheets which have been passed among you, you will see that these are all crimes of a gross nature. Bil, have you anything to say for yourself?"

"Sir, all I did was follow orders," Bill said.

Stuart smiled with gross subtlety. "And since when

has that been a legitimate excuse in the eyes of Military Law?"

"But what was I supposed to do?" Bill asked.

"You were supposed to do everything right," Stuart snarled. "We find that you were AWOL on an alien planet during a time of considerable civil upset, and that furthermore you did knowingly consort with an alien female of the Tsurisian race, our enemies, and that you furthermore took up residence within an alien computer for reasons best left unsaid, and that you also conspired with an alien general from another time period, one Hannibal, who was unable to be here for this trial due to pressing engagements with the Roman General Scipio Africanus. But we do have Hannibal's deposition. Since it is written in Carthaginian, we have had a little difficulty deciphering it. But we think it says, "This trooper is guilty as hell of everything he's accused of and he ought to fry painfully in the worst you can give him.""

"Hannibal is my friend." Bill said. "He wouldn't have said anything like that. You must have gotten it wrong."

"See for yourself," Stuart said. He gave a meaningful nod and one of his clerks hurried forward carrying a large baked clay tablet with cuneiform characters inscribed upon it.

"I can't read this," Bill said.

"Of course not," Stuart agreed. "It would have been strange, not to say treasonous, if you had been able to. Since that is the case, how can you deny our interpretation of the message?"

"My guess about what it means is as good as anyone else's," Bill said.

"Oh, is it now?" Stuart said. "We thought you might take that line of defense, and so we have brought to this court an expert on interpretations of unknown scripts. Will Professor Stone please take the stand?"

Professor Rosetta Stone was a tall and skinny spinster with a cold and imperious manner. She looked contemptuously around her and sniffed. "An expert at languages such as myself can always be expected to make a more reasonable, not to say pertinent, guess as to the meaning of a dubious text than can a lay person such as the barely literate trooper here."

And so it went. Various witnesses were brought in to testify. Bill had never seen them before. He later discovered that they were professional witnesses, who appeared in cases in which the prosecutor knew that the plaintiff was guilty as hell but lacked supporting evidence.

Bill thought it unfair when one of the witnesses, a clergyman of the Albigensian sect, swore under oath that Bill was responsible for the sacking of Rome in 422 A.D. Bill vehemently denied this. Since there were sufficient other charges against him to warrant whatever sentence the judge pleased, that particular one was dropped.

When it was his turn to speak, Bill asked for time to prepare his case. The judge smiled. "That is the sort of thing the guilty always say. Listen, trooper, this case is a foregone conclusion. If you want to waive your right to speak, it will be held in your favor that you saved the court valuable time."

"And if I don't?" Bill asked.

"Then we won't let you prepare your case and your asking will be held against you."

Bill's shoulders shrugged. He had been here before. "You've got it all set up against me. What can I say?"

"As little as possible," the judge said. "You have no idea how tiring it is for me, sitting here and hearing criminal after criminal perjure himself in the name of a law which he took all too lightly when he perpetrated his various and heinous offenses. Any final remarks? No? You're learning. Now let's get on with the important part, the punishment."

"You forgot to ask the jury how they vote," Bill said.

"A mere formality," the judge said. "I think we can forget all about that little bit of nonsense.

"No!" Bill cried. "I want to hear what the jury says!"

The judge looked disgusted. He had a busy day ahead of him. Three rounds of golf were scheduled that afternoon with important personages who would not take it kindly if the judge's game were not up to its usual high standard. They hadn't traveled all this distance to this remote post to have a crappy golf game. It passed through the judge's mind that this trooper was being very difficult. No one else had ever insisted that the jury be heard. It just showed the disadvantage of filling the military personnel with new-fangled ideas. He toyed with the idea of pulling out his laser pistol, which he always carried in a cutaway holster under his judge's gown, and saving everyone a lot of time, expense and trouble by blasting this goniff straight to the hell he so richly deserved for even having taken on enough of the shading of guilt to be brought in front of the court. But then he calmed himself. He already had several demerits for shooting prisoners out of hand. The lily-livered bastards back at Military Command liked to do it all by the book. Until he could prove that they were engaged in a conspiracy to undermine the entire justice system, he would have to accede to their wishes.

The judge turned to the jury. Nine robot heads (and three thoraxes) swiveled to look back at him. Their blank eyes and shiny metal skins reminded the judge of juries he had served with in other cases, some human, some robotic, some Simian.

"Robots of the jury," the judge said, "have you listened with care to all the evidence?"

"Indeed, your honor, we have," simpered the foreman, a deviate robot with a shiny purple face and granny glasses.

"And have you had time to weigh the evidence and come to a verdict?"

"Oh, indeed we have, your honor."

"Then how say ye?"

"We find the defendant not guilty in any degree whatsoever and deserving of a medal, maybe two."

The judge gave them a look in which consternation mingled with rage to terrifying effect. "Did I hear right?"

"It depends what you heard," the foreman giggled.

"Did you find this trooper not guilty?"

"Yes," said the foreman, "that's how it looked to us. Don't forget the medals, either."

There was pandemonium in the courtroom. Mothers wept and clutched their children close to them. Strong men lit cigarettes. Robots of various kinds and descriptions who had been in the audience as spectators gave cheers of applause, as well as the high-pitched yelps that robots emit when in a state of elation, for reasons that are still under investigation. The judge swelled up like a chicken under pressure. Several bailiffs fainted and had to be revived with strong drink. Reporters for the military newspapers rushed out to telephone the scoop. Bill rushed down from the stand and embraced his friend CIA, who had been in the crowd rooting for his friend.

"Bill, it's wonderful!" he cried.

"But why?" Bill asked. "I never heard of robots not voting the way they were supposed to."

"Everybody! Stop! This court is not dismissed!" So shouted the judge. In response to a wave of his hand the doors were barred. But just before they were barred, a messenger in motorcycle leathers, his goggles still in place over his eyes, gouts of sweat bursting from his forehead, rushed in and approached the bench. He handed the judge a slip of paper, then collapsed on the floor and had to be revived with powerful drugs.

There was silence in the courtroom as the judge read the slip of paper.

The judge pursed his lips. He cleared his throat. He stood up, glaring at Bill.

"It seems we have some extenuating circumstances," he said. The courtroom waited.

"Report to your base commander," he said to Bill. "This is a circumstance I had no knowledge of. The jury however seems to have figured it out beforehand."

His expression said that he did not like this, and would probably do something drastic about it.

"Case dismissed!" he cried. And the MPs gathered around Bill to take him back to base.

CHAPTER **71**

THE MILITARY BASE LOOKED THE SAME AS Bill remembered it. A group of one- and two-story buildings in the middle of a swamp. The MPs brought Bill directly to Headquarters Building. Here they removed his handcuffs, wished him luck, and departed.

Bill sat on a bench in the waiting room of General Vossbarger, recently appointed supreme commander of Sector South. It didn't take long before the clerk at the reception desk signaled Bill and told him he could go in.

The General had a nicely appointed office. Wall-to-wall carpeting, Danish furniture, bad paintings on flocked purple cloth, a whiskey decanter, the usual stuff. He was a big man who seemed larger because of the rolls of fat around his neck and nose. What hair he had left was blonde, thus lending credence to the rumors of the Blonde Beast that had preceded his posting.

"Take a seat, Bill," Vossbarger said. "Cigar? Care for a drink?"

Bill considered turning them down; after all, they might be poisoned. On the other hand, it might be a military offense to turn down cigars and drinks when offered by a general officer. He was in a perplexity which was resolved when Vossbarger poured him a drink and put a cigar beside it.

"Go ahead, Trooper, drink up. Take a puff. There's good leaf in that cigar, unlike the junk you enlisted men get in your PX or canteen or whatever the hell you call it. So you're Bill. Well, now, I've heard a lot about you. I'm mighty pleased that trial turned out in your favor. In fact, it's a very good bit of luck for us. We couldn't use you if you were dead, could we?"

Bill realized that was what lay behind the robot jury's unexpected acquittal. There was a reason, of course. In the military there's always, no matter how cynical, twisted or warped, a reason.

"I'm very pleased, sir," he said cautiously, wondering what was coming next.

"Now, Bill, about the Disruptor you were ordered to bring back—"

"I'm sorry about that, sir," Bill cringed. "I practically had it, but then a lot of stuff came up . . ."

"Never mind that. We think we know where we can get one."

"That's good news, sir!" Bill said.

"Yes, isn't it? And the cost won't be too high, either."

"Better and better!" Bill said thickly as his suspicions began to grow.

"Unfortunately, there's one hitch."

Bill nodded. Somehow he wasn't surprised that there was a hitch. What interested him was how the hitch involved him.

"The Tsurisians," Vossbarger said, "have indicated their willingness to provide us with what we need. But there is one stipulation."

Bill groaned. Not only was there a hitch, there was also a stipulation. This was getting worse and worse. He puffed the cigar furiously and drained his glass as he waited for the news none of which would be good.

Vossbarger nodded understandingly and refilled Bill's glass.

"Well, Bill, they want us to send an emissary there to be trained in the use of the Disruptor. As you can understand, an advanced tool like that requires careful study.

"Yeah, sure," Bill said.

"You'd have to volunteer for this mission, of course," Vossbarger said.

"Now wait, no, impossible!" Bill cried aloud. "I'm all finished with all that volunteering bowb."

"Too bad," Vossbarger said. "There was some talk of reinstituting the charges against you. This time you wouldn't be up against anything as easy as a robot jury. One jury would decide the entire issue. Me."

"Ah," said Bill.

"However that will not be necessary. There is no time to waste on that kind of rigmarole. I am ordering you to volunteer." He took a large gun from the desk drawer and pointed it between Bill's eyes. "Are you disobeying my order?"

"Excuse me, sir. You wouldn't like to tell me about this mission I'm volunteering for?"

"That's what I like to hear," Vossbarger said, smiling like a vulture over an elephant's corpse. The gun vanished. "Go ahead. You have fifty-five seconds to ask all the questions you like."

"Why me?"

"Good question. Well, there's the fact that you've already had some experience on the planet Tsuris. That weighed in our considerations."

"Yes, sir."

"But most important is the fact that the Quintiform computer, which, as you know, governs Tsuris, specifically asked for you."

"It did?"

"Yes, it did. It was really quite insistent about it. Said something about unfinished business between you two. Since we want that Disruptor, we saw no reason to turn the computer down. Especially since the woman added her demands as well."

"Woman? What woman?"

"I believe she said her name is Illyria. She's become the new president of Tsuris."

"How did she manage that?" Bill asked.

"We don't have all the details yet. Something to do with her new body."

"She's always getting new bodies," Bill sighed, feeling the trap jaws closing. "You wouldn't happen to know what does this one look like?"

"I haven't seen her myself," Vossbarger said. "But she requests that you be informed that her new body will be quite a surprise for you."

"I've had enough surprises."

"And she also informs us that she has your old body ready for you to occupy."

"But I've got a body!" Bill cried.

"It will have to be returned to the computer," Vossbarger said. "It was only a loaner."

"But what sort of body has Illyria taken now?"

"She did say that it's quite small. So as to fit inside the computer."

"I don't want to live inside the computer!" Bill moaned.

"Try it, you'll like it. Otherwise . . ." the gun quickly appeared again.

"Aye aye, sir," Bill sobbed.

He thought about it later, drinking in the enlisted men's canteen. No sooner had he gotten back to the dear old military than he was being shipped out again. Back to Illyria and the Quintiform computer. After a few drinks, it all started to feel better. The Quintiform computer wasn't a bad sort of machine. And as for Illyria . . .

Yes, on second thought, Quintiform was decent enough, he conned himself into thinking. He'd like to see his friend inside the computer again. And as for Illyria, it would be nice to see her again, too. When you're in the military, you take what comes up. And he could take it!

Then why were tears running down his nose and dripping into his drink?

CHAPTER **72**

WHEN BILL REACHED THE PLANET TSURIS, the preliminaries were few and far between. There was the usual array of Tsurisians present, in their familiar three-sphere form. The doctors who had treated him during his earlier stay on the planet were all there. They waved pleasantly as Bill's little space launch landed. He was led inside with shouting and cheers, and taken to the special chamber beneath Tsuris castle where the computer had set up headquarters.

"Hello, Bill," the Quintiform computer said. "Good to see you again."

"Hi," Bill said suspiciously. "You don't sound sore at me."

"Of course not, Bill. You and I have always gotten along well."

"Why did you send for me?"

"Well, that's a story in itself," the Quintiform computer said.

"Tell me it; I got time," Bill said.

"In fact, it was the request of my wife. She desired that you be returned to Tsuris for her wedding present."

"Your wife? Since when do computers have wives?"

"It is unusual," the Quintiform computer mused.

"But you don't know my wife. She is a determined woman."

"Is it any machine I may have met?"

"It's not a machine at all. It's Illyria."

"Illyria?" gurgled Bill.

"Did somebody call me?" a feminine voice asked. Although Bill had never heard it before, he knew at once it was Illyria. You just can't be wrong about a thing like that.

Then Illyria entered. Bill had never seen the body she was wearing. It was gorgeous, especially if you like them a little plump, as Bill did.

"I still don't get it," Bill said.

Illyria turned to the computer screen. "Quintiform?"

"Yes, my love."

"Don't listen until I tell you to again."

"Yes, my precious. Anyway, it's time I checked to see how things are going on the planet." It began humming to itself. The hum diminished as though the computer was going away, which, in fact, it might well have been, and then it died away altogether except for a faint aftertone which also diminished and died.

"Illyria, how could you have married the computer?"

"It was the only way I could get you here, beloved. I told the computer he would have to bring you back."

"Now that you're married," Bill said, "I don't see what you want me around for."

"Bill, the computer is a dear, and he's very interested in human emotions. But with him it's all talk. You know what I mean?"

"It figures, I guess," Bill said. "But I'm still a Trooper, you know. I've got some leave for this job, but..."

"If time is limited we must make every second count," she sussurated as she reached for him. "Let's start this way..."

Bill's last thought, as the warmth of embrace enveloped him, was that he had been ordered to do this.

War sure is hell.